the underbrothers

Simon Hacker

Copyright © Simon Hacker 2023 Cover image: Simon Hacker. Illustration & art © Hope Hanni Eva.

The moral right of the author has been asserted. No part of this publication may be reproduced, copied, stored in a retrieval system, or transmitted, in any form or by any means, without the prior written consent of the copyright holder, nor be otherwise circulated in any form of binding or cover other than that in which it is published and without a similar condition being imposed on the subsequent publisher.

With thanks, as ever, to Neil Lyndon.

For witches past, present and future.

part one ~ the father

Whitecross Hall   Friday, November 1st, 1782

Fear infects this night. Fixed in ink, I pray God it shall be banished. The Master is away, all servants given leave. From the library, I observed the frost silvering the lawn. Save the fire's embers, all was still. But then came noises.

    To these I ascribed the scratchings of mice, yet thereafter, footfall, my candle shifting in the air. It is a fancy of the village that one night, three score years ago, a curse was laid, a malediction upon three sons of this house. Of this, my Master, setting faith before the idleness of praters, utters nothing.

    Despite my agitation, peace resumed. Yet presently, a new draught ruffled my papers. Flinging down my quill, I sped to the hall, shouting to the chambers above – "Reveal yourself!" From the stairs, I paced the gallery to the corridor for my Master's bedchamber where, rubicund with rage, I pushed the door. There, in my lantern's flicker, I saw… a form, lying a-bed, 'neath a movement of the linen. Albeit fearful, I advance to grasp the cloth, but a shadow enrobed me, cheating my light of its air. In blackness, fear fixed me as, all around, feet scurried, this way, that. As in a merry dance.

    "In the name of King George, begone!" I called. "For if you are not the work of Satan, you will soon make his acquaintance!"

    Struggling with my lamp, feet encircled – I some maypole for their darksome revel-rout. Yet once lit, nothing, save from the corridor, behind – a soft bump. There, I found a loose panel of the wainscot, cold sifting through.

    Next morning, I will nail this foul portal shut.

    And pray it so remains.

C.B

inklings

The monster stirred. Black eyeballs popped from their sockets, a studded tongue chainsawing its target. From above, the girl smiled.

"Steady!" she breathed, dropping fruit into the glass chamber. "Save some for your sister."

Exhausted, Scarlett Wycherley flopped back down. Summer holidays, day one, time stretching forever. Maybe start a blog? She pondered her life: good, bad, ugly.

GOOD
Derek and Daisy. She'd owned her giant African land snails for three years, adoring them, slime and all. Friends? Hundreds. Some she had met. A nice home? No human rights violations. Space to escape her brother; garden big enough for Mum's yoga to remain secret. And the address: the Wycherleys lived so close to London's coolest shops she could smell them.

BAD
Being 15, though GCSEs were a distraction. Weirdly. Beauty? You'd be confusing her with someone who gave a damn. A (clearly) unwell woman on the tube once offered to buy her long, raven hair. But seriously? She loathed selfies. Happy school life? Enough, even if 'happy' and 'school' blended like 'adorable' and 'brother'. Talking of which…

UGLY
Roan. 12. Optimal nerd.

All told, life stacked in a roughly vertical direction. So why no joyful springing into the new day?

That would be your forebodings, her best friend Adeline reckoned. They burden the bones. By day, forebodings sleep, but by night… Scarlett suspected *inklings* a better fit; a word she had read somewhere that now loitered, waiting to glue itself, like a lovesick leech, to her existence. The day she woke with an inkling stuck on her face, at least she'd been expecting it.

Quick mirror check: none yet. Raising her blind, she squinted into the Saturday hum. She might itch for black rain, crows flapping backwards, but maybe pigeon-grey was the best London in July can do. She hungered for escape, but dreaded a rerun of last year's trek to the Dordogne, where people are so bored they literally eat the livers of force-fed ducks. Snordogne, she'd declared, to Dad's dismay. No, this summer, there had to be more? But her parents' plan? As far as she could tell, a big suitcase packed full of nothing.

"Going... going... GONE!" A mile away, an auction hammer cracked down. Onlookers gawped. "Who'd buy that?" a man gasped. Another, raising a card, mouthed "Wycherley".

The day Richard Wycherley bought Whitecross Hall, he oozed anticipation. He hadn't visited the seventeenth-century mansion, but it looked pretty much perfect on paper.

"It's perfect," he told his wife's back as they lay in bed.

Her back said nothing. He carried on, reciting the details. She carried on snoring. Then the fridge door creaked: that'd be Scarlett. Only a Taser would get Roan upright so early. *She'd* listen, she'd surely approve, compared to their routine *vacances en France*?

"Look at this Scarlie," he brandished the details, "it's perfect!" Scarlett slopped oat milk onto her rice crackles. "It's got 12 bedrooms and – "

"– A vast hallway, a scullery, a library... even a tower." Her cold stare fixed on him. "What the hell *is* a 'scullery' anyway – a storeroom for skulls? The joy of life before TikTok, eh?"

"Don't be daft... Hang on, how did *you* know?" He looked punctured.

"Dad, you *never* shut your door."

"Just like your ears then, eh?"

"Okayyyy," she groaned, "Roan might enjoy somewhere to store skulls, but maybe you're just a property addict? Why not be an estate agent, instead of shouting at screens all day?"

"Ah... still listening to your mother? Well you're both wrong: this was a chance discovery – to think we nearly missed it!"

Crackling cereal or Dad: Scarlett weighed up which was less dull. Sensing the apathy, he flicked the kettle on and traipsed back to his wife.

"Perfect? I thought we'd got that," she grunted, "here!"

"Yes, Joanna, I was just telling Scarlett... there's a huge kitchen... a scullery, *must* Google that... even a library... and look, there's a panoramic view, up from the 'north tower'. Just imagine!" he grinned, his vision breaking free, "our very own tower!" Joanna thumped her pillow. "Hopefully the bid clinched it," he added. She was asleep.

Despite August's lull, plans moved fast. Dad's money, Scarlett's mother advised, worked in mysterious ways. But the timetable was simple, breaking, as Scarlett instructed Roan, into just three phases:

1: Move from Point A. All furniture in lorry. Which they obediently follow into green wilderness, beyond the M25. Wherever, whatever, this is Point B.

2: Stranded in Point B, Dad sorts relocation to Point C – his mystery place, close to Point A and in London. Crucial bit, this. Obviously.

3: Point C, their new forever home, sorted, everyone (having avoided inhaling too much disgusting, clean air) returns to London and... relax, back where having six fingers isn't a personal achievement.

Tolerating Scarlett's apathy, Roan remembered his mother's advice: roll with it. Accept Dad's plan or he might run away to become a TV presenter on a ghastly daytime property show nobody watches. Hopefully.

With little time to focus, here they were: on the lane towards Whitecross Hall. In drizzle. From her window in the back of Dad's careworn Volvo, Scarlett swiped the condensation. If emotions were baggage, she reflected, they must be still in London.

She dropped the window a crack as the gateway loomed. A brace of eagle statues scowled from beneath cloaks of moss as the driveway lurched ahead into dense woodland. Reaching for the brochure, she wondered: could Whitecross be anyone's cup of tea? She pictured a brew served cold, a dead spider beneath the surface. Damn, she hated being so inklingist.

"Gently does it," Richard mumbled. As the greenery swallows them, Scarlett sensed nausea that had little to do with his driving. Behind her, Mustard, their three-year-old mongrel, woke from the undulations. Ordinarily, she loved observing Mustard, but she fixated on the removal lorry, scraping a path through the branches. Roan tutted. The incessant wobbles were ruining his book.

"I keep reading the same line!"

"Maybe your eyes are too fast for your brain? Or you're worrying about your stick insects?" Her dark eyes widened, smile feline. "Couldn't blame you for that... all that *bumping* and *rubbing* together... What happens, when sticks rub? Don't they get hotter, and hotter, until they burst – "

" – Enough, Scarlett!," Richard snapped. "Don't listen, Roe, poor girl's like her mum – thinks comedy's a bloodsport." Joanna shot him her headteacher look.

Yet Scarlett was equally worried. Lodged in their case, behind her, sat Derek and Daisy. Maybe they wouldn't miss London, but surely this green desert would be too suffocating, even for molluscs?

Finally, it emerged. Grey, giddy, a mansion to thrill – if you weren't sleeping over. She smeared more steam aside. Under an insomniac moon, black windows stared back; in one, the reflection of the lorry. They had followed its slogan all morning: *Colby and Son – we deliver dreams!* Stepping out, her father approached a man, waiting in the porch. Dangling from his hand, an absurdly large key.

Omens began earlier. At the M4 services, Mum said she was excited. But Mum never did excitement – an emotion that requires being open to change. Loyal to the same TV, food and fashions, how could she feel anything besides trauma at being *here*, where all the fur coats were still breathing?

She re-checked the brochure. The main picture was taken months ago, before the leaves blocked the sun. Lot 131 required 'updating to maximise the charm of this 12-bedroomed Baroque 17th century mansion which enjoys the benefits of original bla, bla, bla...'

Charm? To whoever wrote this, bubonic plague was a mild rash. Here, today, Whitecross was something maximised with dynamite. It enjoyed drainpipes with rickets, walls erupting with acne and a rooftop toupée of weeds. It didn't stand, it loitered with intent to collapse. Opening her door, she stepped out, feeling her heels slowly sink.

"This... this *pit* is our holiday home?" She could barely croak. My gob, she decided, is 100 per cent smacked.

To be fair, Dad seemed subdued. Feeling the key's dull weight, he paused to trace an insignia of intertwined initials within its circular head. Most bankers buy boltholes. Weekend retreats, he'd joke, so cute you could welcome guests "while never lifting your bum from the loo seat". Being tall, he once returned from Ireland, forehead bruised, cursing cottages as a "leprechaun conspiracy". He preferred the airspace to swing an average-size giraffe, he said. All of which, Scarlett knew, made Whitecross Hall a flame. And Dad, dear Dad, a big, idiot moth.

As he turned the key and shoved the towering door, Scarlett abandoned hope. Pushing again, the hinges whinged and, with a shudder, finally gave way. Stepping forward, he led. In his wake, Scarlett saw nothing.

All said, she'd settle for that.

terms & conditions

"It's been empty since the year dot," Richard shuddered, blowing dust from a wonky grandfather clock. From the look of it, Scarlett guessed, it tocked its last before electricity came along.

He clicked the light on, the echo searching up towards unseen corridors. Like surly men in raincoats, shadows shuffled away. She pondered the arched summits of the hall's ceiling. Festooned with cobwebs, a grand chandelier hung from a chain thickened with rust. Webs were everywhere, some thick as trampolines, some drifting like the tresses of a drowned crone's hair. It smelt of dead memories. Her skin puckered.

"Maybe we can order an IKEA catalogue," she whispered, "and Mum can batter you with it?"

But Dad was already fussing around the removals men. Their furniture was suddenly absurd, in this space, their belongings now salvage from a doll's house. Having rescued Derek and Daisy's case, Scarlett overtook her dressing table halfway up the broad staircase and artfully wove ahead, turning left for her designated room.

Whitecross must have been designed, she guessed, by a control freak. The landing, little more than a wide balcony, encircled the hall below. Apart from the master bedroom and a few more rooms off a corridor that ran to the north tower, it felt like each bedroom could be monitored from downstairs. Having found hers, overlooking the driveway, she resolved to think positively. Her snails' case secure, she plugged in their heating lamp. Oblivious to their new world, they nosed chunks of cucumber. For a while, Scarlett stacked a few books before perching on a sagging armchair – from where she finally noticed the mirror.

Standing seven feet tall, in an elaborate frame, the glass bluish pale, its reflected image uneven, it had certainly seen better days, but she shivered with anticipation. Stepping closer and clasping her hair into a thick tress, she pursed her lips to blow away a sheen of dust.

"Mirror, mirror…" she pouted. Shaking her hair loose, her instant witch felt perfect in the mottled image. Maybe one day I'll crop this all off, she thought, holding her hair back. She itched to take the scissors and be gone with it. Mum and Dad would be traumatised. Perfect: had they not done as much to her? I'm more certain of my legs, she decided, contemplating her tatty jeans, but maybe now's the time to search for some lame pinafore? Standing back, she focuses on the mirror's surface. It felt unreliable. Staring deeper, her heart dropped a beat, its stumble an impulse to move. Closer.

Scarlett reached out, then withdrew her fingertips, fearing the glass might fracture, as if it marked a gateway to a place where this frail version of herself could be forever trapped. She shrugged, her pupils drawn deeper into the reflected room. And there, something moved.

A figure, looming closer.

"You might knock!" She spun around.

"Scar!" Roan exclaimed. At least he was real. "Come and see this!"

Rushing to the other side of the landing, he leaned over the balcony. While hers overlooked the driveway, his room opened onto the ramshackle gardens behind. She wondered if *he* had a mirror. As if he would notice.

"A-hoy!" he yelled. The echo was impressive. "Who'd have thought it'd have this amazing hollow space?" Brothers, she reflected. They really are such a commitment.

"Don't tell me, Roe, you'll fritter your summer here, lobbing paper aeroplanes." His mind roamed, immune to Mum's warnings of Scarlett's "negative energy".

"It's like the balcony... in a theatre." He gazed up.

"Or a prison?"

Scarlett scanned the walls. Varnished wood smothered the house. The particulars said 'heavily wainscotted', which could only mean one thing: a minibeast hotel. How many generations of pests had chomped these acres of oak, walnut and elm? Was a living army crawling inside? Deathwatch beetles scuttled across her mind, their lazy click an omen of death. Running a fingertip along the worm-eaten handrail, a peppering of tiny holes resonated like unknown Braille.

More boxes of commitment reached her room. From her window, Scarlett saw the men were preparing to go, making thoughts of stowing away irresistible. But her father blocked the doorway.

"Troops demobilised, Sergeant Scar? Snails happy? Right-o... next item, family conference, five minutes!"

Conference? Dad was a deluded headmaster. As he breezed off, his shoulder bore the empty shell of a spider that must have crawled off to become bigger and scarier still.

"Be in the kitchen ASAP. I'll get the tea on," he added, from the stairway. "Oh, and I've got a bit of news..."

News? As her gaze settled on the elephantine four-poster bed in the far corner of her room, Scarlett realised she didn't care. After all, today couldn't hold more surprises.

Could it?

"Retired!"

She was used to Mum yelping, but the tortured sound from across the kitchen table was no reaction to a proposal. He'd already done it.

As bankers might, Dad had been creative with the truth. Sure, he'd *intended* Whitecross as their holiday home. After all, he'd insisted they'd soon be moving to a proper house, just streets from their original address. They'd move everything back to London come September, by which time the decorators would have sorted the bla-de-bla-de-bla. But, like Mum, Scarlett couldn't believe her ears. The decorators hadn't touched the new home. Because there wasn't one. Not in London. Not anywhere.

Bla-de-bla-de-bloodyhell.

Slowly, everything made sense: so that's why Dad insisted their future home remained a "nice surprise": in reality, there was just this. Nice had legged it, leaving surprise all alone. In the thick silence, her father simply stirred his tea.

"This isn't easy... and I'm truly, sorry, but hear me out." They'd no other option. "My project, my deal, to secure our original plan backfired... instead of a windfall I was counting on, I was trading on a loss. A large one. In the end, all I got was a 'retirement offer'."

She caught random words... mortgages, sufficient funds, more waffle. When he finally paused, he folded his glasses, as if he'd prefer not to focus on the firing squad. Scarlett senses he might cry, and her heart stopped. She could beg him to order the lorry back, but logic, damn logic, told her he had no choice. My family, she realised, is quite literally inside a snow globe being violently shaken. By a crazed monkey.

"They just wanted an excuse, the swines! There are younger, cheaper talents baying for the blood of old boys like me. I'm Jurassic." No arguing with that. "That's why I took the money and hoped for a better time to explain. There hasn't been one, and the truth can't be sat on any longer."

Everyone stared at the table, the truth sitting on them.

"But what about school?" Roan asked, voice cracking. "How do we get back to school, every day?"

"School? School! Yes, Roe." Had he forgotten? "I'm afraid this does mean a new school... we can't afford those fees – and you'd hate commuting. There's a good comprehensive in Whitecross – with all the continuity you both need..." He sounded like a Ferrari salesman forced to flog mopeds. "It won't be too bad – you'll make new friends; you'll both bed in, given time."

Time... Scarlett's stomach was a tumble drier, her life tumbling inside. More than Dad, she was shocked at herself – surprised that finishing GCSEs in an alien world didn't mean she'd already begged Mum to magic an Uber for three. But Mum had simply remained silent. Maybe she still needed to unpack her backbone?

The Aga groaned. Paws twitching, Mustard slept at its base as Joanna gazed towards the window, tears welling.

"Hot water... the boiler needs servicing – if there's any money left?"

"Of course, dear, we've enough, for now." Dad was a general who's been told the enemy's closing in, but on the plus side there's just enough cyanide to go round. "And something'll come up!" He thumped his empty mug down. "Yes, I'm sure we'll all be fine!"

bedding in

Date: September 2
From: scarlettwycherley@whitecrosshall.com
To: adelinebenn@74lincolnvale.co.uk

So, Adi... We finally got here and – ta-da! – velcom to Dracula's Castle. My room's like the school library – lined with wood, my bed's a huge four-poster with side curtains to trap you inside. And when I say vampires, forget swoony, think skanky home for retired bloodsuckers. On the first night, it sounds silly, but it just felt like I wasn't alone, like eyes were on me. When you come, you'll see. Oh, and this is now my home – <u>FOREVER</u>!!! Dad overlooked that one little detail.

    Negatives first. The nearest town's three miles, there's no shops, no cinema. Here, the main entertainment seems to be just a huge maze to explore, but no thanks, I prefer my horror on a screen. And it's so quiet I think I'll go mad. As in chained-up, howling at the moon. Worse still, this means a NEW SCHOOL. I've met our neighbours – they've got a farm three minutes away, maybe quicker when you're being chased. There's this boy, he's called Moreton. He can't actually speak, he just stares, like you're an alien, which I guess we kind of are. His sister's called Isabel – she's intense, though nice enough. Probably superglue myself to her when term starts. She bangs on too much about this house – hinted at an old story, which I won't dwell on now. She admitted it's most likely rubbish, so I'm not going to lose any sleep, if I can help it...

    Anyhow, in order of importance, your packing essentials are: garlic, crucifix, holy water, shotgun. If you still dare to come?
Scar xxx
PS Silly me, I forgot the positives... nope, there aren't any.

Scarlett's message took milliseconds to send, but London felt light years away. If she'd wanted adventure, all she sought now was a time machine back to July. Like the bronzing creeper around her window, she sensed summer withering. Before long, the surrounding trees would harden into skeletons; in days, she faced teachers never met, corridors unknown, a sea of faces that meant nothing. Home was a prison of hedges and fields, her company just cows. She lingered in gateways to feed them bunches of angelica. Life, she read in the subtitles below their chewing mouths, was somewhere else.

Yet life, she soon learned, *had* happened. Roan's discovery came in the shape of a large book, retrieved from a lofty corner in the library. Reading this ledger, which appeared to be a housekeeper's diary, it seemed Whitecross had known busier days.

"Look, it's ancient!" Roan cried from the top of a wobbling ladder. As he wiggled it free, dust cascaded down like a celestial sneeze. "Look, Scarlett! It says 'Household Journal', and some letters…" he held the cover to the light, "well, I think it's a 'C' and, what, a 'B'? Maybe 'CB' lived here?"

She grunted. "Okay, pass it – quick! It's a long way to A and E."

He scrambled down and, propping it up, they turned the first page.

That night, Scarlett slept. Or kind of. Asleep, awake, she no longer knew. Peering through gritty eyelids, she wondered if it was morning. Through a gap in the tapestry that engulfed her bed, a blue-grey glow hung across the room. The mattress didn't help. Whenever one lump shifted, another muscled in. With every turn, everything creaked like a doomed ship, until somehow, finally, she began to drift away. Which is exactly when it came. Like a resonance, emerging from the faintest collection of words. Words spoken with real feeling.

Real irritation.

"I say to thee, we might share, but will ye please stop this wretched a-fidgetin' and grant me my repose!"

Eyes closed, head under the sheets, she slurred: "I'm sorry, I'm trying, but this stupid bed's never going to be comfortable…"

And then she woke. Totally. She'd surely been awake, but now she jumped up like an electrified cat. What in the name of sanity was *that*? Yes, dreams can be convincing, but this was a *conversation*. She'd even apologised. To a talking bed.

Seconds stretched. How could anyone have spoken to her, as if they were somehow under her, mumbling up through the springs? Scar, she insisted, you're nearly 16, this is all in your head. Roan's discovery of that ledger had muddied her mind: a hazy account of noises upstairs, feet running about in the dark, of dancing in a mad 'devilish' circle... crazy stuff: little doors nailed up, self-snuffing lanterns. He'd been unable to put it down. The freak. And when he read a bit about a string of servants fleeing, and 'a curse upon the ancestors, banished forever into darkness', she'd told him: enough, it was just the made-up scribbling of someone stuck here with nothing better to do. Perhaps some part of her feasted on every detail. Just not her stomach.

And then there was Isabel Valance. Or Iz, as she'd been corrected.

They'd met a few days before, when Scarlett tried to trace the footpath that led across the fields from the woods surrounding their driveway. She'd hoped to learn this short cut to the school bus – and might have, had Isabel not collared her from across the field. She'd come out of her garden gate from Valance Farm, where, as the lettering carved in stone above the porch suggested, her family had been mucking about with muck and dying in the stuff since the dark ages.

Picking her way through a minefield of cowpats, Scarlett approached. Isabel was accidentally beautiful, as if she'd tumbled from a 1970s advert for butter. Her glow spilled into her body language: she dazzled, but with a whisper of chaos.

How different to her brother, who shadowed her into the field. Moreton lingered a few paces off, barely nodding on Isabel's introduction. He must have been 17; Isabel said he'd be finishing A Levels next year. Awkward? Arrogant? In a fleeting moment, she sensed his gaze glide through her, heading somewhere more important, though it seemed to finally settle upon the cowpats.

In bounding sentences that swamped the air, Isabel informed Scarlett she'd show her around school. Come Monday, they'd meet by that gap, in the hedge, and get the bus together. Stick with her; she'd nothing to fear. They were in the same year, after all. Three times, she squeezed her arm. That was good? Isabel sensed her anxiety and surely wanted to help? But then an afterthought stirred: maybe this fizzy, frizzy Izzie might be way too energised to be reliable for brave new friendship? Maybe she got through friends like socks? Scarlett gave herself an imaginary slap: she had no luxury of choice, even if Isabel jabbed at her inklings.

Together in that freeze-frame moment, they stared at the disjointed outline of Whitecross, jutting above the trees.

"It must be amazing, actually living there." Isabel's big eyes darted across the rooftops.

"Not sure 'amazing' is the word... certainly *interesting*, if you're not allergic to dust," Scarlett hesitated.

"I guess any old place collects random tales – I mean, there'll be negatives to anywhere?" Isabel ventured, perhaps reaching for a handbrake.

"Negatives? Yeah, we've probably heard them all." Scarlett still hoped to brush the subject aside. But Isabel didn't do handbrakes.

"It's the hopscotch one I remember best, probably because it was a playground thing, back at the village school... "

"No, I don't know that one... " she said, clenching her teeth.

"It's easy!" Turning on her heel, Isabel hoiked her skirt and was away, skipping over the long grass, leapfrogging virtual squares.

By trick of light, they're quick of flight,
But after dark, when moon is bright,
The brothers dance... wahoof!
All... out... of... sight!

Holding back her blonde ringlets, it was as if she had chanted the words a thousand times. When she stopped, they'd charged the air. Amid the static, no one moved. Isabel released her grip as the folds of her skirt broke upon the long grass, her hair shaking loose across her face. Pity the sucker, Scarlett reflected, lured by this solar charm.

"I'm sorry, that was stupid. Like I said, it's just a daft rhyme. I'm sure every village has its witches and curses."

Which was when, to Scarlett's surprise, Moreton finally spoke: "Treat it as nonsense, keep it as nonsense, Iz?"

Surely he was more grounded than his sister, yet both left her baffled. Whatever Isabel said of Whitecross, she could probably add far more. But no way ever was *that* happening. As they stood amid the haze, Scarlett clung to logic: with or without some witch's abracadabra for eternal lockdown, nothing could live all that time – at least nothing actually, properly, real?

Lying in her bed, she repeated one of Dad's threadbare clichés: yes, we have "nothing to fear so much as fear itself". In her clammy baroque prison, she repeated the mantra, seconds stretching to minutes. Tugging the curtain gap shut, she pulled the sheets over her head, pulse pounding, until slowly, gradually, the pressure relented. Yes, she reflected, it *was* a silly dream, a mental glitch. In exhaustion, sleep returns fast. Three hours later, a knock awoke her.

"Morning, sweetheart. Survived the night?" Pulling the bed curtains aside, Dad flourished a tray: two cups of tea, two slices of toast, both heavy with marmalade. His bent hair made her picture some silent movie comic, his faded tartan dressing gown only boosting the effect. Its smell took her home – *real* home, to that far-away dream of London; warm red buses, hot, dirty air in the tube, Hyde Park on wet afternoons. 'Lun-dun', a dull repetition, the rhythm of a distant train.

"Sleep okay, darling?" A strained smile suggested he'd barely closed his eyes.

Scarlett shrugged. "Not too bad... someone was trying to kill me, I ran faster. The usual stuff."

"Ah, you're a born survivor." Placing the tray on the bedside table, he sank into the mattress. "There's a heating engineer coming, so if you hear groaning from the cellars, it's not your mother bludgeoning me. Not yet..."

"How *is* Mum?" As if she didn't know.

"Well, I bought the key to the world's biggest dog house... we need time to sort stuff out. Life stuff." Scarlett opened her mouth only for toast. "She's got her own room, for now." Taking the first half of his slice, he leaned back. "Scar, I know it's a grump of an old pile, but things'll get better – we can get a pulse back into these old bones."

From the hall, the bell spluttered. "Ah, that's the chap to fix the old boiler." He jumped up. "And I don't mean your mother!"

She giggled, ejecting a cascade of crumbs. Dad was so obvious, but he still knew which button made her laugh. Later, she collected their breakfast tray. That's odd, she thought: Dad ate only half his toast. Post-move, his appetite was tiny. Yet there was his plate: empty.

Like it was licked clean.

blank verse

We are the unseen, and, to all of those who dream
To try and find us, blind us with day,
Be warned, for here we have been, years ten score,
And add a few more. And here, all newcomers,
Be ye fearful, be ye tearful,
For here we ever stay.

If you can drown at school, Isabel was a lifeguard. Despite her yearnings to be elsewhere, reports showed Scarlett was adjusting well. If eyebrows were raised in the staff room, they were to be for her brother, thanks to his contribution to the English Language autumn project.

The idea was Miss Kington's. She wanted to combine the talents of year-eleven GCSE Art with the writing skills of year-eight students. A showcase of words and pictures. But it needed a theme.

"I want you to extend the concept of the selfie – think of the page as your mirror," she told Roan's class. "Words about how you see yourself – below that surface image, your deeper essence." The class groaned. "Your *essence* is what gives you your identity, what makes you different from the person next to you."

Slumped in her seat, Sally Shepherd raised a finger, eyes fixed on Roan. "So you mean, like, 'I'm not a bug-eyed nerd'?" Everyone laughed.

"No, you know *exactly* my meaning and we've no place for that, Sally. I expect you to express yourselves more creatively than merely saying what you're *not*. Think of the philosopher Descartes' famous words, cogito ergo sum. Which means?"

Deathly silence.

She typed the phrase onto the whiteboard:

I THINK –

"– therefore, I, am?" Roan volunteered. He hated the attention, but couldn't believe it wasn't obvious. She peered gleefully over her glasses.

"Bravo, Roan."

"Like I said…" murmured Sally, to more laughter.

"This is the key to philosophy – your thoughts make you what you are," Miss Kington added, as the bell rang. "So set your imagination free! Just as long as your imagination's on my desk first thing."

To more grunting, the lesson ended.

That evening, unperturbed by Shepherd and her sheep, Roan thought long and hard. But the appropriate words avoided the end of his pen. Over dinner, he quizzed his shepherd's pie. In the bath, his navel. Neither helped. Finally, lying in bed, he stared at the blank sheet, until he nodded off. The paper slipped away, gliding silently to the floorboards.

"Cogito ergo sum, cogito ergo sum." The words sped him into sleep.

The following morning, he knew. Scooping up the paper, folding it quickly, he'd simply give it to her. Yes – a blank sheet! Wasn't that perfect abstract art?

That afternoon, Miss Kington sat behind the gathered pile, speed-reading, counting, stacking.

"Very good, *very* good… tomorrow, we'll know what's worthy of the final exhibition."

Folded or not, Roan wondered how she's missed an empty page. Yet what followed, later that week, was stranger still.

Obeying a lunch-break summons, he knocked on Miss Kington's study door, expecting a roasting. But she was smiling.

"Ah, Roan, I thought we might have a little chat." She nodded to a chair. Miss Kington had a kind face, but the clock on her desk clicked falteringly. "You do know what this is about?" I'm finished, thought Roan. She's cracked the blank-sheet mystery.

"Well... I can explain, Miss…" he began, but she raised a finger.

"I thought your piece the most interesting one." The clock stopped. "Indeed, the only one to use the collective pronoun 'we', when the natural choice here is the first-person." She paused, holding what was certainly the same sheet of paper. Yet, through the light of her desk lamp, he made out an ornate, spidery script.

What did it say?

Unravelling the reversed scrawl, he wanted to rub his eyes…

We… are… the… unseen?

"In dark red ink, too, as you might imagine blood... calligraphy centuries old… as if with some kind of quill? The content, the concept… this is some imagination, utterly compelling…"

Lost in scrutiny, she raised the paper towards her nose, but quickly recoiled. As if it carried a perfume of poison.

Roan was stumped. Should he admit he wrote nothing? And if he took any credit, what for? He'd suspect Scarlett, but pranks were beneath her. Finally he mumbled "it was nothing", which, after all, was true.

"Nothing? On the contrary! This is all about hidden depth, written with authority and such... attitude!" She looked up, still beaming. He checked her hands. Apparently, they were not activating any kind of security button beneath her desk.

"I, I can't remember *exactly* what I wrote, but if you put it in the exhibition, I'd prefer it if, maybe, you didn't name me?" He could already hear their taunts.

Lost in contemplation. Miss Kington rose from her desk and took the paper closer to the window. Finally, she turned: "Tell me Roan, you *are* happy – if there were problems, here or *anywhere*, you know you can talk to me?"

But the chair was empty, the door ajar.

"There's a spirit driving this pen," she laughed. "Some spirit indeed!"

barking

Scarlett was attempting to watch the TV, despite Roan. In the past few days, he'd developed a new obsession: foraging and faffing in the library. The diary having whetted his appetite, he was desperate to prove something. And now, in the spidery recesses, persistence had paid off.

It certainly looked interesting: a battered portfolio of papers. Quickly, he determined the contents were architectural drawings, each relating to sections of Whitecross and its gardens. Carrying the bundle into the sitting room, he laid them across the floor. She cast a cool eye over his haul; the folder bore no lettering, just an insignia. Catching the light as he opened the cover, a fleeting suggestion in the gilt detailing echoed against something seen before, but *Eastenders,* on balance, was more interesting.

Gingerly, he unfolded the largest paper. Picking through decades of brittle parchment, the plans gave way like filo pastry. Adjusting his glasses, he pushed his mop of hair aside and offered little 'hmmm' noises, as if he was cracking a code. For anyone nearby, it went beyond irritating.

"Roan, have you ever considered getting a life – somewhere else?"

"Huh, since when was soap addiction part of a meaningful life?" he scoffed. "We've been here more than a month and we haven't even seen all the rooms. D'you want to know this house, Scar, or just lodge in a bit of it?"

He had a point. Deep down, she felt like a guest of an invisible landlord. As Dad grumbled, many rooms had keys that didn't fit. And an old bell-pull system in the kitchen suggested each door was numbered, yet most doors either weren't, or were so caked in paint their keyholes had disappeared. It *was* an issue, but Dad was too busy persuading the Aga, and Mum, to function. Begrudgingly, she'd admit to herself alone, keys might be key to something.

"It's fascinating," he continued, ignoring her pout. "If you look at this layered floor plan, you can see cellars, attics... so many corridors and stairways, but we've no idea how much exists today – and," he paused, "call me weird, but I want to know."

"That's just it though."

"What?"

"You are."

"I'm what?"

"Weird! I mean, we no longer have to make our own entertainment." She flung the remote control down. Seriously, what was so odd about an old mansion having tucked-away rooms? And far more importantly, a cliffhanger was playing out on *Eastenders*: a pram rolling directly into the path of a car. As they converged, the thundering beat of the final credits rang out.

The commotion jolted Mustard awake, launching him into a blur. Scarlett muted the TV and jumped up, trying to calm him. Eventually, silence returned. Or almost.

High above the ceiling's plasterwork, they could hear it.

A scratching, a scuttling.

Their eyes scanned the ceiling. The noise lasted seconds – long enough to realise no rodent could create such volume, over such distance. Strangest of all, Scarlett could see that, tracing where it began, it moved in an ever-tightening circle, spiralling towards the centre of the room. Where it came to a rest, the silence was only more perplexing.

"Where's Dad?" she whispered knowing she'd glimpsed him mowing the lawn, minutes before. And Mum was miles away at the hairdressers.

Roan reached for the relevant plan. "That's the *fifth* bedroom, the last one directly off the hall, before the corridor. And it's locked." He layered the diagram over the ground floor. "What you really need is a three-D model. It'd make it all much clearer…" he faltered.

Even in two-D, the evidence was stark: the walls of the room above exactly matched the room they were in. Roan dropped the papers.

"Maybe it's time we went in?"

The thought was tempting as an open grave, but she followed him towards the stairs.

what's the matter?

It was an heroic effort, but Roan's technique was pure comedy. As Scarlett watched in disbelief, he grabbed the knob, unleashing his seven-stone force. And what if he succeeded, what then? They wrestle and detain whoever – what-ever – they'd heard scuttling from below?

Mustard, meanwhile, played detective, snout jammed into the sliver between door and floorboards. Snuffling the air, he processed it with a series of growls. Lungs and spirit deflated, Roan slumped to the floor, resignation forcing a reverse-thrust of his elbow. It wasn't like this in films.

But the force of his elbow changed everything.

The key, tucked above the doorway, dropped neatly into his lap. Astounded, they locked eyes. Without hesitation, Roan jumped up, inserted the key and pushed the door.

A gasp of stale air enveloped them, but with the shutters across two windows at the far wall, all they could make out was a forest of white sheets. Roan expected Mustard to plunge in like a bloodhound, yet his paws marked an invisible line across the threshold, hackles taut, growls rumbling. With a tut, he pushed by to reach for the light switch. It was dead.

Undaunted, he followed the gap down the side of the room. Scarlett took a few steps as lifeless cold prickled her bare arms, but Roan was already at the far end, grappling with the shutters.

At the first, the handle broke clean off. The second squeaked open but jammed half way, suspended like a maimed pterodactyl. Bad light, he reasoned, was better than none. A slash of sunlight dissected the room. And seeing more, they gazed, with dropped jaws.

It was a sea of furniture – chairs, wardrobes, dressers, tables, hat stands… even what looked like the hulk of a grand piano, each covered by a dust sheet. Roan began rushing from one mystery to the next, teasing back covers, making mental notes. Slowly, some sort of order emerged: from the windows, a narrow aisle veered right, heading through the mountain ranges, towards the centre. With Scarlett in reluctant tow, he realised the path wound inescapably into a helix of dead people's stuff.

Finally finding courage, Mustard followed. But just a few feet in, a passing cloud momentarily cast the room into a monochrome light. He growled and scuttled for the door, which groaned on its hinges and slammed, with a paint-splintering whack.

"I'm not so sure this is a great idea…" Scarlett whispered. "I mean, there might be rats. They can jump at you – latch onto your neck."

Roan shrugged. "No way, that was no rat – keep going – it's got to be just two more corners. Maybe there's some answer, and we'll sleep better…"

A jittery rabbit behind a valiant mouse, she advanced. But two corners on, it was finally there: the dead end. And there, covered by a sheet, a tall shape loomed.

The height of a man.

To Scarlett, it harboured some ghastly Victorian artefact, a monster that would snap to life and claw at their frozen faces. She'd have pulled Roan back, but he was out of reach, a hand already on the cover.

Gently, he pulled.

She staggered back and, reaching to steady herself, felt her fingers close around a covered shape, a complex roofline, one corner rising proudly above, suggesting a tower. Like a miniature mansion.

"Wait! Something's *here*…"

But he wouldn't be stalled. "Another time, Scar – whatever's *here* has to give us some answers."

He pulled again. The sheet fell away.

"A bird cage!" He laughed.

"Is there anything *in* it?" She was still cowering, but at least it was just more lifeless junk.

"Well, the door's open, so anything captive would never have stayed. But wait…"

Delving inside, he retrieved something. A black feather.

"Feathers… loads of 'em. And poo, down here, so some type of corvid… crow, jackdaw? Oh well: it's empty now."

Scarlett's mind reeled. How could birds get in here? No open windows. And even if they got in, who was tending them?

"Roan," she whispered, "I'm freaking out here."

But fear was not her only feeling: had they finally discovered their home came with a squatter? Coming and going, just as they pleased? How dare they?

Her brother leant close to the cage floor, inhaling deeply.

"The poo's pretty fresh."

"Oh my God, I'm literally going to…" Scarlett's gag reflex rose as he pocketed a sample feather.

"Exhibit A!" he declared, but as he closed the cage, he stopped. There, on the latch, was something he'd not noticed.

Something dangling.

It had the appearance of a slug – silvery black, hanging by a thin membrane. Without hesitating, he clamped it between finger and thumb. It came free from its sticky anchorage and, with a sheen when held to the light, felt dry to the touch. Remarkably like skin.

"Look, Scar! Maybe our intruder left a piece of himself in a hurry?"

"Eurgh! It looks like a huge wart!"

Roan eyed her thoughtfully as he nestled his second find into a piece of tissue paper and, from a pocket, produced a magnifying glass.

"A wart, you say? For once, Scar, you might be right."

"Well, maybe not. I mean, it could be part of a bird?"

"Well if it *was*, it'd be a first. Look…" He held the crude nodule towards her pinched face. "No, this bit, at the end…" It was millimetres from Scarlett's nose. And there, at the end, she saw it, sprouting proudly.

A silver, squiggly hair.

"I mean, maybe I'm wrong, but hairy birds are yet to evolve, eh?"

By now, Scarlett was gasping. From his jacket, Roan calmly took a matchbox. Exhibit B was his for future analysis.

"You know what?" he beamed, "We're finally onto something."

brooding

"Half term in the sticks." Scarlett dragged her spoon through limp cornflakes.

Roan, at the sink, was scraping burnt toast so obsessively there'd soon be nothing left. Knowing she should tolerate him made her feel even more ratty. She had reason to be happy: today, Adeline was coming. At last, someone who'd see how cut-off she'd become, someone who'd understand?

But she also feared her visit: what if Adeline found it all so grim she did a runner, hitch-hiking back to London with a grim message for their shared social network? Who'd blame her? Less than three months after their move, her inner gloom was very outer. But Dad was having none of it.

"Come on, Scar, there's heaps to do," he said, wrestling with a knot in his bacon. "Mum was saying there's horse riding at Valance Farm – remember how you both adored hacking on that school trip?"

"I was 11, Dad! Shall I change my name to Cressida and join the Pony Club?" He looked deflated. She felt bad. Mildly. "Sorry, but *horses?* – been there, done that. And Isabel says we can go with her any time for free. I was thinking more having some space with Adeline, one-to-one… going to the shops, you know – being normal?"

"Well, we'll see." He was so predictable she lip-synched his words.
"Okay," he adds, "as you say, Scarlett, what-ever, but as it happens, Adeline's father and I have business to discuss. Maybe I'll get him to stay."

"Business! He's your mate, drop the excuses, Dad!"

"Okay, a pint might come into it, but Tom's a big wheel in building circles and he's picked up some work that's not too far from here…" He faltered. "I can't say more, but it's probably great news for 15-year-old girls… it might just mean a brand-new shopping mall, conveniently situated."

He failed to mention how traders in Whitecross High Street were already fuming over the project but, as Tom explained, there was no stopping it. The same company had bulldozed through many similar protests and Tom Benn Developments knew just what to do.

After all, Adeline's father owned the JCBs.

Perhaps because the light bulbs now worked, Adeline's introduction to 'Castle Wycherley', as her father guffawed, seemed less negative than Scarlett's. Breezing in to the hall, she stopped at the motif in the middle of the mosaic floor, a feature Richard's elbow work had revealed just days before. Dropping her bag, she gazed skywards.

"Oh. My. God!" She span 360 degrees, her long, red hair flying free. "It's not like Dracula's Castle at all, Scarlie... I mean it's just a really fun place to live – it's so, so... " she fumbled, "epic!"

Richard scowled. He'd hoped his daughter might have depicted some fairytale palace, not Nosferatu's crib. But Tom Benn had his attention. Like a human-size Lego Minifigure, he filled the doorway, firing a granite handshake. Given their need to discuss 'business', he took little persuasion to stay over. In fact, he'd already booked a local pub, don't you know, for a cosy dinner. To Scarlett, the man was a magnet for repugnance; she pitied Adeline.

But Adeline was oblivious. Without speaking, she'd moved across the hall to a large painting, shadowed beneath the staircase.

Beneath its jaundiced sheen, a man with bouffant hair wore a long coat and black riding boots over vaguely preposterous breeches. He grasped the reins to a gleaming, black horse while behind him, a familiar outline loomed: the Wycherleys' new home.

"Scary, eh?" Scarlett whispered. "Sir Robert Boxwell... Roan says he built this house – about 1680. He's the resident librarian..."

Adeline giggled. "His eyes," she said, drawing closer. "So sad... he doesn't look happy... Good looking though? A bit Harry Styles? I mean, it's like what they say, about eyes, following you..." She stepped aside, testing the theory. "It sounds freaky," she whispered, "but I like it."

"Styles? Don't you mean Dracula?" Adeline drew closer, eyes inches from his face. For seconds, she was lost, but then suddenly recoiled, flinching from the painted stare.

"What is it, Adeline? It's only a freaking picture!"

"Sorry!" Someone stepped on my grave." She shrugged. "I meant to ask: what's the bedding plan... you said there's loads of rooms, but we've *so* much catching up... can we share?"

Scarlett laughed. "I decided to put you up in the tower – but you're lucky, seeing as we can't find the key." Adeline's eyes widened. "Oh go on, my bed's big enough for a party."

"Excellent! Show me, I'm dying to see the fairytale bedchamber!"

"Fairytale? Yeah, it's certainly brothers Grimm, but at least you'll see how my snails have grown."

Lost in conversation, they climbed the stairway, oblivious to their fathers who, having quickly settled in the library, were already clunking glasses over a bottle of whisky.

From a slit in the wall, a watchful eye swivelled.

"So in principle, it's agreed." Tom gazed around the pub.

"Hold on, chap!" Richard shifted in his chair. "Sure, but I must consider *everyone*." The Forest Inn was the poshest night out for miles, but he was fully aware the menu was blackmail.

Tom ran through his argument again.

"Look mate, leaving London was probably wise, if you have the means to put this Whitecross idea right." He broke off to ask the waiter why *in the name of sanity* chips weren't available. The man looked confused. "Maybe fluent English wasn't a specified requirement. As I say, Richard, you're in a *good* position. If your family have gone full-on rural, I fully understand you staying put."

That was clever, Richard reflected: since Tom's wife talked to Joanna, Tom surely knew rural life was *not* her dream. But what of Roan and Scarlett – what of their future feelings? Yes, they'd been dislocated, but now that they were bedding in to a new school? They might jump at life back in London, but would they really thank him, 10 years on? Wasn't one fracture, already healing, wiser than two?

"I can only say what *I'd* do," Tom continued, as the starters arrived. "For God's sake, man – you'll get *t*wo point five million pounds!" Having lowered his voice, it was only the diners immediately next to them who revealed what was in their mouths.

"You'll have six months, maybe longer, if you had trouble finding somewhere new. Maybe make it a surprise for the kids, though equally you might whizz them off to a decent school – bish-bash-bosh!"

Whizz them off? The words jarred. Pack them off, more like.

"And boarding obviously didn't do *me* any harm!" He drained his glass as two tiny bowls filled with a gourmet foam appeared. Richard peered in, watching the unknown substance slowly deflate. "And if my Adeline's anything to go by, Scarlett would adore being back in town… you'll be wealthier than ever and, if you're back, there could be the odd consultancy position," he added, the side of his glass pressed knowingly to his nose.

The main course arrived. With chips. Tom beamed at the waiter.

"Bravo! Dig in, Dickie boy!" he laughed. "It's so good getting exactly what you want, eh?"

blackout

If Adeline was sad, Scarlett was heartbroken. That Thursday afternoon, her father's Range Rover barrelled into the driveway, a spaceship primed to abduct her oldest friend. During their goodbyes, he mumbled furtively to Richard, though she noticed nothing.

As Joanna recounted, they'd had a fabulous time: overdosing on fresh air, exploring bridleways on horseback (thanks to guidance from Isabel) and escaping to Cheltenham where, Scarlett reported, shops had not, after all, been a figment of her imagination. They even attempted the overgrown maze, but reversed when realising Roan's diagram suggested they'd be lost forever.

Adeline waved as they spun away in a flurry of leaves. But just before the gates, she gazed back and caught a glimpse of Whitecross's roofline. How odd, she thought: Roan must have dashed from the front door to the highest part of the building. Wasn't he standing beside Scarlett? Yet there he now was, at a window, in the tower.

It had to be him, a vague shape, a thin arm, describing a slow arc.

Richard's brash exhaust faded into birdsong Scarlett nursed a pang. She called Mustard, put on her boots and headed out. It looked like rain.

"Perfect," she sighed.

In his room, Roan had the diagrams strewn across the floor, the matchbox safe in his pocket. Now and again, he would cup it, through the cloth. There was something thrilling about his first specimen, known only to him and Scarlett. Sometimes, he aired it in the secrecy of his room, never questioning why it didn't change: plump, wrinkly when squeezed, odourless. Showing no natural willingness to decay.

Slouched upon the floor, he leant against the panelling opposite his bed. It was growing dark, but he stared obliviously at the fading images, the mass of measurements jumbling together as his eyelids drooped and he drifted towards sleep.

Moments later, the closest wood panel began to move. Near silently, sliding sideways by a fraction. Barely enough for an object the size of a hand to pass through.

Scarlett wanted to venture further, but after minutes trying to figure where the footpath goes, she realised it was getting dark – properly. One bonus of living in a tall house, she reflected, was that it was easy to find. Beneath the swaying trees, she traced her return. Reaching the limits of their woodland garden, a swirl of leaves elevated into a vortex. Eager for supper, Mustard plunged on.

If he'd been awake, he'd have recognised it as a hand. Technically. A spatula of papery flesh, five bony rods, inhuman as sundae spoons, splaying, straining forwards. Grey fingernails, clawing for the rug's edge. Then, as if detached, it crabbed forward, with arachnoid stealth, closer to the edge of Roan's jacket. But the hand was not detached: with it followed inches of wrinkled wrist, then more flesh; flesh the pallor of raw pastry; a spongy, yellowing pastiche of skin, stretched bubblegum-thin over porcelain bones.

    Blind as any eyeless limb must be, it locked to its target. As roots seek water, the fingers reached Roan's jacket, fingernails encircling the shape of the matchbox. Roan stirred; the hand froze. But he slept on, legs folded under his knees. And quick as it came, the limb retreated, the panel remaining ajar.

In the wind, Scarlett almost missed the call. She fumbled to answer, as Mustard looked back, tail down in disappointment.

    It was Adeline. So she till wanted contact.

    "Hi you! Home already?"

    "Nah – stuck on the M25, Dad's getting petrol. Forgot how far it was."

    "Don't remind me… it was great seeing you though." Scarlett's eyes roamed to the dancing tree-tops. She'd never anticipated feelings for the M25.

    "Maybe come up next weekend?" Adeline ventured. "I hear your dad's coming on Friday to see mine about something? Oh, and that Hallowe'en party Amanda had last year… there's another."

"What? As in when Sean Mason tried to snog you but couldn't get your mask off?"

The line distorted with her cackles. "Yeah, he never got over that on Snapchat. Nor did I, come to think. Okay, no masks this year – something more practical?"

"Sounds good – I'll work on Dad."

"Cool. Just one other thing, though it could wait… " The line sizzled.

"Don't be dumb, Adi – you know I can't wait if you say that?"

"It's nothing, but when we were going… I saw Roan… waving, from up in the window."

"Maybe he's got a thing for you?" she laughed.

"Hilarious. Thing is… the window… he was there, up in the tower."

The word poured into her ear like cold water.

"No… I said we can't unlock it, it's been driving him nuts finding a key and… " she faltered, "this is a wind up, right?"

"Oh *God*, I shouldn't have said. It could've been just the light, or – " her voice shrank into static. Scarlett checked the signal: one lonely bar.

Whatever Adeline's motivation, she'd talk to Roan the moment she was back. But the wind in the treetops was gaining force.

The hand returned, holding the end of a rope. No longer interested in Roan's jacket, it scuttled to his left foot, delicately threading the end beneath his ankle, bringing it around, twisting it into a knot. Then, so caringly, the fingers prised enough space to open the gap beneath his right foot. Finally, they push the rope through, ensnaring his other ankle. With a satisfied pat, it withdrew.

"I cried at the hairdressers," Joanna said. Richard steered into the supermarket car park. "She asked after our holiday plans."

He understood: holidays had somehow become something other people do. He turned off the engine.

"Darling, you'd have every right to cry... I bungled all this. Magnificently." He squeezed her hand. She closed hers around his.

"Oh, don't be sorry for me – be sorry for *them*: our children need to be part of decisions that affect their lives... and holidays? Talk about touching a raw nerve."

He knew that nerve well, tracing back to a childhood and a career-first father who had dragged his children around the world.

"They just need calm now, they need to know where they're going – no more surprises?"

"Absolutely," he said, pushing images of Tom Benn aside.

By the time Scarlett reached the porch, it was totally dark. She shouldered the door – a knack she was developing well. The hall lights didn't work.

Funny, she thought: it *was* windy, but enough to knock the power out? She called out to her mother, towards the kitchen: no reply. She checked her phone. Still no signal. Finally, she remembered: they'd gone to Whitecross; a late shop. So where was Roan?

By instinct, she hadn't let go of Mustard's lead. Now she was grateful. Luckily, she remembered the torch, in the cloakroom. Fumbling past the coats, she elbowed aside images of someone hidden within them. It was there, but the batteries were feeble.

From the foot of the stairs, she called up: "Ro-an?"

He could be plugged in to music, but even on battery power, he'd have noticed the dark?

"*RO-AN!*" she bellowed. Mustard's eyes twinkled in the dim beam. "Let's find him!" she whispered. Together, they climbed, turning right from the top step to walk past the bedroom doors: one, two, three... all closed. Room four, ajar, bathed in moonlight... room five, now locked, that vile chamber stuffed with someone's past. She moved more quickly, eyes locked ahead. At the end, square on, room seven. Roan's.

Reaching for the handle, she saw the beam trembling. Mustard nosed the door; it moved with a low creak. Taking a small step inside, she raised the light. The beam ricocheted off a mirror and sliced through... nothing.

Roan's not here.

Rushing to the window, she tugged the sash open. The wind was stronger, flits of moonlight bathing the gardens.

"ROAN!" she yelled, panic mounting. Maybe he'd gone for a walk, too? Or tagged along with Mum and Dad? But Dad would have texted her, he'd surely not leave her alone? She called out again. Nothing.

Pulling the sash down, Scarlett rested the torch on the ledge – just as the beam died. There's nothing for it, she decided: she must get back to the kitchen to find fresh batteries, a candle – anything. Gripping Mustard's leash, perhaps too tightly, they approached the landing. If he had a menacing side he'd never displayed, she hoped he'd finally show it.

She could see as far as the stairs, but to step through Roan's doorway into the pale perspective felt like trespassing into a painting. In the faint moonlight, this cold expanse was Whitecross in its naked truth. With clenched teeth, she stepped ahead, floorboards graunching, her pace measured by a pulse pounding in her ears.

At the topmost stair, Mustard remained close. She turned her head instinctively, fearing a sudden push from behind. Resisting the urge to bolt, it took eternity to reach the bottom, but finally she was down – just a few paces, now, to the kitchen. Maybe Roan had left a note?

It was her final thought before hell broke loose.

once bitten

It wasn't until she read the payment card that the woman blipping their shopping snapped from her trance.

"Mrs Wycherley? Oh, aren't you the same lady what's moved to Whitecross Hall?"

"Uh, yes, I am," Joanna nodded. "Just settling in… sorry, this is my husband, Richard."

"Oh my, forgive me; I'm Isabel's mum? Margaret Valance – we're neighbours!" she beamed, adding, as if to clarify, "From just over the field."

"Of course!" said Richard. "You have an adorable daughter in Isabel, she's been so kind, helping Scarlett adjust."

"Ah, yes, our Izzie…" she trailed off, as if saying anything more might be problematic.

"Well, we must get together some time!" Joanna said, folding her receipt. Somehow, Richard suspected his wife was just being polite.

Close to the kitchen, the lunge came: a black force through black space. A tall shadow, arms sweeping from behind, enveloping her like a cloak.

"Gotcha!" the voice boomed. Mustard reared up, all tail and teeth in a spill of moonlight. Her heart hammered as the shape bound her still. Though not still enough: with enough room to twist her head, she swivelled to locate the forearm enclosing her neck – and did Mustard's job for him. A cornered wildcat, her teeth sank through cloth to reach their soft target.

"Argh! Get off!" A hand grabbed her hair and yanked her head, but the pain was too much: the figure let go, stumbling back into the moonlight. And in that instant, the truth dawned on them both.

"MORETON!" she exploded, as Mustard barked at his ankles. She couldn't decide to laugh or cry.

"Scarlett? I'm so sorry! I thought you were a burglar!"

"And I thought…" She didn't know what she thought he could be. Stepping back, she collapsed onto the staircase.

"What are you even doing in here?" Her voice was hoarse.

"I'm sorry, the front door was open… " he gasped, "I was locking the chickens up and I heard someone calling – I saw you had no lights on. I guessed you were all away, but then… I didn't know what, I just ran."

In the dim light, she studied his eyes. Unsurprisingly, they were preoccupied with his left forearm.

"Well I'm glad you did, I guess," she said, now calmer. "I was looking for Roan… I'd been for a walk, but when I got back, he'd vanished. And the power cut just made things 10 times worse."

"I don't think there's any power cut, not anywhere else? Maybe it's your fuse box – probably in the kitchen?"

She found matches at the side of the Aga. By candlelight, Moreton, still rubbing his arm (excessively, she decided), traced the box. Balancing on a chair, he flicked a switch. The bulbs over the table flickered on, the fridge coughing into life.

"Something tripped it all out – condensation, a power surge?"

"I know how it feels," Scarlett sighed as she unfastened Mustard's leash. "I'm totally tripped out. And I still need to find Roan."

The lights of her father's Volvo snaked into the driveway. "At last! I expect he's with them – they went to the shops," she explained. "I'll stick the kettle on."

Moreton pulled out a chair. She'd never contemplated him as the brave hero, but after tonight? At a squint. The front door slammed and, at the sound of their voices, Mustard scampered to the hall, tail flaying.

Yet no third voice.

"Hello all," beamed Richard, hoisting shopping onto the table. "Interesting evening?" Scarlett was impressed her father's brow didn't furrow at Moreton's presence, but before she could reply, Joanna yelled from the hallway: "Good God, Richard! There's blood out here!"

"Oh, it's nothing," said Moreton, "I heard shouting and ran over…"

"Oh no! Don't tell me our beastly dog bit you?" Joanna gasped. "I'm so sorry Moreton," She scowled at the innocent hound as Scarlett resolved to let that little detail go. Her eye caught Moreton's; was that a glint of a smile?

"Yes, Moreton was trying to help, but ended up getting a bit of a nip. I got back from my walk, the power was dead, I couldn't find Roan – "

" – What d'you mean?" Joanna froze.

"You what?" her father echoed.

Scarlett raised her palms. "Well, he's not upstairs – I've shouted the flipping house down!"

Joanna rushed away, Richard following. Their footsteps stomped across the landing, then past Roan's creaking door. After a brief silence, voices mumbled before Joanna headed to their main bedroom, directly above.

Richard soon reappeared. "He's in bed – must've been fast asleep; says he had a headache. Beats me how you didn't see him." Scarlett wondered if he suspected some prank.

"Well, that seems sorted?" Moreton said. "Sorry if I, you know, shocked you, Scarlett."

"Oh, don't be, you did the right thing, I'm sure – but look, you need something for that arm."

"It's okay, I've had my share of animal bites; it'll heal quicker, if it just breathes."

By now, Richard was standing by the doorway, willing Moreton's departure. "Yes, thanks for coming, Moreton, and do say hello to everyone – we saw your ma at the Co-Op, seems a lovely lady," he said, patting him a cursory farewell.

At the front door, Moreton crouched to jostle Mustard. Scarlett suspected he connected better with animals than people. His eyes met hers and self-consciousness pulsed between them before be sloped off, bearing the imprint of her teeth into the night.

"For the record, Dad, Roan wasn't there," Scarlett sighed, as he unloaded the dishwasher. "I wouldn't just make stuff up."

"It's fine, Scarlie. Could be a thousand things. I don't think he's too well. Your mum thinks he's got a temperature. Maybe he was sleepwalking, or it's just something about us all being somewhere new…" He yawned. "I'm gonna magic up some toast and cocoa, fancy joining me?"

It'd been a long day. But what was that parting look from Moreton, she pondered, as she blew on her cocoa. That Scarlett Wycherley bit harder than any dopey dog?

electric

The more he struggled, the tighter it drew. A jab to his leg had stirred him. Eyes wide, all he saw was a hand, disembodied in the fuzz of confusion, a ramshackle collection of claws and bony knuckles, the shape covered in skin reptile grey. But it was not detached and, as adrenaline sharpened his focus, he made out the entire arm, stretching through a hole in the wainscotting. Like a sick joke, it was making a signal: a long forefinger curling back and forth. Beckoning. For seconds, he was transfixed. Then he cried, "No, no way!", jumped to his feet and ran. Or tried. Within two paces, he was flat on his face.

Snap!

The rope, threaded around his ankles as he'd slept, pulled taut. And by the force of whatever lay at the other end, began to draw him back. Towards the outstretched hand, now trembling. Roan tried to grasp the chest of drawers. Fingernails scratched varnish, glassy splinters pinging into the air, but within seconds the furniture was beyond him and his feet were already inside, sliding into the blackness.

"Come in! Be not shy!" came a voice from beyond the woodwork. A sound lumpy as cold gravy. "Tut, tut... struggling never helps. You're already in trouble, let us make this easy."

"Scarlett!" he cried, knowing she'd left for a walk.

"Screaming like a baby, dribbling for his sibling, what a way to be! Come, boy, be calm..."

The wainscotting reached his waist. "That's it, we'll soon get you *comfortable*." That voice, deep and flowing, breaking into laughter: could it be separate from whoever, whatever, was hauling him?

Then he was inside. The hand, reaching to check the bedroom, smoothed the rug before shutting the panel. For an eternity, fear rang in his ears. Then the voice came again, gigantic in the pitch black.

"Ooh, indeed it's time we had a word." Lips puffed so close he felt each syllable: "Master Wycherley, welcome to our... domain. And don't fret – it is as if you were never even there."

As knobbly feet pinned his arms and a bag of rough hessian was forced over his head, Roan began to hyperventilate, the hood so snug one ear was bent forward. Then more rope, as the slack, after he'd been hauled in, was looped around his body. This is it, he realised: I'm trussed like a spider's supper. Finally, all movement ceased. Silence prevailed, except one sound. He'd shut it out, but it was close enough to smell. Amid the smell of something surely dead, yet active, suddenly the truth was bright as day: a papery rasping, it was the sound of lips being methodically licked.

"Your room's super disgusting. What you been up to, stashing cheese?" Scarlett was perched on Roan's bed. Bad weather having blown over, the morning's sun leant the room's ripeness a fruity edge. "You and me need to talk," she added, trying not to inhale.

"You and I. It's you and *I*, unless this place is infecting you." Even half awake and puffy from trauma, he remained the champion of grammar.

"Have a day off, Roan. And stop avoiding the rhino in the room."

"Elephant!" he gasped. "I suppose you mean last night?"

"Obviously: I come back, the power's gone, I try to find you, I get the fright of my life off Moreton..."

"Moreton!" Roan laughed. "If you two have a thing, just get a room." He stretched like a starfish. It was a fair bet that hinting about Moreton might repel her. You only had to look at his face whenever Scarlett was near; he was hooked. "Look," he finally offered, "I'm not hiding anything; I can't tell you what 'happened' last night. I was looking at those plans," he hesitated, as if he was connecting fragments. "I felt tired... and I think I fell asleep, and then, the next thing I know, Mum and Dad are here, looking like I'd grown another head... Then, I slept and woke up to this, the Spanish Inquisition. Did I maybe miss something?"

"Just your vanishing act. So you're pulling a stunt or..." she stopped suddenly. "Where's the matchbox, Roan?"

"Oh, it's safe."

"So where is it?"

"You misunderstand what 'safe' means."

"So it's a secret from *me* now?"

"For pity's sake. In my jacket – on the chair. Check, if you must."

She reached to pat the nearest pocket. The cloth felt flat. "Not in this one, is it the other?"

"No, it's *that* pocket..." He sat up. Scarlett pulled the empty pocket inside out.

"Call me paranoid, but if it's gone... maybe someone wanted it back?"

Aghast, his focus wandered to a distant point, beyond the chest of drawers, beyond the wall. His mind had an unscratchable itch.

"Oh well," he sighed, "maybe we're better off without it."

At dusk, Scarlett suggested a walk with her mother. She arrived sporting a pair of pink wellingtons, looking as local as an L.A. YouTuber.

"Who'd have thought it?" Joanna laughed as they head out. "It's like we're turning into a proper rustic family." Scarlett felt queasy.

"*You*, rustic?"

"Go on, it's not so terrible here? Just different?"

"That's one word. Alien's another. I suppose we're getting used to it, kind of," Scarlett added. "And Dad – "

"Ah, Dad. Bless. Yep, he screwed up, but he knows. And worse things happen – it's not like he ran off with his secretary." Scarlett wondered if that might have been preferable.

"He seems happier, now?" she half asked, aware she was playing hopscotch in a minefield. In truth, she had just one question: were they both okay, or at least functioning? Joanna's vague reply encouraged her to steer clear. Changing the subject, she breezed: "I was thinking I could see Adeline next weekend, back in London? Dad says he's got to see *her* dad anyway... maybe we could all go?"

"All those autumn sales," she drooled. "The body is willing if the credit card isn't. I'll think about it."

If Adeline's idea now had its boots on, Scarlett knew exactly the boots to get. Not that she needed London for that. Leather-free Doc Martens. Deciding she'd hung out with too many cows to enjoy wearing their relatives, they'd be fine for everything. Throw in some self-hairdressing and, who knows, maybe she'd feel more at home – in Whitecross and her own skin? The wind tugged harder, sending leaves cascading.

Joanna smiled. "It's been tough on Dad, to be fair..."

Scarlett had no answer. "Maybe Whitecross was a shock to us all?" she offered, "I mean, it can't be easy, after so many years in his job?"

"Yep, maybe he'll surprise us all. And anyhow, he's forgiven – ish."

Parents of today, she reflected, they're such a responsibility.

"And I have a feeling," Joanna declared, snatching a leaf as it corkscrewed down, "we're all through the worst? I mean, lightning can't strike twice in the same place?" She hugged Scarlett and they felt closer than any time since she remembered. The sky rumbled.

The rain held off until they reached the stile to the field, the carelessly arranged windows of Valance Farm visible through the gloom. Scarlett sensed something in the air: at first, the wind slowed, but soon gathered speed. And with it, the rain descended like a year's supply. Thick, cold rods connecting cloud to ground.

"Perfect Hallowe'en weather!" her mother laughed.

As they turned back, towards the agitated mass of woodland, instinct told Scarlett to seek clear ground, but the storm made no difference to her mother's pace. The gusts gathering, she lengthened her stride. It'd take three minutes – two if they just focused.

"Come on, Mum!"

But the rain intensified, pushing Scarlett on. She was just metres ahead when a crack rang out.

Like the slap of a hand on a giant's thigh, it compressed the air, shaking the ground. Scarlett looked up – just in time.

"Get back!" she screamed, but her mother was right in its path.

With a tearing of wood, everything turned green as an enormous bough slammed to the earth between them. Tumbling back amid an explosion of leaves and mud, Scarlett realised that she was somehow unscathed. But the path has vanished, replaced by a wall of twisted branches.

And there, at the bottom, sticking out beneath the tangled branches, lay a pair of pink boots.

Soles splayed in opposite directions. Not moving.

Scarlett screamed, tugging helplessly at the branches. Cursing that she'd left her mobile charging in the kitchen, she turned to run forward, only to find the path blocked by another shattered limb from the bolt-struck tree. There could be only one hope for getting back quickly: she had to take the long way around. Diving left, she stumbled through the undergrowth and reached a barbed-wire fence. This she cleared in one jump, running flat-out along the edge of the field, towards Whitecross's gardens.

It was an entrance she'd never used, a gate slouching in the wall, framed by a pointed arch. It *had* to be the most direct way. With one push, she blurted through, then froze.

The maze.

Ahead stretched what once were corridors of delight but, in the fading light, she saw only tunnels ebbing into menace. Wiping away rain and tears, she plunged on, ducking straggling branches. The wind and rain eased, but the foliage tugged at her jacket like meddling fingers. Determined and moving quickly, she watched for hidden turns, left, right, left, right . . . none. She reached the furthest point, but it was not until the last yard that she saw a way through: two ways, in fact, both densely overgrown. The house lay somewhere right, so right she turned, into a new corridor that looked… exactly as before.

Panic welled. Think, you idiot! Think! Roan had studied a diagram from those plans. What did he say? To get back, turn right every time, except left every fourth time? That's it!

She moved swiftly, taking two more right-hand turns. Then a terrible thought struck: what if it was keep *left*, then *right* every fourth time? At the final, fourth turn left, she dared not look.

Straight ahead was a sullen square of grass. Empty save, at its centre, a stone obelisk, perhaps 10 feet tall. Staggering forward to the base, she slumped down, knowing she has merely discovered the heart of the maze. And all she saw, as she closed her eyes, was a pair of splayed, pink boots.

It was darker now, a numb tranquillity replacing the storm. From the gloom, something swooped through the open space. Moving silently, a flash of white beneath its wings, an owl inspected her before fading into the black. Scarlett studied her mud-encased boots and slowly lifted her gaze. Strewn like funeral confetti, all across the clearing, feathers. Hundreds upon hundreds. Black, glistening in the pattering rain, dabs of velvet on canvas.

Time lost all sense as she curled against the foot of the obelisk and closed her eyes. Shut tight against the sea of black petals.

breaking news

The lost minutes felt like an hour, but a last-ditch recollection proved correct: it *was* three lefts and a right. Scarlett stumbled past the police car, barely noticing it. At the porch, her father was talking to an officer. He rushed to pick her up in a single scoop.

"You're alright, you're alright!" he repeated. "It's okay, Scarlie – Mum's okay. Just scratches and bruises. Moreton must have carried her back and then rushed off to find you, though we're not sure – she's a bit muddled."

The officer spoke into his radio: mother and daughter both now accounted for.

"I'll stop by at Valance Farm," he said, clipping his radio into place. "Just for our records."

"Good-o," said Richard. "But just one more thing... my wife's flustered about her boots – if you spot any, they're bright pink, so I guess they might jump out, so to say."

As the patrol car left, he carried Scarlett to a bath which had been run by a bewildered-looking Roan. Soon after, she found herself wrapped in a blanket, tucked on the sofa, next to her similarly swaddled mother.

"Cuh, this place is like a wartime hospital," Roan huffed. Hugging her mother, Scarlett sobbed.

"Hey Scarlie! It's all okay," she croaked. "My feet feel like an elephant stomped on them, but it's nothing two weeks in a spa won't sort."

"I thought you were crushed, I couldn't get to you and..."

"Shush now." She rubbed Scarlett's back. "It appears I was saved by some knight in shining armour."

Scarlett pulled back. "So you *did* get knocked on the head!" she giggled, face glowing in the firelight.

"Well, all I remember is these manly arms heaving away the branches and lifting me. Next thing, I'm wrapped in Mustard's old blanket from the porch and your father appears, looking like someone getting the weirdest home delivery... whoever put me there just vanished – maybe to find you?"

Only one name explained this: it had to be Moreton. Again? Did he scarper out of embarrassment? Scarlett felt a rush of something uninvited. Pride, she guessed? He's a natural-born hero, she all but said aloud. At least the soft firelight hid her blushes.

"Yep, that Moreton's got sponsorship from Weetabix," said Richard, his gaze fixed on the TV. "Schoolboy, farmer, part-time 999… must make sure they're on the Christmas card list."

"Yeah, lucky you didn't need him on Saturday morning – that's when he's all caped up and refreezing the ice caps," Roan added, though he sensed Moreton was now officially untouchable.

But Richard was distracted by the TV. The sound muted, the local news showed Whitecross village, the words "Storm hits sleepy village" rolling across the screen. But this was no weather report: a graphic showed the outline of a shopping complex. Roan raised the remote as a local campaigner began to speak. Immediately, Richard snatched it away.

"Not now, Roan! Maybe we've all had enough drama tonight?"

"But Dad, it's that shopping mall – you said Tom Benn's involved?"

"All in good time, Roan!"

Richard flicked over to an old black-and-white movie. A woman lay sleeping as a ghoulish hand appeared through her bedside wall, fingers advancing towards her throat. "Terrific – remember this classic, Joanna? *The Cat and the Canary*? Must be a Hallowe'en special… made before the war; all about these guests in a haunted mansion, and how they began to disappear… " he trailed off. "Excellent!" he added, switching channels, "Looks like an an old *University Challenge* repeat on BBC2. I got three right once."

"Yeah, if it was a repeat, Dad. I'm off," Roan groaned, "think I'll do a bit of Fortnite."

"A *bit*? Not too late, mind," Richard called after him, "or the WiFi's off in one hour."

Soon after, both exhausted, Scarlett and her mother headed for the stairs. Richard watched TV briefly, but diverted to the library before turning in. In semi-darkness, he perched in his revolving chair and lifted the phone receiver. He knew the London number off by heart.

"Tom, it's Richard – hopefully you'll pick this up early. I trust you've read my letter? Look, I know I've not signed yet, but it's warming up here – looks like local TV's onto it…" he paused, lowering his voice. "So listen: if you can get things in place for my visit next week, this is a *done* deal. But my bottom line," he insisted, whispering closer to the receiver, "is for all my terms met before your JCBs come near this driveway."

divination

Date: November 1, 14.15PM
Email from: Scarlettwycherley@whitecrosshall.com
To: adelinebenn@74lincolnvale.co.uk

Friend-a-mine, oh Adeline… I should be able to make the party on Saturday, though we had our own Hallowe'en event already… A bolt of lightning, literally, hits a tree, knocking off this huge branch. And guess who's under it? Yep – Mum. She looked like an instant panini – her boots sticking out like the Wicked Witch of the East. I run for help, get lost and end up going gaga. Well, almost…
Anyhow, nobody died, but things keep getting weirder.
Rewind first to the day you left: after you'd gone, there's a power cut – during which Roan decides to disappear. And while I'm trying to find him, fumbling in the dark with Mustard, Moreton appears – and grabs me! Okay, maybe that's not so bad, but I thought he was a ghoul, so I bit him. As in with my actual teeth. Fortunately Mustard got blamed. Good doggy!
Anyhow, turns out Moreton is more a hero than a dog snack – not only did he pop up when the power was out, but maybe he rescued Mum? When the tree got zapped on Hallowe'en, after I ran off for help, I ended up lost and stuck, yep… in that spooooky maze. Dad meanwhile found Mum dumped in the porch, all in one piece but like she'd been fried.
And in other news… Roan's weirder than ever. The day after he vanished, he told me I was fussing about nothing and – this is the odd bit (and maybe I should have said before) but he had this disgusting thing we found, what looked like a black wart. He went full Gollum about it. But the morning after he'd disappeared, the container was gone. And then it's like he doesn't even care about it any more. Or care much about anything – he just wanders round like a ghost or sits staring at screens. Am I over-analysing?

Scarlie XxX

PS And I finally cut my hair. See pic. Radical?!?

Date: November 1, 15.47PM
Email from: adelinebenn@74lincolnvale.co.uk
To: scarlettwycherley@whitecrosshall.com

OMG Scarlie…"Aliens in our attic made my brother a zombie!" And Moreton!? Love at first bite! Get past the farm fragrance and those brooding eyes… hello Farmer Charmer!
Speaking of eyes, I had the weirdest dream. Maybe it was all from that painting, in your hall. Whatsisname – Robbie Boxwell? Did I dream it, or is there a woman in the pic – standing at that window, up in the north tower? I don't want to spook you, but my dream was as if I was at the front of the building and Boxwell was ahead of me, with his horse. The wind was blowing in the trees, and then I thought, kind of mixed in with the sound of the wind, there was a woman's voice, like wailing… Boxwell's horse reared up… he tried to calm it while waving to the window, waving to the woman to get back, from the bars… That was what was strange – the windows didn't have glass, just bars.
God, I shouldn't say this. It's just something's bugging me, about Whitecross – like it's trying to tell a story, if you found how to listen? Anyhow, forget it – come to London and we'll blast away the country cobwebs?

Lotsaluv, Adi x

PS Massive OMG! You DID it! Six inches off? And one side's shorter… I guess deliberately?! Cool! They'll be choking on their porridge!

Scarlett logged off. Yes, Adeline, she wanted to reply, you *shouldn't* send this. She couldn't care less what she thought about her hair – she wasn't hugely sure about her DIY work herself. If it was 'inappropriate', mission accomplished. But as for everything else, what was Adeline doing? Setting up shop as a ghost hunter?
Adeline could mash up hallucinations of Roan and Boxwell all day long. I have no such luxury. Nope, for me, this is real. Every. Single. Day.

no recall

"Rapscallion, *rap-scallion!*"

The rasp was close enough to be moist.

"I know what you want – it's in my pocket," said Roan, voice muffled by the hessian covering his head. He'd passed out but was now intensely awake, and aware – though he saw nothing – that he must be in a chair. Bound to the frame, he realised it must be bolted to the floor. No way out, he reckoned: stuck like filling in a pie. Yet strangely, a part of his mind knew he had nothing to lose, so *he* might as well ask a question.

"Who are you, what are you doing here?"

An arm outstretched, a powerful thumb and forefinger, the same beckoning finger he'd first seen in his bedroom, minutes before, clamped around his throat, kinking his airway like a heel on a hosepipe. For seconds, breathing was impossible. The voice returned: "Questions? He dares ask *questions*? Oh, gallant boy. How magnificently foolish."

The hand dropped away and Roan sucked at the cloth.

"Yet what delicious irony." The figure moved around the room like a strutting headmaster. "Since the same question I now offer you. As this is most unequivocally *our* abode, pray, enlighten me: what circumstance leads your kindred to contaminate it?"

He neared again.

"My father bought this house, and we came here because…"

A hand punched the chair's frame, shaking Roan's body. "We know, we know *everything,* proud fool! My question seeks not to drown us in the minutiae of your tedious lives. Moreover, I desire to know why you seek to know more about us?"

"I don't underst… I mean, who are 'us'?"

Again, the fist slammed: "I counsel nary a question to which you may be fearful of the answer, errant boy."

The figure retreating, Roan sensed busy hands. Fumbling with… a box? At a workbench? He cursed his imagination while logic suggested what he most dreaded: a tool box.

"Wretched lid!" the voice spat. "Who locked this? How am I supposed to affect credible torture without my instruments?"

Roan jolted against his bonds. "No!" he screamed. "Please! There's no need, I'll tell you anything. Just ask – anything!"

The voice chuckled as he loomed again, with a padding and a clicking of sockless feet and long, curled toenails.

"Anything? What use is anything? Dear boy, what I am in the business of needing is some-thing."

Again, Roan heard the hands, now picking through what must be a different box. Then he stopped.

"Aha! At last. The key!" The lock released, the lid clanked open.

"Let's see... spanner? Yes. File? Aha, here... Hand-saw? Now where is it? Ah, silly me, here, with the chisels. Oh, I nearly forgot, my new blowtorch. We're very modern here," he laughed. Edging closer, he whispers: "I think they call it oxy-acet-ylene... Should be good for the warm-up. But first a game! Oh *do* cheer up! Children love a game! This one's called 'guess the temperature and I'll let you go'."

"Of the flame?" said Roan, voice quivering.

"Most certainly, boy. Try me... to the nearest 10 degrees."

"Two thousand."

"Two thousand? Genius!" But Roan sensed this was not to be a moment when knowledge was king. "But none of your Celsius nonsense, Fahrenheit, please. We have no decimal tosh here, we're true imperialists. Thus, *wrong* answer!"

He clicked the burner on and a sword of flame slashed across the space between them. Hood or no hood, Roan yelped and pleaded again. The feet pad away, back towards the box, where eager hands lined up tools, as if planning an order of use. Then the rush of the flame increased. Through the woven threads, Roan watched the blue scythe.

Even worse, close by, the illuminated face finally appeared. Grinning.

Not bearing to see more, Roan closed his eyes as the figure jigged in excitement, toenails clickety-clacking.

And then, drawing a dagger from his waist, Roan's captor stooped to slice the bonds around his ankles.

"Master Wycherley, you will tell me all we need," he grunted, massaging Roan's calves with wretched delicacy, "as comprehensively as you will find no memory of today."

Gently, his fingers loosened the shoelaces.

"But first," his round eyes blue with the flame, "As you have such cold feet…" Clunk, the first shoe dropped. "Would you like a local anaesthetic? If preferred, I can numb your toes with this hammer. *Very* local – crafted here, in the village."

He rocked back with laughter and already, the second shoe was off. Guffawing like broken pottery in a shaken bucket, the figure nearly keeled over as Roan's head dropped forward, chin to chest. Seeking the only available escape, once more, he had passed out.

"Zadoc, what on earth is this?" a voice boomed. The newcomer stood a few yards away. "Barely do I turn my back! I told you secure him, maybe instil fear, not kill the wretch. And where the blazes is that from?" A long finger pointed at the flame.

"Oh really, Edmund, don't fuss," Zadoc wheedled, "I acquired it from that plumber they summoned to attend to the boiler. Heavens, I was merely warming his toes."

"You witless oaf!" Edmund brushed him aside and crouched at Roan's feet. His spine creaked like wicker but he moved quickly. Carefully replacing his shoes, he secured the laces neatly.

"Have you got the box?" he hissed, "Zadoc! Do not test me. The box! Is, it, back?"

"Oh yes, t'is here, in his pocket. I merely wished to establish his motive." Zadoc delved into Roan's pocket and offered it to his eager companion, like a sacred relic. "See, no damage done: he will be complete again, surely?"

"Praise the heavens." With a hand less gnarled than his brother's, Edmund reached to take it.

"But wait!" Zadoc blurted, his fingers still clinging on. "What if we were to essay an idea?"

"Are you demented, brother? You know that this is his poor flesh. I take it back to him or he is, by imputation, destroyed."

"But indulge my heresy: ask yourself, would that really be so bad?" Zadoc held fast to the box. "Do you want more than 300 years of living like this? Like timorous silver fish, never able to endure the light?"

Edmund stepped back. "Zadoc, if you would end this excuse for a life we have, on the basis of some expression of genius from that cavity where your brain once resided, then do so of your own behest, but you know, as well as I, what lot awaits us. And while such heart that I have still beats in this memory of a chest, I shall not let her win. For my part at least, this story ends not now."

Zadoc sighed, as if such words are simply more volleying in a game played down decades and centuries. "Your valour is above question; you will always be the eldest and wisest. But listen: I have another idea, one that might be a pathway for us to be free, to walk in the sun, step out into daylight, breathe virgin air. The three of us."

"Oh?" Edmund groaned. "And pray, what now? What blessed miracle do you propose? That we fashion wings from cobwebs and flit free into the autumn night? Meacocks made peacocks?" His words diminished into a sardonic wheeze.

"Nay, I speak of science, not fancy. Come closer," Zadoc whispered. "After all, we are not alone. Of this, let even the churchpigs not be party."

To underline his words, and with button pupils fixed upon his brother, he stretched down, fingertips delving into the dark. Immediately, his hand returned to the blue light that bathed their faces. Between forefinger and thumb, a fat woodlouse coiled.

"No one can hear of this." He set the insect between his teeth, pursed his lips, and crunched.

Crouched at Roan's inert feet, Edmund groaned but drew a reluctant ear close to Zadoc's twisted mouth. His bleached eyes opened wide in the gloom as, not for the first time in 300 years, he listened.

part two ~ the sons

of termagants & talismen

"Wow! They. Are. Mega!" Scarlett liked her reaction. "The biggest snails ever – they make the ones behind our cowsheds look micro. Proper monsters…"

"No, not monsters!" She wrapped her arm around their case. "Derek and Daisy wouldn't hurt a fly. Look!" She stretched a fingertip close to Daisy's head. Two tentacles extended, exploring her skin. "It's like a kiss."

Isabel tested the theory with Derek. "Not quite a snog," she giggled. "But they have beautiful shells…" she paused. "Don't they miss Africa?"

"They're no more African than us, they're Londoners! I think they like it here, though. London's a bit fast, maybe country life's more their pace." Scarlett immediately realised her blunder, but Isabel looked unoffended.

Despite her wild reaction to her self-cut hair, she was glad Isabel had come. For the past two days, she'd been sniffling with a head cold, probably triggered by the soaking in the storm. Despite what she'd done to her hair, her mother agreed that she could take time off. But how she had missed Isabel's random conversations.

Sinking down into the duvet, her visitor produced a bar of chocolate from her backpack. "I brought this to help you get well, or get well fat," she laughed, "though it apparently won't work unless it's shared."

Scarlett rubbed her palms. "The best medicine… but tell me: I think the police headed your way – so it *was* your brother, then, the secret hero, out there rescuing Mum?"

"Eh? Nope. We didn't have a clue what the police were on about. Something about lost wellies… Moreton showed his… Dad offered an ID parade of all the farm's boots," she laughed, "I think they've left the case open, for now at least."

Scarlett frowned. "I'll update Mum – the mystery rescuer and the missing boots…" lost in thought, she trailed off, then added: "It's probably just another one for the list."

In a lull of silence, Scarlett realised that if Isabel might offer any insight to Whitecross, she'd need to mirror her transparency. "Iz," she ventured, "did you come here much, before *we* got here?" She tore the wrapper and broke off another row. "I mean, who actually lived here, before? Was it empty – did you know anyone here?"

"Questions, questions!" Isabel laughed, rolling foil wrapper into a ball which she flicked, with perfect accuracy, at the bin. "We never knew of anyone, not living here, no," she chewed. "Though I used to prowl about with Moreton to peep through the windows. Sometimes, we'd dare to go into the basement – the door was always open, though it was all boarded up. Don't actually think it's been lived in, like a family home, not for yonks."

"Blimey, all those years, just empty." The bedroom door creaked gently in a change of draught.

"Yeah, but my gramp used to say it *was* busy, back in the second world war – it became a makeshift hospital, for American soldiers. Before then, he says it sat empty, but if you rewind to the first world war, it was used in a similar way – a place to patch up the wounded before they sent the poor souls back to the trenches."

"Wow, I need to bring Roan up to speed. He's the historian." She paused. "But before all that, what was it you recited from that old rhyme – about how 'the brothers dance'?"

Isabel stoped mid-bite. "Oh, I dunno, Scarlett. You know the thing with nursery rhymes – mumbo-jumbo."

"Really? I thought *Ring o'Roses* was all about the black death – don't they all have hidden truths?"

She sighed. "If I say what I know, all I know... d'you promise not to hate me?"

"If you don't tell me, I'll make you laugh in every lesson so much you get excluded."

"Okay! So, from what my family's always said – and the tales that go around..." she bunched her unruly hair, as if it might deviate her thoughts. "It all goes back to the time before the local squire built the house, back in the late 1600s. Before he built Whitecross, there was actually a different house, a farmhouse, right here. And the tenant here, he was called Jeb Tow. So he would've been the original neighbour of whoever lived back then at Valance Farm. Maybe old Jeb was some twig off our family tree, seeing as my family tree goes back forever. But anyhow, this Jeb Tow... he suddenly got evicted – turfed out."

"Who'd have done that?"

"Robert Boxwell, of course. The same bad-boy that's cloaked-up and staring out of that painting in your hall. And he did it 'cos he could. He owned the land; he was going up in the world and he fancied this location for a mansion. And here," she turned her palms to the ceiling, "we sit, in the fruit of his dark deeds: Whitecross Hall. They say someone stuck a white cross in the rubble of Jeb's farmhouse, a symbol, sympathy… the name just stuck. He probably relished it: apparently, he thrived on being a bad-ass."

"But that's terrible! Our home was literally built on a grudge?"

"Maybe, though my dad says it happened everywhere – half the country houses were built by profit through slave labour, or just stabbing people in the back, sometimes the front… " she swilled her words with the chocolate. "And *our* farm belonged to Boxwell too, so lucky for me he didn't fancy that corner of the map, or I'd not be sitting here now."

"Okay, so he cleared the spot and then he wanted to build, what? A family home?"

"Not *exactly*... he was your classic playboy, Squire Boxwell. He even had royal connections – if *Hello!* existed back then, he'd be a regular story. He lived in London and only came back here to hunt foxes – when he wasn't hunting women." Scarlett pictured Boxwell in a clichéd period drama. "So Whitecross," Isabel added, "was just a bachelor pad – for him and his mates whenever London got dull and they fancied a romp here, pillaging women and wildlife."

She thought of her own father – at least *his* plan hadn't been quite so panto. He'd been underhand, but he surely had no black heart.

"So," Scarlett shrugged, "Squire Boxwell chucks out the tenant, flattens the farm and builds this…" She paused to snap what remained of the bar in two. "Let's get to episode two. There is an episode two?"

"You bet. I'm no history expert, but it's said poor Jeb Tow had a hard time… he was banished onto higher ground, to the north – all Boxwell gives him is this barren patch – but he has to pay the same rent. He's forced to clear the land of stones, and he uses them to build a small cottage, up where the Tump is."

"The Tump?"

"Yeah – sorry – it's on part of the land we farm, half a mile from here. You just take the footpath by the bus stop and walk straight up, to Starvecrow Field, up to the far corner, where three fields meet."

"Hang on, so he built a house, but now it's a tump? How's that work?"

"Quit rushing! Sure, Jeb builds his hovel, but then the poor bugger dies – collapsed one winter morning while fetching water from the well in front of our farm. When the doctors cut him open, all his stomach holds is scavenged cob nuts and blackberries. Worked himself to death trying to keep his wife and baby. Boxwell's deal just wasn't enough."

"Ah no... a wife and a *baby*?" Scarlett winced.

"Yep, but the baby dies, not long before him."

She held her breath, sensing that worse awaited. "So, that leaves his wife... alone?"

"Exactly. His widow, Rosamond. And Ros is not happy, amazingly..."

"But she couldn't exactly take him to court?"

"No, she was powerless. Too poor to afford a proper burial, and Boxwell wouldn't help, so she buries Jeb with her own hands, piling a cairn of stones on top, at the side of the cottage. Next to their child's grave. And then, they say, she gets weaker, and weaker..."

"And what, dies?"

"You'd think so. That's where the real mystery begins. She disappears, just before 1700. Rent collector finds the cottage empty; they lock it up and leave it. Nobody wants to take it. Anyhow, next time Boxwell's back from London, he brings his mates for the usual binge. Soon they leave him though, and on the last night of his stay, Boxwell is there – well, here, come to think – alone. And there's a knock, on the door..."

Sitting bolt upright, Scarlett grabbed her hand tightly: "This a wind-up, isn't it? Isabel?"

"No wait, cross my heart... He goes to the door and there, standing back in the porch, in a hooded black robe, is this beautiful woman. I mean, we're talking super-high cheekbones, crystal-blue eyes, perfect teeth, Disney-blonde hair... "

"So what does she do, break into a catchy song?

"She says she's a nanny... she's come about 'the job'; she'd heard in the village the Master had lost his wife, and that he needs a nanny to oversee his boys."

"But wait, he had no children?"

"Yeah, even Boxwell's pretty sure of that. I guess he decides she's been pranked, but he brushes this aside – it's too late. He's spellbound."

"So... he brings her in and bla-de-bla happy ever after?"

"He certainly falls for her. At first, he makes her housekeeper. Then, whenever he goes away, he realises he just wants to be back here. For a while, Nanny – somehow the name sticks, though he knew her first name – seems to change his life; he visits London less and less; his friends say fate's snared him with the perfect woman. He never asks how or why she appeared that night; it's as if he's bewitched –"

" – Oh dear, oh dear." Scarlett cut in. "Stop! No, keep going."

"Yep, so bewitched he is, he gives up his playboy status. She gets promoted to wife, he gives her a beautiful ring, their initials linked: two Rs, back to back, stitched together," she hesitated, looking around, "I'll draw it?"

Scarlett passed a notepad and, using a pencil, Isabel fell silent as she sketched the shape. Two Rs, the first written backwards, its back square to the second, began to emerge. Scarlett studied the shape, the initials dancing upon her retinas. Alien, until they finally shifted to be something more familiar.

"It's like the shape of a headless woman, waving her arms, with her skirts billowing out…"

"Maybe…" said Isabel, "or upside-down, like this," she inverted the paper, "it's maybe a fork coming up, through a hole in the ground, like reaching up?"

Scarlett shuddered. "How d'you know all this?"

"Duh? If it was his idea or hers, he must have loved this symbol… he put it all around here, if you just open your eyes."

In a flash, Scarlett sees the day they arrived: that key her father collected… and in the hall, when Adeline first walked in, the shape, at the heart of the mosaic.

"Perhaps it was some symbol for protection?" she ventured, "You know, what's the word?"

"A talisman?"

"That's it! Well no bad seemed to come, not immediately," Isabel added. "She gives him three sons: first one, then twins. All boys. And though she's their mum, they always call her Nanny."

"So finally, all's well that ends well?"

"You can guess the answer to that. As the boys grow, she begins to act more and more strangely. Her past was murky, which Boxwell maybe likes, but there are moments, like flashes of danger. One time, they're out hunting when she yanks her horse across his. He's lucky to survive. She swears it was the horse's fault. Other times, she tries to harm *herself*. Whatever she did, Boxwell starts locking her up, claiming that it's all for her own safety."

"God, he sounds like the monster."

"So they grow apart and, by the time the boys are teenagers, he's eaten away by doubt. He suspects she's cheating, whenever he goes away. Maybe his jealousy is an excuse to keep her prisoner – it all just turns into a marriage from hell."

"Wait: 'lock her *up*,' you say… where?" She craved details, even if she knew they might never again be packed away.

"I dunno," Isabel faltered. "Anyhow," she continued, "he'd swan off to London, leaving her like a prisoner. And then one morning, when he's let her out, when she seems calmer, maybe his guard is down, she tells him her work is done, and it's time to go home."

"Home?" Scarlett stopped breathing.

"Yes, to where she belongs. Boxwell's stumped. But he follows her: she just wafts out, down the drive, across the lane and starts to tramp across Starvecrow Field, to where those three fields meet… And when she reaches the hovel Jeb built, she walks in – even though Boxwell had ordered it to be locked up. She shuts the door, climbs the ladder to the loft bed and draws the ragged old sheets over her head."

"Ah God," Scarlett shuddered. But Isabel was locked on like a terrier, dragging her onwards.

"Boxwell kept his distance, but knows where she's gone. When he reaches the door, it's locked. He holds back, but he has to know. He pounds on the door. He kicks it: no reply." Scarlett braced as Isabel drew breath. "In the end, his temper boils – he kicks the woodwork in, finds the room empty and storms up the ladder. From the top, he can make out her shape, in the bed. Under a sheet…"

Her bedspread tight around white knuckles, Scarlett's pulse raced.

Isabel leant closer: "Boxwell steps forward and challenges the hidden shape: 'What are you doing, Nanny?' but there's no movement. And then, as you'd guess, he steps closer again, ripping the sheet clean away. And what he sees literally shocks him to death… " Scarlett covered her ears, tresses from the remaining long side of her hair falling over her eyes, like a feeble screen. "Lying under the sheet was no woman, but a withered, dried-out corpse – with the leering, decayed face of an old hag.

"He can't tear his gaze away: hag or no hag, he sees those perfect teeth, that long, blonde hair. Even the staring eyes make no difference... she's a bag of dry skin, but he knows that moment whose bag of skin she is – his wife, his widow. His avenger!" Triumph glinted in Isabel's pupils. "In his panic, he turns and whacks his head on a beam, falling back and landing beside his crispy wife. And when he tries to break away, her clawed hand's on his jacket like Velcro... and there, on the *third* finger of that hand, dangling on the bone... he sees it. The same ring he'd given his wife to cherish. Death finally caught him in her grasp."

"Oh. My. God!" Scarlett squealed, "Isabel! That's disgusting!"

"Yeah, but that's not all." She was in her stride now.

"Okay, I want the whole story, I guess... but," Scarlett interrupted, "I need to show you something... "

Scarlett in pyjamas, Isabel still in her school uniform, the two made a curious couple as they slunk past Roan's silent room and on, beyond the door marked 12. Ahead, a doorway at the end of the corridor marked the entrance to the north tower. Scarlett turned the heavy key in the lock, and pulled the door a fraction to reveal the foot of a spiral stone staircase.

"It's the way up, to the tower; Roan's been in, at long last he found this key, but I haven't wanted to go up, not alone..." she faltered. "Remember when Adeline came, the other day?"

"Yeah, she was a good laugh."

"She emailed me after; she said she'd had a dream, about a woman locked up here – it sounds mad, but it's some coincidence, isn't it?"

Isabel stopped. "A dream? Yeah, but two plus two never equals a hundred, Scar."

"True, but when she came up, as she was leaving with her dad, maybe she saw something, something that put an idea into her subconscious? Come with me, Iz: I need to check what she told me – and I'm never doing this on my own."

Isabel paused, but any question remained unspoken. Scarlett pushed the door further ajar and, together, they stepped into the cold.

Tom Benn was in his usual chair at the Mayfair club when Richard was led over. Brimming with glee, he jumped up.

"Dicky boy! How marvellous!" he bellowed. "I trust you bear good news? No wait, how rude… waiter, can you fix me another brace of these?"

Nodding meekly, Richard sunk in the opposite armchair, thighs squeaking on stiff, button-back leather.

As ever, the mood in his old London haunt was expensively subdued, he reflected, as he gently compressed his left arm, feeling the paperwork concealed within his jacket.

room 13

The climb twisted like an argument in stone, fifty steps, their limestone centres hollowed by countless feet. As their path turned, the sound of a window flapping grew stronger, a wince of cold metal against stone. The temperature dropped with every step, sucking warmth from their clothes; Scarlett wished she'd grabbed a dressing gown. Pyjamas didn't cut it here.

Near the top, a ceiling of mesh grating blocked their path. Scarlett shoved it upwards and the frame shuddered, peppering them in rust. They emerged in the centre of an empty space.

There was no switch, but the sunset still offered enough light to reveal the room's reaches. Someone, some time, had swept it clean.

"So... the thirteenth room. Unlucky. It does feel like a prison, of sorts." Isabel wondered. "But the view's amazing!" She stepped cautiously past each opening. "Not that it would be much compensation, if you were locked in. It ties up with something else I heard..."

"About Squire Boxwell?" She spoke his name reluctantly.

"Huh? No... more recent stuff: in the first world war they'd bring wounded soldiers up here. Dad said one of the old boys at the pub had an aunt who was a nurse; she said they took some of the patients up here. The ones who'd be a danger to themselves. They found it calmed them, because of the view. Better than a trench, I guess?"

Scarlett checked each window. One sat ajar, at the far corner, overlooking the driveway. The air streamed in, carrying a scent of rain; she secured the handle, as best she could. Standing back and rubbing her hands, she took out her mobile, checking for a signal. Two bars. It'd do.

"I'm gonna call Adeline."

Isabel raised an eyebrow. She answered immediately.

"Adi? Hi, it's me... yeah... well, I should be okay for the weekend, still feel a bit yucky... Listen, I know it sounds mad, but you know that email you sent, about your dream?" She did. "And in this dream... you did say there were bars, on the windows?" She did. Isabel gazed out as a cluster of crows wheeled around the tower, tumbling and cackling their secrets.

"Okay, well that's a relief. Yeah, I'm up there now, with Iz, just scoping the place out. I reckon it was all a bad dream, a coincidence – perhaps something that picture triggered, under the stairs... it did freak you out?

Anyhow, that picture, it definitely has no woman shrieking from the window – I've checked it... And best of all – well, best for me – there are no iron bars, not up here."

That painting must have jumbled her brain, she told herself.

"Sorry, Iz," she said, pocketing her phone. "Adeline told me something, after she came up. It made me sense a connection... with all of these stories."

She turned to run her hand along the ledge of the closest window. Nothing, just welcome dust. "To be honest," she said, holding her fingertips to the fading light, "if there *had* been proof of iron bars, I think I'd be telling Dad to call an exorcist – and bin that creepy painting."

Looking northwards and down through the thinning trees, she could just make out the stone eagles that guarded the gateway. She remembered the day she first saw them. Was she still ill at ease? Definitely. Yet that wasn't everything. She resisted it, but if Whitecross were a locked box, she wouldn't be backing off now. She'd prise it open, shake out the contents, force them into a meaningful shape. Wasn't that the only way to put this to rest?

Lost in thought, she stepped forward to the next window. From here, looking beyond the gates and across the lane, she could see the land rise to a distinct bulge. Like a tumour. The highest corner of Starvecrow Field. So that's it, the tump, or as she now knew it, Nan Tow's Tump. But if it was a *cottage* 300 years ago, how did it change into little more than a mound? Turning to ask Isabel that very question, she swished a careless fingertip along the window ledge.

Something cut her skin.

In the fading light, she raised the finger to her face and watched a bead of blood grow. Stooping closer, colour drained from her face: there, in the masonry, protruding enough to present a rough edge: a sawn-off stump.

The stump of an iron bar.

Quickly, she searched above. There, too, on the corresponding recess... With mounting unease, she revisited the other windows. Every casement, the same. Despair and bewilderment surged: how had she not used her eyes?

Isabel seemed oblivious. Or already knew. Leaning on the opposite wall, her knees began to give way. Slowly, she slumped to the floorboards, hands flat, fingers splayed. Beneath heavy eyelids, her eyes darted, as if watching a tragedy unfold.

"You know he locked her up here, when she began to behave untoward?" she slurred. "The boys, they hated it, but he says it is for her own good. 'The only way she'll understand,' he told them. So much for *trust*!" In a tone of confession, her face contorted, her features a bloodless mask. "And then, my sweet, is when the words were written."

Scarlett drew nearer. "What do you mean, 'the words'?" Kneeling before her, she took Isabel's hand as a tether to the here and now. Her skin was cold as the air, her breathing shallow. Like some Pre-Raphaelite beauty, she was transported. When she finally stirred, her breath and words felt relayed from beyond and her eyes snapped wide, ugly flashes of a face behind her own.

"Squire Boxwell, he got his dues, all right!"

Scarlett recoiled as a hard bark replaced Isabel's voice. "Went the same way as her, in the end. They found him, 'neath his sheet, in his bedchamber. Lyin' still, just like he'd found Nanny beyond Starvecrow. He'd stopped eating," she rasped, "after he found her, up at the hut: he needed no food for his journey. No one ne'er got no sense nor meanin' off him again. In short days, t'was all over…"

The final words escaped like moths, tumbling from her lips into the pale light. Scarlett anchored Isabel's body with her hands, but sensed her moving away, moving out of reach, and this body, her route back, stretching to snapping point.

"What do you mean, 'she *wrote*'? You're scaring me now, Iz… Iz?"

For a while, the form said nothing. She tried a different approach: "Tell me, then, if poor Nanny was locked away up here, how could she write anything? It makes no sense. Did she leave letters?"

"I, I," Isabel struggled, her legs flexing straight, as if yanked by chains invisible. "When you have no choice, there is always a way. I… *she,* she took a splinter, from the floor." Isabel's eyes roamed the boards, as if she was seeking the place. "And she used it first, to draw her blood." She held the invisible splinter to a point just above her wrist, to skin that bore the marks of so many linear scars Scarlett had never before noticed. "And then she wrote it, all across this wall."

"She wrote *what?* You have to tell me. We need to know, Isabel…"

"He didn't find it 'til after she was dead. He just used to push her in through the door, lock her in. Day upon day. Just a bowl for her kitchen and a bucket for her needs. Not so much as a blanket and the wind just whistling,

whistling through the bars. Here is where she died. Her body lay here… t'was not her flesh and bone, t'was her spirit what drew him home."

Scarlett stared aghast. Across the room, a loose pane shuddered in its decayed frame, humming to the wind's breath. Isabel's eyes closed. But in no peaceful slumber.

"No… tell me, Iz, stay with me…"

"What was written out, all across the wall, was what was always sung, when she was singin' them boys to sleep. Boxwell always thought it just that, just a lullaby." She laughed, but her eyes remained shut and Scarlett felt a thousand tiny hairs stand to life.

But then the form fixed on her with a piercing gaze. Scarlett flinched away: in the room's pallor, her pupils were shot with the steel of a winter moon. She strained to escape, but in her grasp she could neither move nor look away as the voice within Isabel began its song:

> I buried my love, by the ol' broken wall
> And I buried my heart, o'er the loss of them all,
> But my heart will be free as the wind in the trees,
> And all life that I give, will be here, never leave,
> Will be here, never leave…"

Behind Scarlett, unseen, the words glowed fresh across the wall, fading instantly as the voice stopped, all breath spent, pupils devoid. Transfixed, she watched as Isabel's eyes slowly returned to their familiar green, like pools of thawing ice. Bit by bit, her aura returned to her flesh.

"He didn't find the words," she gestured, across the room, "until the day after she died, after he followed her in the hovel, but found her body here. He might have scrubbed them off, but their echo stayed, like a rhythm that would only stop with his heart."

WHAM!

They flinched as a door, far below, slammed shut. Scarlett jumped as the air buffeted around them, the force jolting Isabel to her senses.

"It's just the draught." Her hand calmed Isabel's brow, voice steady, though her skin was drum-tight. She helped her to her feet and, dusting their clothes, they move towards the steps. But then another sound. A key, in a lock. Turning forcefully, as if a hand were righting a mistake.

In a bundle of confusion and fear, they rush headlong and Scarlett was first to the bottom stair: she grabbed the handle, tugged it and pushed. It was solid. They both screamed and kicked against the frame.

"Let us out!" Scarlett yelled. "Roan! Open it! Roan! What the hell?"

But there was no sound, no footsteps.

And Scarlett knew already: Roan was nowhere near.

necrosis

Scarlett knew her parents had gone out but still pressed HOME. After 10 rings, Roan finally answered.

"So funny, Roan, *completely* hilarious," she spat.

"You what? *What now?*" he mumbled.

"Just LET US OUT!"

"Where are you? I thought you were in your room. Wait, I can hear you… I mean, not on the phone… what? You're in the tower? I'm coming."

"*Someone* locked us in," Scarlett declared, as he turned the key.

Roan ignored her. "Sorry about that, Isabel. Maybe it was the wind, maybe the lock wasn't fully turned and a draught blew the door, so the jolt turned it and – "

"– Yeah, that well-known thing when wind locks doors."

"Well, don't look at me, it's not strange, not for this place."

Slack shouldered, he turned back for his room.

"So what's eating *him*?" asked Isabel. She wondered if Scarlett was in denial: wasn't it obvious he'd not done it?

"No idea, but he found that key, *he* matched it to this door… it's not rocket science."

"Everything alright, Scarliebabes?"

Scowling into her phone, she huddled close to the Aga while her mother unloaded shopping around her.

"Isabella not staying for supper then?"

"Nah, she had to go. And it's Is-a-*bel*. She's not a *'Bella'*, thank God."

"I consider myself corrected."

Scarlett contemplated adding that Isabel's departure *possibly* had something to do with the fact that she'd popped round for a cosy chat, but ended up being sucked into a dimension where the ancient spirit of a woman – probably, yeah, definitely a witch – floated by for a chat… that same spirit, perhaps another – who knows? – subsequently locking them in the north tower. But, on balance, she decided, maybe best keep it to herself.

"So... you're alive enough, for going in tomorrow?" Joanna raised a sarcastic palm to Scarlett's taut forehead.

"I suppose, if it gets everyone off my back... "

"Oh that *poor* back of yours, darling," she pouted. "There's no need to do anything for *us*... it's all about you putting in an effort for *yourself*. You know all this," she urged, squeezing her unyielding arm. "As your dad says, a day missed is crucial at this stage in – "

"– My *edu-ca-shun*... yeah Mum, for the *millionth* time," she groaned, but added: "At least it'd be a change of scene."

"Absolutely! It's bad for the soul, wallowing in this fusty hole with all your unhealthy relatives. Speaking of which, where's Roan? Don't tell me, he's *still* on that screen?"

"I guess."

"Well could you give him a 10-minute warning? Dad'll be back soon – he's bringing a Chinese."

"Cool. Will do."

She cleared the chocolate wrapper from her bed and checked her snails before trying Roan's door. Now she'd calmed down, she felt guilty. A bit.

No answer. She knocked again, louder. Still nothing.

Gently, she peered in. He was on his bed and, in a bluish light from his computer, hardly looked in good shape.

"You okay?"

Looking at her, he didn't speak. Moving closer, Scarlett made out a gleam of sweat on his brow. Reluctantly, she took his hand. It was limp, like room-temperature meat. In her mind, an alarm bell sounded.

"Roe, can you *hear* me?" Surely two people couldn't go transcendental on her in one day? Roan struggled as if he couldn't move his arms, an invisible pressure on his windpipe. Then the hand that felt so inert shot out, clamping her by the arm. Hard.

"Get out, we don't need you here!" he hissed. Stumbling backwards, and quick as her legs could go, Scarlett fled.

⊙━┱

"So no recent holidays... school trips abroad?"

Perched at the edge of the bed while her parents fretted, Doctor Cramley peered into Roan's throat and ran through what Scarlett presumed were scripted questions. Diagnosis-wise, Roan was either off-colour, properly sick or about to become a full-on zombie.

"No, nowhere," said Joanna, pacing the room. "I made him tea, he's taken a few sips with a couple of pain killers since we rang – I guessed that couldn't hurt?" Richard tried, and failed, to calm her.

"There's a little fever, his body's fighting something," the doctor added. "It's sensible to start him on antibiotics – keep a close eye and that's all good, for now."

For now: that was a cold comfort, Scarlett sensed.

"With the course in his system, I'm sure he'll be right as rain," the he concluded, giving his patient a gentle farewell pat on the leg.

But the pat was no help: Roan flexed as if a needle had been recklessly jabbed deep into his thigh.

"That's curious. There's no rash on his torso, but best check his legs – maybe there's something specific."

He began to remove the bedclothes. For his dignity, Scarlett turned away, even if her brother was beyond caring. So all she saw was her father's face, turning shroud-white, as her mother gasped.

"It's okay, I've seen worse," Dr Cramley said. "A local infection was making you poorly, young man."

He fingers a saucer of dark skin which surrounds what could only be a large, glistening wart.

"Where the hell did *that* come from?" Richard asks.

"My guess is your son had a small growth, most probably harmless, maybe he knocked it, and it got infected," he added. "But he's been rejecting it: if you look closely, his system's been fighting, isolating the area. In fact," he took a tissue from his bag, applying it to the protuberance and affecting a bold twist, "presto! See, there was barely anything anchoring it."

Clenching his teeth, Roan convulsed with the tug, but seemed instantly relieved at divorce from the alien parasite. Glimpsing roots of flesh dangling from the wart, Scarlett felt her gag reflex tighten. Unfussed, the doctor held the object to the light and fished in his bag for a specimen tube.

"You've made an interesting start to my shift, young man, a welcome change to bad backs and migraines."

Scarlett wondered which was more queasy: that familiar slug of skin, or the enthusiasm of someone enjoying such work a *bit* too much?

"I'll send it to pathology, in Gloucester." With an audible slop, the moist lump dropped into the tube, which he stored in his briefcase "But not to worry: this kind of necrosis is common – just let the area breathe, keep it dry and don't skip the antibiotics."

Yet Scarlett knew this wasn't 'common'. How otherwise would their lab explain it?

Dr Cramley readily accepted the offer of a nightcap, although he would have nothing stronger than tea. Joanna dunked his teabag before dropping it into the bin; soon after, the doctor's curiosity got the better of him, his new patients agreeing to take him on a brief tour of Whitecross. Any previous occupants must have been exceptionally healthy, he said: no colleague could ever recall visiting.

The kitchen empty for 10 minutes, there was time enough for the wart to be retrieved for its rightful owner, an act so stealthy no one, not even Mustard, suspected anything, although his nose twitched in the wake of the air's disturbance, alerted by a whiff of living archaeology.

Pathology didn't report back, the technicians chalking it up as a bizarre error. Either that, or they would have been forced to record Roan Wycherley as the planet's first human to grow a teabag.

conclusions

"So much for your science, Professor Zadoc."

Like a praying mantis, Edmund crouched before the fireplace in the smoke-blackened room, warming his slender limbs on the evening's last embers. Watching Zadoc return through the panel, the brief spill of light from the Wycherley's kitchen illuminated his face, framed by a tangle of hair that hung in greasy tails.

"Ah, mock me as a jolly, but at least I had the heart to *try*," Zadoc declared, holding up the trophy of regained flesh.

"Mockery? Verily, you make infinite material. But pray, little brother, what will you now tell your dear Jacob? That your sick experiment, which risked greater proximity to death's door than any of us has known, was a spectacular flop?"

"Edmund, you were there; *you* agreed to my hypothesis: had the implanted flesh survived upon the boy's body, had it not decayed in daylight, we would know something new. Verily, it *was* an experiment, yet no harm is done." Zadoc growled, but Edmund would not let go.

"Fool! Did you earnestly believe that allowing even the slightest part of ourselves to be exposed, in *raw daylight*, beyond these walls..." he faltered, as if suffocating, "that the survival of this pathetic morsel of flesh, stuck to the body of a young boy, would determine we could walk free?" Tresses of his hair danced against his threadbare velvet collar.

"Stuck? I implanted it with the utmost craft. Had the boy remained well, yes, it could have proved her words no longer hold binding force. And yes, then, we might have encouragement to walk free."

Edmund hissed. "Deprived as they are of connection to a reasoning brain, I nonetheless trust your eyes still have the sense to see that, *by our slow decay,* we are always and ever dying? All that we know, all we've ever known, is that the only way to preserve our chances and resist fate is to keep ourselves together. Jacob made a mistake when he fled and thereby scagged himself, an error compounded by your reckless science, leaving the wretch a-bed, his soul leaching from the loss. Who knows how long his recovery needs, or if he may ever be restored?"

Spying a woodlouse at his feet, he paused to cup it in his palm, before softening his tone: "Well, if there is a lesson, losing that morsel of himself might illustrate the folly of crow husbandry. I always said you can't farm the poor wretches."

"But isn't that it?" asked Zadoc. "Did Jacob not merely wish to prove he could be of more use? What if *you* fell ill? Would it not be wise for one of us to acquire such skills as you possess?"

"Why fix a scheme never broken?" Edmund laughed. "We all know the only way to harvest a crow is by moonlight, when they are drunk with sleep. 'Tis quick, 'tis noiseless; I have them plucked, prepared and all you need do is cook, open, chew and swallow. If he hadn't been nearly caught with his caged livestock, this fiasco would never have happened. Who knows how much damage such separation of flesh might bring?"

Zadoc grunted. He knew he alone was a master with a scalpel; a skill learned through two world wars, spying on surgeons; watching through a spy-hole, he would painstakingly replicate their work on stolen joints of meat. Had Master Roan felt any pain from his supple blade? Besides, was it *his* fault the infant failed the experiment? A surgeon's lot was to keep a steady, quick hand. Beyond that, nature was the nurse.

"Perhaps you'd have it we live on churchpigs for eternity?" Reaching out, he plucked the woodlouse from Edmund's palm and flicked it into the back of his throat. "Like eating ourselves, is it not? They scuttle around, hide in the shadows, cower in fear." Chewing the gritty mass into a paste, he adds, clacking his tongue: "And their taste? A cannibal savour of diddly-squat. Remind you of anything?"

"That this 'life' lacks flavour? Indeed, Zadoc, we've endured 300 years to illustrate that, but enough banter, get to him! Speak no more of this. Repair the wretched bit whence it came, and let us hope his flesh conjoins with our hopes."

"'Tis all but done," Zadoc sarcastically bowed. "But indulge me, Edmund: although we have always deferred to your seniority, perhaps ask yourself *who* will play the fool here? You speak of keeping us from death's door, yet today we are practically licking the varnish. How many more score years shall we hide, avoiding death's shadow so much we are terrified of our own? Sooner or later, we will decay; death shall finally take us: not even *her* curse can conquer that?"

Edmund stared into the glowing ash as Zadoc threaded his limbs through the narrow gap, disappearing into the corridor that leads to the ladder. He listened as feet clambered up rungs, a muffle of words. Zadoc and Jacob's voices blurred, rendering it impossible to know one twin from the other. As ever, he sat apart from their cosy symmetry. But he knew Jacob would be relieved for his flesh returned. And angry or not with Zadoc, he savoured that reassurance. Their constant wish must be to be fit for today; tomorrow could taunt its threats, but tomorrow, fate showed countless times, never came.

"We will not fight you, death," he spoke to the embers. "But you shall not consume us, not *before* we taste real life."

His mind drifted to an image of walking free, not by night, not on legs that trapped him in a kaleidoscope of pain; a dream of breathing sweet summer air, of seeing through eyes that felt no scourge of sunlight. It felt brief, but the encroachment of death freed a surge in his heart: he sensed a rising resolve, fuelled by certainty that the three of them had less and less to lose. A glow kindled in his eyes as his leathery cheeks tautened into a smile his ancient face rarely knew.

"As brothers, we have already known eternity, hidden brothers, living beyond natural law, starved brothers, shut away without hope of kindness, under brothers, banished beneath the shadow of a poisonous will. Is this how our story ends?"

With a final flurry of sparks, darkness enrobed the room, but still he spoke – louder, more sure than ever.

"The time for suffering our guests is finished," he laughed, his thorax flexing like a basket.

"The time for children's games is over."

sacred texts

Sun Nov 8 20.15pm
From: adelinebenn@74lincolnvale.co.uk
To: scarlettwycherley@whitecrosshall.com

Hi Scarlie, Gutted you missed the bash. Guess I overdid the Hallowe'en make-up – didn't manage a snog. Hope you haven't been having more horrors yourself… Sorry about the tower stuff – I was definitely seeing things. So any more dates with Mr Heathcliff, or you playing it cool? He must have noticed your new look? Questions, questions… meet up soon? I can jump in with Dad when he has an excuse for escaping – he's making noises about seeing your dad. Keep me posted!

Love ya heaps, Adi xxx

Sun Nov 8 21.09pm
From: scarlettwycherley@whitecrosshall.com
To: adelinebenn@74lincolnvale.co.uk

Yay Adi, Yeah, sorry about the no-show and lack of party thrills. Moreton's playing a waiting game, if he ever liked me… don't know if he'd make a move, seeing as I'm mates with his sister – all too nextdoorsy? Maybe he just doesn't fancy me, hair/no hair. All quiet in house of horror. Be great to see you… tho my dad's usually desperate for an excuse to get to London, so will see what's possible… Scar xx

Closing her laptop, Scarlett knew she was shutting Adeline out. Not that she didn't trust her, but her old friend's imagination, her willingness to conjure up any sort of scenario, made her dangerous. The whole story of Nan Tow, as much as she knew of it herself, she'd happily keep to herself. And as for self-locking tower doors and that vile growth? She shuddered to picture Adeline feasting on that.

    And what was all this about Moreton? She pinched her leg at the thought. Somehow he had skulked into her thoughts. Yet what thoughts? Nice ones, she'd admit. Just Isabel saying his name sent something ricocheting.

She knew she liked him; she just never wanted liking to waft into *expecting*. As she said to Adeline, even if – and that was a massive 'if' – he was ever interested in her, wouldn't being mates with Isabel ward him off? And then there was Moreton himself. He was so shy, damn it. All of which made the alert from her phone, as she got into bed, more head-spinning:

Hi Scar, Isabel gave me yr no. Just checking all OK? M

As she reads, another follows:

Sorry M = Moreton… Anyhow this is my number. PS cool cut.

Scarlett smiled; he'd even written 'Scar'. And he'd noticed, not that her hair was that easy to miss. So maybe he wasn't shy? At least not by text. Well *she* wouldn't be.

Hi M. No, all Okay-ish. Hair = experiment. More follows? Or less. CU tomorrow ;) SCAR x

She pressed 'send', then panicked: an 'X' and a winking face? seriously? Too clichéd, too… romantic? She screamed for unsend. The escape of sleep took ages, but she was in deep when the knock came.

slow food

"Jacob needs sustenance." Zadoc lifted the fireside pot and sniffed the familiar stale gruel. "Something to rouse his appetite, a restorative concoction. Ingenious as I am, man cannot live on corvidae alone."

On the table lay a battered tome borrowed from the library. It appeared he was in search of nostalgia: *The Epicure's Guide to Family Cookrie* being a 1797 publication.

Oaty beef? Admirable, yet no oats, no beef. The Wycherleys' refrigerator was scandalous, the contents of their bin even worse. Half the comestibles he couldn't even recognise: most were shrouded in foul plastic, making it difficult to sample without betraying their meddling. Nevertheless, he had discreetly swilled his tongue through what purported to be 'Greek' yoghurt, pronouncing it more palatable than Mrs Wycherley's staple diet of cottage cheese, not to mention the infernal chaff in the larder labelled 'breakfast cereal'.

At page 85, he paused. Devilled kidneys. Offal? Workhouse food. Onwards he leafed, to the desserts. Perhaps a posset, syllabub or spunge might not be impossible? He rolled his furrowed tongue at the promise of gooey dessert. Delicious, but a distraction: what of the meat?

He raised his eyes to the ceiling. All was quiet. Jacob slept, tucked in his cavity beneath the girl's bed; by now, it was dark enough for Edmund to be abroad, checking his traps, creeping well-worn paths. Oh well, perhaps curried crow tonight? But he knew how that would go down: his brothers loathe anything exotic, their ancient plumbing convulsing at the mere aroma. In despair, he returned to earlier pages. *Peppered gammon?* Succulent, but pie in the sky. It had to be something within gathering distance, bagged by stealth, before the sun's savage curfew. Light of finger as Edmund may be, he couldn't picture him felling and portioning a pig. Not after the last time.

He flicked to the index. A few notes on the pretentious palates of the French made amusing reading. But wait: here. Something extraordinary. And untried in living memory. Frogs' legs may have been a disaster when they had attempted them (a pragmatic substitution of toads being part of that gristly dilemma), but escargots, surely, were easily foraged? Plenty of stones unturned in the gardens. An idiot could do it, so why not Edmund? And oh, what relief from a thousand ways with woodlice?

"Yessss!" he exclaimed, "By George! This looks splendid!"

The heading read: *Garlicked snails in cream.* By curled fingernail, he guided his sight along the text, licking crinkled lips at the promised revival of ancient tastebuds.

"Heavenly ssssssnails," he drooled.

"What *exactly* do you read?" a voice asked. He'd been so engrossed he hadn't heard the rungs, or the soft pad of his brother's rag-bound feet.

"Nothing Jacob! Well, it was to be a surprise. I thought something less mundane than crow might enliven your flesh."

"That is thoughtful, Zadoc. Sorry I startled: being abed can be so dull." He blew feebly into the fire, the glow illuminating the bandage on his forearm. With no sign of blood seeping through, Zadoc judged the misadventure safe to forget.

"It is eternal consolation to have been blessed with a brother who has always remained human," Jacob mused. "Eternity is quite a long time to be stuck with the... *alternative.*"

Zadoc chuckled. "Oh, Edmund... he means well. I saw the humanity in his eyes these past few days, it survives, beneath that crust of melancholia." Their laughter was shorthand for a single frame of mind.

"So, a grand supper of *snails*, eh? It's certainly *different.*"

"Yes," said Zadoc, "and an easy task for our hunter-gatherer. Snails from the garden and, if we are lucky, cream – Edmund's light fingers can coax sufficient milk from the Valance herd as they sleep."

"Bravo, dear brother. But what of an easier, more grandiose feast?" Jacob's milk-white eyes darted as, drawing closer, he whispered: "I picture something more *meaty.*"

"How so?" Zadoc quivered.

"Come! See!"

Barely deeper than a coffin, Jacob's bedroom, a compartment that formed the base beneath Scarlett's bed, was pitch black. Clawing his fingernails, Jacob located a loose knot in the wood. Wiggling it free, a shaft of light pierced the chamber. Silently, he urged his brother closer and, with his better eye, Zadoc drew focus.

"It's no good! Afford me a better view."

"Certainly." With a deft blow from Jacob's pointy elbow, the entire panel popped loose. Carefully, they angled it free, their blanched faces bathed in the room's electric light. Zadoc extended a hand to move the overhanging duvet aside as his brother jabbed excitedly with a finger towards a point, near the window.

"What need for eyes? Just follow your nose!"

Zadoc inhaled and squinted. A glass tank. Finally, he knew.

And the idea was delicious.

a house, moving

"What the hell? It's the middle of the night, Roan!" Scarlett glared across the landing at his dishevelled form.

"I'd ask the same question of *you!*"

"Well *you* knocked on *my* door!" she snapped.

"Seriously? Maybe you're sleepwalking – that knock was on *my* door. End of."

Both knew their mutual wake-up call would never be explained.

"What time *is* it, anyhow?" Scarlett shivered, peering down into the cold hallway.

"Five thirty – not quite middle of the night. I'm gonna make a drink, I'll never sleep now." He shambled towards the stairs. "D'you wanna come?"

Hot chocolate by the Aga felt better than lying in, angsting about Moreton, course work, Mum, Dad, Mum *and* Dad and the small matter of her home being possessed by a door-locking, door-knocking, spirit. But as they neared the kitchen, the curtain across the front door billowed up, a balloon of air blasting from beneath. They stood transfixed.

"Hello! How are you two up so early?"

Richard looked gaunt, but hardly matched their expectation of a phantom. All the same, he was ghostly enough.

"Must have been something we ate," Scarlett offered. "You're back early – how was London?"

"Ah, you know, the usual. Never liked sleeping in hotel beds." He stooped to pick up the local paper, tucking it beneath his briefcase. "Well, as we're all ahead of the sparrows, might as well get breakfast on. I thought I'd surprise you... obviously not."

Scooting past his sleep-deprived children, Richard dumped his bag, the local paper concealed beneath it on a kitchen chair. Favouring a lamp to the overhead light, he strode across the room. It clicked on, and all three jolted at what awaited, there on the table.

At its highest point, it was just over two feet tall, perhaps three across. Built on a wooden base, only a strong light would later reveal what lay beneath its layers of paint: an entire structure made from matchsticks. Yet there was something compellingly real, in every detail. They circled it like awkward gods, pondering the mortals within.

"Blimey, I guess you didn't whittle this up in a spare moment, Roe?" Richard gasped.

"Er, no, not *quite*," Roan stuttered. He didn't look to Scarlett, but knew she would agree: someone, something, was playing a game. One they'd never asked to join.

"We *found* it, actually, Dad," Scarlett blurted. "Yeah, up in that old junk, the fifth bedroom… we thought it'd make an ornament… and brought it down as a surprise?"

"Yeah," Roan added, "and it got *me* thinking: maybe I could adapt it into a, er, nice lamp? Or even a Christmas decoration?"

"Well hold that thought, Roe, let's not rush." Richard's eyes roved across the front door, up to the bedroom windows, then to the tower on the left-hand corner. Scarlett wondered if he doesn't look a little sad as his fingertip lingered on the tower windows, tracing their delicate frames. Then he drew back. Quickly.

"It's so fragile," he whispered, "if you start fiddling, it might just – "

"– Fall apart?" Scarlett snorted, "Like the real thing?"

"Well, I suppose…" He yawned, straightened his back and mumbled about the urge for coffee.

"How about you whisk up breakfast and Roe and I get sorted for school?" Scarlett suggested.

"Scarlie, that is a great plan."

"What the hell was *that* all about?" she hissed, as they retreated upstairs.

"I know, *I know*… I thought *you'd* put that model there, after all, *you* found it, but I knew you'd not go into that room again. Not alone…"

At the final stair to the landing, she paused: "Roe, it sounds crazy, but it's like someone's trying to talk to us."

"Well they're using a very odd language. More like trying to scare our pants off."

Scarlett grunted as they continued towards Roan's door. "Listen Roe, I know you can't remember what happened, but all of that strange stuff with that *thing,* in the matchbox… we've got to keep our heads together." He looked bemused. "There's no point telling Dad – not about the wart, the dollhouse – not *anything*. He'll think we're making up rubbish because we hate living here," she whispered. "And as for Mum, she's angsty enough as it is…"

"Yep, she's the über-angstmeister… So what do we do?"

"Simple. First, we need *evidence*. Hard facts."

"How?"

"We need to *record* whatever this is: get it on film."

"Okaaay," he faltered. "So technology… motion detection? I can sort that out."

"Brilliant! At last, a point to being a geek."

"I've got those birdwatching cameras somewhere. We need to download an app, then leave them running."

"Cool. And if we get something solid, *then* go to Mum and Dad?"

"They'd *have* to believe us."

"Oh my God, can you imagine? Dad will probably rent the place to ghost hunters."

"Or just flog it?"

Wasn't *that* his sister's dream come true? But glancing at her watch, Scarlett's eyes widened: if she wasn't going to meet the bus looking like a corpse, time was running out. And *he'd* be on that bus.

Standing before her mottled mirror, guessing how much make-up would trigger a detention, Scarlett thought of nothing but Moreton, realising she did so most of all when actively trying not to. She wondered: could she confide in him? He'd surely be safer to talk to than Isabel. After her trance in the tower, she feared his sister was susceptible to any energy that came her way – good or bad. Did Isabel thrive on trouble? Did trouble thrive on her? Maybe it was in her blood? After all, if some murky ancestry showed the Boxwells and the Valances locked in a perpetual historical dance, did whatever lingered in Whitecross also flow in Isabel's veins? And Moreton… he shared that blood. But no, not Moreton?

Sure, he was intuitive in an emergency, but he didn't give an impression of someone with *more* than five senses. Sometimes, she reflected, five seemed a push.

"Oh *sod!*" Time had stood still, but only in her head. Eyeliner like drunk spiders, she flicked off the light and rushed from her room, forgetting to top up Derek and Daisy's food. Finally remembering, she doubled back to their case, peeling and lobbing in a bruised banana from the bottom of her school bag. "A treat!" she called, over her shoulder.

The garden gate clanged as she jogged the short cut to the lane and Zadoc, from his crevice, salivated over the final checklist of ingredients.

Derek and Daisy in a rusty bucket at his feet.

sins of the father

"A little reading matter," Richard whispered.

Placing the details on their bed with the breakfast tray, he opened the curtains. A dream house, near London; she'd had to love it. Pulling the curtains apart, he took no notice of the intricate pattern of frost, etched across the window pane. The children having left, now seemed a good moment to test his wife's reactions.

Joanna fumbled for her glasses. "And why would I want to look at *house details?*"

"Sorry, dear?" He browsed his newspaper intently.

Chewing her toast, she remained silent, even if what she saw *did* look amazing: a house so immaculate, rooms so white you'd need sunglasses. Tidy gardens, even an infinity swimming pool, all within walking distance from the tube... who wouldn't drool?

"It's great," she finally said, "but what's it to us?"

"Nothing, except the price: it's what we could *afford*, if you put your name next to mine."

"Aha!" Joanna laughed. "The fog lifts. This smells of *Tom Benn.*"

"Oh, and this, too." He placed the legal papers in front of her and retreated to the kitchen.

Within seconds, a scream rang out.

Richard rushed back, dressing gown flapping around his ankles.

"What is it, what is it?" Surely the flipping contract wasn't *that* terrifying? She was beneath the duvet, a wavering finger jutting out, pointing towards the window.

"There was this cracking sound, the window pane, there... look! It just split apart!"

He followed her gaze. A zigzag in the glass runs from top to bottom, through an entire pane, dissecting the frieze of ice.

"It's nothing, maybe some frost got into the old glass and forced it apart?" He reached out to smooth away a protruding shard of ice.

But ice it wasn't.

"Ouch!" he yelled. Holding his fingertip to the light, he teased out a long splinter, then sucked and blew on the cut, his hot breath blasting against the pane. As he focuses on the bright ball of blood, his breath melted the glaze of frost that surrounded the cracked glass and he was oblivious to the disappearing initials.

Carved within the tracery of ice, a matching pair of Rs, the first reversed, their swooshing tails curling into the suggestion of an incomplete heart. Slowly, the insignia faded, only the cracked pane remaining.

Scarlett held her distance behind Moreton on the last stretch to the bus. He hadn't noticed her. She'd thought to call out, but if they got talking, what if there was more time to the school gate than their conversation might cover?

She focused on his back. Maybe all that farm work had given him a certain maturity that might not be typical of a year-twelve boy? She liked his gait, not swaggering with a weight of imagined muscle, like some from his year. And then there was the way his rucksack dangled from one shoulder. His hair was certainly, to her taste, too long. She'd make an exception, she decided, before telling her inner commentator to clear off.

God, she sighed, is there anything of the existence of Moreton Valance not to like? The liking exhausted her. Before long, a neon sign would sprout above her head, I ♥ MORETON. She disdained any use of 'nice', yet here it was: subtle as a clown at a funeral. Nearing the bus stop, she tried to divert her thoughts. They surely had many places to go.

A plaster on his finger, Richard stacked the dishwasher and contemplated supper. He checked the larder; somehow they were down to their last clove of garlic. Didn't they have more? He added in to a mental list: Things That Keep Disappearing. Leaving the kitchen, he remembered the local paper, tucked under his bag.

He straightens the front page. As predicted, Tom Benn's schemes were now an open secret:

MALL PLAN DEFEATED!
VILLAGERS in Whitecross are celebrating halting a bid for a retail mall. The plans, from London-based Western Mall Developments, looked set to transform the centre of Whitecross.

But a community campaign paid off when district councillors ruled that the project was too big.

"After this battle, we're confident this developer won't come back," said one campaigner.

However, the council won't confirm rumours the same developer is negotiating an alternative site nearby.

Framing the page, he took a picture and texted it to Tom:

So plan A's dead – plan B now raring to go?

Then he safely filed the paper.
In the bin.

Isabel's trip

It was not until the bus home that Scarlett spoke to him. Slumping his backpack onto the adjoining seat, Moreton perched beside her. Feigning calm, she scrolled through her phone.

"Heard anything from my sister?" He took his own phone out.

"No, nothing… I thought maybe she's off sick?"

"Sort of. Last I saw she looked like she'd spent most of last night out."

"*Out*? Where? At a party, with friends?"

"Not with friends… more like she just disappeared."

Knowing that he wasn't really burdened by any gene for chat, Scarlett sensed his fear and clicked her phone off.

"Last time I actually saw her, she was coming back in, just as I left for the bus," he said. "Don't know where she'd been, though I've got my suspicions."

"Well she wasn't at ours – maybe she's got some secret boyfriend?"

"Nah, they're never secret." His stare made her feel both pleased and on edge. "Should've seen the state of her: no shoes, all clammy – like she's been under a hedge."

"No shoes?"

"Wouldn't have been the first time; she'll often sleepwalk in the house – if it *was* sleepwalking."

"So… you're not convinced?"

"When I went to feed the chickens, first thing, the back door was unlocked, plus, her footprints were clear enough, in the frost. They led out for the gate, to the back field. They didn't wander – she was focused."

"But when you saw her, coming back, why not just ask her?"

Moreton snorted. "Chat with Iz first thing? Sooner cuddle our tomcat. And he's a vicious git."

Yeah, you and animals, Scarlett almost replied. "So where might she have gone?" She tried not to slide into him as the bus slewed through a sharp bend. The corner meant they were close to their drop-off.

"Maybe she'd been *that* way?" He nodded towards a field, to their left.

"What, towards that tump? She told me some things about that."

"Dare say."

"What she said, it's been bugging me."

"Save your energy, Scarlett, whatever she said – it's just a stupid old mound. Pain in the arse – steals a great big chunk off our field." His smile was broken. "Okay," he half-sighed, "maybe we'll go up there... if it puts your mind at ease? Let's get it out the way, it'll be too dark if we wait."

For discovering the past as much as Moreton, she has no reason to disagree. Telling Roan she'll be home later (and ignoring his *yeah-right* face) they climbed the stile in hedge's gap and moved wordlessly through the damp grass. Up to Starvecrow Field.

unhinged

Whitecross Hall   *Monday, December 13th,* 1788

Christmas is in hand, yet not all is in order. Amid complaints of 'intolerable interference' at the hand of persons unseen, I have before me the resignation of another servant. No matter how many the master assigns, their tenure is uniformly short-lived.

    With this departure comes the burden of seeking what will be the tenth assistant housekeeper – in four years. I give no credit to the protestations of those who quit, yet there is repetition in their words. Some question whether the master is, during the times declared, genuinely away; all insist on an unknown presence. I would not add weight to idle gossip, and besides, my Master tolerates no slander of his predecessors, living nor dead. But despite the calumny of villagers who would not grant his great uncle and three sons the peace of the grave – where, they do demand, are the graves? They pour scorn on claims they were buried in another parish, and there is resonance in these doubts. They dwell in me.

    My only relief lies in the prospect of temporary leave. Verily, I have considered remaining forever abroad. Perhaps what tethers me is that there is also strange reassurance in the word of God. Those who say all the happenings attest to one fear – that some 'witch' unfettered has freedom to menace our lives. I counsel they heed this greater truth: that they would study Exodus, 22,18. And read it well. C.B.

Roan tried to digest the words. As he thumbed through the journal's tortured calligraphy, his eye paused on the date: CB's log had been made on this very day, he realised, 230 years ago. He returned the journal to the bottom drawer of his bedroom cupboard. In the same place, lay the diagrams of the house, his focus for hours of dry-eyed gazing.

    An itch he shouldn't scratch was now a stinging scab he was compelled to pick, his recovery, a grey patch of lost memory. In its aftermath, he was sapped, although he sensed his parents were more preoccupied by Scarlett's next hairstyle than their son's turmoil.

The light faded. Thankfully, Monday was over – hockey first thing; blue-limbed torture. Then English, Miss Kington snooping over his shoulder to see if he might scrawl more prophesies.

A furtive moon cast a chrome sheen over the fuzz of the maze below. He pictured Scarlett, out there somewhere with Moreton, risking raised eyebrows come supper.

He knew his curiosity for Whitecross should have faded. Up until Zadoc's amateur vivisection, his curiosity had been the same as that of any boy parachuted into alien surroundings. But after being dragged into the brothers' world, a restlessness for answers, like the wound on his thigh, kept throbbing. And there, on his chest of drawers, was a new trigger for new questions. Aside from what the model even was, who had moved it up from the kitchen?

He stepped closer, tapping a finger against the front door, staring, like a giant door-to-door salesman, through the windows. A few details could be made out, the odd bed, a dressing table. Pressing one eye to a first-floor window, he studied the vaulted ceilings. Why had it appeared? Why now? Would the inside offer answers? Try as he might, every place failed: no hinges, no hidden locks. He pushed and levered the roof. Maybe some section slid apart? It was less Whitecross, more high-security prison. Irritation boiling, he strutted to the bedroom window, slid the clasp aside and rammed the frame upwards.

"You know what, you can keep your freaking mysteries!" he grunted, as he lifted the entire model and staggered closer to the opening.

But balanced on the ledge, the jutting tower made the house too tall, by millimetres, to pass through. With a free hand, he tried to budge the raised sash higher. But it was solid. Using his shoulder as a battering ram, he hoped something might give as, despite cramping muscles, he pictured the splintering crash and the joy of saying good riddance to the stupid piece of tat.

Then something *did* give.

The obstructive tower moved, a fraction. With his face against it, Roan watched incredulously: with a mechanical click, the entire house, along a seam of roof and walls, hinged open. To his horror, half of the model pivoted out, into the open air, the balance shifting against him. He clung on, but had neither reach nor muscle. Inch by inch, it tilted forward and, having refused to let go, he now couldn't: more than half of the model beyond the frame, his watch strap was caught on a finial sticking out from the model's lower floor.

More and more of his meagre bodyweight drawn forward, he had no time to consider the irony: directly below, he was destined to land with a pile of matchsticks on the same real-life finial that jutted into view. Bit by bit, he felt his body lift. To the point of no return.

a mortsafe

"These early nights are a curse."

Moreton moved ahead as they reach the top of Starvecrow Field, following the edge of the plough's furrow. From what knowledge Scarlett had, she knew they were close. He was right: nightfall had been rapid, but she welcomed the gloom drawing them closer; all else shut out.

In the last yards, before the hedge and fence met, she felt keen to absorb any secrets this place might reveal. It hardly looked promising: a gentle bulge, at the corner of the field, marked by a scrub of brambles and a few outcrops of hazel. Then the soil beneath their feet changed, the uniform brown flecking with splinters of limestone, some large as broken bricks.

"Bits of the cottage, apparently," Moreton replied to her unspoken question. "Isabel might say more, seeing as she always listened to what's been handed down. Boxwell went crazy, after his wife died. After he'd discovered her body."

"But how did he demolish it? I thought Iz said he was good as dead?"

"Well, he didn't die before he'd bent the ear of the Duke."

"Duke? Iz never mentioned that. I didn't think there was anyone else in their story, and not someone *above* Boxwell?"

"There's always someone above," he laughed. "The Duke sent a gang of labourers, to level Jeb's home."

Watching the sun's vestiges play on his profile, she wondered if she ought to feel uneasy, yet was comfortable. Perhaps it was Moreton's lack of small talk; something in it she read as an encouragement.

"So come on, Mort," she urged, "all this legend of curses and ghouls… you're sure it's not all just fake news?"

He puffed his cheeks. "The truth's maybe somewhere in-between, between the fantasists and the realists. What I'm not so sure of is if this is really a tale of a 'witch'… probably more about witch-hunters."

Scarlett ran her fingertips along the twist of the barbed-wire fence. "So you think the story of her being actually buried here is true? How would that have been allowed?"

"Huh! There's your so-called Christians! The church wouldn't have her body on consecrated ground, but even if there hadn't been outrage about her being possessed, she'd have been kept out anyhow. They'd have chalked her death up as a suicide – that alone guaranteed she'd never get in a graveyard."

He seemed the voice of no-nonsense truth.

"She *is* here, then…"

"Sure. Come on, I'll take you to see her… if you like?" Moreton sensed her hesitation and, despite the dark, Scarlett was all too aware of that piercing stare. "Scar," he stepped closer, "you *do* want to do this?"

"Yeah, sure, though it's not a case of *wanting*. Ghost-hunting was never my career goal. But I'd like to understand." She felt her skin tauten where it met the December air, but the last impression she'd let Moreton take home was one of weakness.

He held out his hand. "You'll need to hop over," he said, stomping the barbed wire down. "And watch your skirt." By the lack of it, he guessed it was unlikely to snag. Once over, they climbed, a walk of maybe forty feet, a rise of perhaps ten.

"Did Isabel *really* come here?" She pictured bare feet among the nettles and brambles.

"If we're betting on it, yes. Don't get me wrong, she's an odd one any day, but she mentioned your tower. Going up there was something she's always wanted to tick off, though you weren't to know that. And she's been restless ever since – bodyclock all jumbled, not eating, hardly herself…"

Scarlett pondered his words: appetite loss, mood swings, messed-up sleep patterns… wasn't Isabel ticking the classic boxes for a crush? After all, being loved-up could surely happen to anyone?

They reached the the crest. Standing at the fringe of an open circle of ground, Scarlett tensed as a flush of instinct urged her feet to stop. A step behind, to her left, Moreton weighed her hesitation. Gently, he moved his right hand into the curve of her own. Their fingers fitted like a habit.

"It's okay, I've got something…"

Too right, he has: wasn't it obvious, all along? He's superhuman. It explained *everything*. As he extended his left arm ahead, she was completely comfortable about the imminent shaft of light about to irradiate all before them, beaming like a cosmic supernova from his palm. She was almost more shocked that it was merely the torch on his phone.

Roan didn't process the hand on his shoulder. Or the other one, wrapping around his arm, tugging him back. But then, recognition burst: that grey skin, almost scaly… those fingernails, like ammonite shards… a blur of velvet sleeve. And a strength bordering on brutal.

In the turmoil, he crashed to his bedroom floor. And though he was saved, he fought to breathe. The presence of a huge model house on his chest didn't help, as a memory burnt firework-bright in his mind, a string of images unfurling.

That first beckoning hand…
The tautening rope…
The rough sack on his head…
Being bound to a chair…
And that putrid, leering face…
The longer he closed his eyes, the more he saw.

Moreton's beam was narrow. He aimed squarely where he judged most would be revealed. Tied in a small cluster, wilted from the day's sun, the light picked out a bunch of flowers, bound by a ribbon to the iron railings. And among them, something familiar.

"Forget-me-nots!" Their blue clusters twinkled with an unreal quality.

"How're you so sure?" Scarlett asked.

"Mum's got some plastic ones. She must have pinched them."

"So it's what, a grave? I can see railings, I didn't expect that…" She gazed at the ironwork that reached upwards.

"Not railings, not exactly..." he replied, as if the vision has jolted his memory. "But, come on, we need to get back. I've been a bloody idiot!" he cursed. "Maybe she's already gone again, in this new night?" He shuddered with the thought that Isabel could easily come and go, neither of their parents likely to take notice.

Scarlett struggled to keep up as they abandoned the field's edge, steaming directly towards Valance Farm. Soil gathered to her soles like glue.

"So if they're not railings, what *are* they?" Physically and mentally, she couldn't keep up.

"If you have to know, they're what was put over her. To keep her in."

"Keep her in?" she gasped.

Suddenly, he stopped. "Yeah, that's what they thought they had to do, when they buried a 'witch'. They didn't trust death. The bars loop over the top, then back down. They were driven down, all around her upright coffin, like a net round a spider."

As he spoke, he took both her hands, her eyes shining with the night's balm. Drawing her closer, his mouth was so close her senses hummed.

"That's what they did, Scar, to Old Nan Tow, to his fair Rosamond. They put her in a cage."

a table for three

"Say buddy, what's cookin'?" Jacob poked his head around the corner of the fireplace as blue flames licked the belly of Zadoc's pot.

"I wish you'd remember you were born *this* side of the Atlantic," Zadoc groaned.

Ever since they had invaded their home in 1942, Jacob obsessed with all things American, his ear eager for slang from the nation Zadoc dismissed as the land of the loud. When the first colour TV arrived, via a short-lived tenant in 1975, he had relished every opportunity to watch what Zadoc cursed as "that lousy box". Unlike his impressionable brother, Zadoc's tongue remained loyal to the Georgian of his youth.

But Edmund differed again. Being the eldest spelt responsibility, though his speech, seasoned by words snooped between Victorian servants and the banter of soldiers and nurses of two world wars, was far from stiff. But what united both in dismay was Jacob's yankee slang.

Which was exactly why he used it.

"If you *must* know, although your olfactory skill should have foretold such truth, tonight we will dine on snails," Zadoc sighed.

"Hot damn it!" He rasped his palms.

"I've soft-fried the onions while Edmund did the honours with the cream, the Friesian didn't stir; his fingers retain the finesse of a maiden."

"That's as may be, yet I can't smell me no searing meat?"

"Just a short delay; giant snails are best prepared with alum. And *alum*," he rolled his eyes, "appears to escape the Wycherley's list of resources. No matter: citrus juice will suffice, in sufficient quantity."

"Lemons?"

"Indeed. As many as possible. Edmund is searching the kitchens."

"And meanwhile, those finger-lickin' snails?" His nostrils flared.

"Rest assured, they're here." His foot tapped a bucket, beneath the table. "No point cracking them open yet – trust you prefer 'em fresh?"

"Indeed! You've got me droolin', bromeo."

"Then begone!" Zadoc scowled. "Find your best garments. Tonight will be a capital feast."

Kicking off muddy shoes in the porch of Valance Farm, Scarlett rushed up the snaking staircase in Moreton's wake. The air smelt of baking and ripe fruit – warmer than the mustiness of Whitecross. As he edged Isabel's door open, a rustle of bedclothes reassured him that she was there. At least physically.

"You okay, Iz? He spoke gently. "I brought someone, to see you."

Scarlett approached. Isabel was clammy, tresses like crushed springs, eyes half-open.

"Scarlie," she smiled, a hand emerging. "I'll be myself by tomorrow, just came over all… I dunno, maybe it's a bug."

Drifting back into reverie, Scarlett retained her hand as Moreton perched on the bed's edge.

"Sleep is probably what she most needs," she said. "Might anything else help?"

"What d'you mean – sleeping tablets?" He looked confused.

"No… I was just thinking, maybe you had best lock the doors?"

But before he could reply, Isabel's inert hand clamped around Scarlett's wrist. She jolted upright, eyes ablaze: *"That'd be just the answer, wouldn't it? Fiddling with your little keys in your little locks!"*

Scarlett recoiled as Moreton leant forward. Taking Isabel's shoulders in his hands, he urges her back down. But her grip was fast. "Lady laa-dee-da-dee-Scarlie, flitting all over as she pleases, proper princess of Whitecross, thinks she can declare what she likes, be who e'er she likes, *have* who e'er she likes!"

"Enough, Iz!" Moreton insisted. "Come on, it's okay Iz, no one's locking you in, not now, not ever. You're always free, you know that," he soothed. "She's never been one for containment," he whispered to Scarlett, as Isabel drifted back to sleep. "We turn the locks, but the keys stay in them. After all, if you can't use a door, maybe you'll choose a window?"

Scarlett felt thoughtless. Isabel breathed heavily as he tucked the covers around her. Watching his hands, she coveted their tenderness, a closeness she struggled to comprehend as she thought of Roan. Then, eyes closed and with no sign of consciousness, Isabel spoke again. This time, in lifeless monotone.

"You must help them, Scarlett. You *must* help those boys."

Eyes writhing beneath shut lids, Isabel's words were a trail of thought that tracked a pathway into a fog of sleep. Both sensed what the words meant, as Scarlett finally understood exactly what Moreton has known for years: sometimes, Isabel was literally not herself.

minute 35

"Dinner's in the oven, lover girl!" Joanna called out, though she was too occupied by the TV to cross-question her daughter's late return.

Leaving her mother's creation to dry out, Scarlett was heading straight for her room.

"I took Roan's up on a tray – you could eat with him?" she added, as her daughter flitted past the sitting room. "He's still not right, poor boy."

"Okay Mum, okay, I'm on it."

A familiar thin light diffused from his room. Minecrafting or Roblox, she guessed, though as she got closer to her own room, something felt amiss.

She flicked the light switch back and forth. Dead. Would Roan unscrew the bulb? Roan pre-wart? Definitely. Roan now, skulking on the fringes of family life? Whatever the reason, she didn't fancy entering alone.

"Ro-an?" She edged his door. He was at his PC, but not gaming. His room was freezing, food untouched, window half-open, curtains shimmering in the draught. How could he sit there, in just a T-shirt? Then she noticed: the model, the house.

No longer in the kitchen, it was on the rug, in the middle of his room. It had been in the wars, a thin crack running top to bottom.

"What happened, Roe... did it open?"

"You could say everything's opening. Maybe mark this date: Monday thirteenth, Sesame Day."

Wondering if he had lost the plot, she realised what was on the screen. The spy footage. She'd *totally* forgotten.

"It turned up. In here." He jutted a sharp finger at the doll's house. "It likes to get around."

She stepped closer.

"I'm running through the last 24 hours." He nodded towards the spycam, high on the bookcase, the lens overlooking his doorway. "We should have got a better app – it was only supposed to film if it detected motion; it's like it ran non-stop." Shutting one file, he opened a new one. "Each flipping one of them's an hour long."

"It's very fuzzy." Scarlett squinted. How could a film about nothing be so mesmeric?

Roan hovered the cursor over a list of files. "I put *this* one aside; it came out shorter, ending just before I got home." He clicked on it. "There's an error code ... might as well bin it," he added, dragging it towards the trash. "I watched it up to minute thirty-five... nothing. It just flickers and dies."

"Wait!" Scarlett grabbed the mouse. Roan huffed: if *he* couldn't get anywhere, she wouldn't. She clicked towards minute thirty-five, then let the file play. Eyes glazing, they watched the same sequence of nothingness.

"Duff software."

Scarlett ignored him. "Maybe, but... look!"

In the last two to three seconds, the file went blank. Yet slowed down, and tracked back several frames, they saw the lamp, on Roan's desk: flickering. It was obvious: the lamp died *before* the images stopped.

"And that suggests?" Roan squinted.

"That it *wasn't* your software that failed – that the mains went off?"

"Let's look from where the next file picks up," he said, reclaiming the mouse, "though the light goes off, it comes back on, minutes later."

"So you've checked the file immediately *after* this?"

"Not yet." He slid the mouse back to Scarlett.

It showed nothing amiss: the lamp was back on.

"So... if there *was* a power cut, it was just a blip?" Roan half asked. They watched the empty images resume. Empty, except for one change.

There, on the chest of drawers, where up to that point sat nothing more than a few of Roan's books, it now stood: the doll's house. Both know the power failure coincided perfectly. Too perfectly.

"Whoah! *That's grim!*" Scarlett exploded, as Roan calmly marked the time on his notepad.

"So, the doll's house appears *just before* I got back. I guessed Mum moved it here, but there's no sign of that. Maybe she came in when the power tripped? Though who'd drag that around in the dark?"

Scarlett was lost, until she remembered her own laptop. She didn't relish retrieving it from her room, but Roan volunteered. From its screen, more empty scenes unfolded as he worked towards the time that matched the power failure.

The camera's view, trained on her doorway and a section of landing beyond, was empty. Maybe Roan was reading too much into the model's relocation? He could always just go and ask Mum if *she'd* moved it? But then everything changed.

"Yes! Look, it's Mum!" Roan punched the air. It *might* be her, Scarlett reflected, watching the frames as a vague blur swept past her doorway. And she – it had to be a *she* – certainly was carrying something. But the motion was so swift. Perhaps they must leave it at that: the frame speed wouldn't slow any further.

"So that's the end of it?" Scarlett asked, as Roan froze the sequence on the figure.

"Of the file? No, there's a bit more."

"Let's see it then."

Seconds later, the figure appeared once more: across the landing, back turned to the camera, gliding into the darkness of Roan's room. With their faces close enough to see every damning pixel, they recoiled, the truth lancing into the air like a spike. Neither spoke as Roan froze on the image.

It was not Mum. Not unless she had somehow acquired a wig of flowing, silver-blond hair.

"Scarlett's left her supper! That dog's going to need a gastric band."

"What you on about now?" Joanna asked, as Richard returned, balancing logs for the fire.

"What's she living on, Coke and Pringles? Factor in all this messing with her hair... something's obviously not right?"

"Right? Have you *seen* the state of girls in her year? Apparently, it's called ad-o-les-cence."

"So you say," he grunted. "And as for Roan, he might as well donate his legs to science. We only see him when the WiFi's off."

"I know, and it's nice you're *so* concerned."

"Meaning what, exactly?"

"You tell me: you're the one who dragged their lives a hundred miles and dropped them here."

"Oh for pity's sake, Joanna, change the flipping record."

"I'm only repeating myself because you can't expect your kids to live through change and *not* change themselves. Wherever they are, it's called growing up!"

"Okay." He drained his glass. "So I guess that means you'll happily sign the contract?"

"Darling, I've thought of nothing else," she sighed.

"And?"

"And I suppose I've realised that, on balance…"

"Yes?"

"On balance, I *should*."

"Now?" he asked, producing it from his pocket.

"Whenever, whatever."

"Here then…"

He had a pen prepared.

The nib was kissing the page when the scream rang out.

memory jog

That was a proper scream, Roan decided. Enough to have him scrambling for Scarlett's room. Moments before, she'd borrowed his torch and pinched the bulb from his desk lamp to fix her overhead light. Despite the phantom image, she'd insisted on sorting it alone.

So when he heard the cry, he guessed it was the result of either a fall, electrocution, or both. Yet her light was working. And Scarlett didn't look injured, though she was pointing, wide-eyed, at her glass cabinet.

"They're gone, Roe, they've *taken* them!" Fire glowed in her tears.

"What, your snails? Who do you mean, *'they'?*" Roan asked, though the evening's bursts of recollection offered him enough clues.

"I'm not having this. Not Derek. Not Daisy!" she spat, her knuckles white with rage.

"Woah! Deep breaths Scar," Roan eased her shoulders as if she were a bomb. "First, are you *sure*? Maybe they crawled out? You've checked down the back?" He began to search around the room.

"*Of course* I've checked! The lid was secure. They're *massive* African snails, Roan!"

"Okay okay, let's just think this through…"

"Think *what* through?" a voice interjects. "What's all the noise about?" Mum stood in the doorway.

"It's Scarlett, she – "

" – I'm *fine* Mum, I just landed badly, on my ankle . . . the bulb blew, and I fell off the chair, after I'd changed it," she gestured at the still-swinging lampshade. "It's just a bruise."

"Okay, but maybe leave bulbs to your dad, eh? Doing something useful might stop him fretting about you. Your supper was ruined, by the way – it's in Mustard. Again."

"Oh? That's fine, I ate at Isabel's – dropped by as she was off today."

"Isabel? Ah yes, *Moreton's* sister. And how *is* Moreton?" she asked, a smile playing on her lips.

"Let's not do this now, eh? I'm exhausted."

"Of course, precious," she said, retreating.

"Why didn't you tell her?" Roan hissed.

"Exactly *what?*" she hissed back. "That a bunch of gremlins are skulking around, stealing stuff, locking doors? You want me sectioned?"

"Yeah, or Dad'll just say you're undermining him… or they'd think it's your age…"

"And what's that mean, exactly?"

"You know, there's masses of stuff online about poltergeists, telekinetic energy, how it happens around teenagers – usually girls."

"Yeah, yeah…"

"Google it: as you get older, you gain this aura that triggers weird stuff. Kind of like girl power, gone bad."

"Well that's just the kind of trash Mum laps up," Scarlett scoffed, though she immediately pictured Isabel. "And anyhow, how does all that square with my snails?"

"Or, to be fair, that black thing being stuck to me…"

"Oh, and that skanky doll's house…" Her thoughts swarmed like death watch beetles.

"I *hate* that thing, I wasn't going to say, but…"

"Say *what,* Roan?" He avoided eye contact. "If there's something you know, maybe now is a good time."

He spoke as if he was coughing up a parasite: "I know more than I did, I know that, uh, well, I saw his hand."

"Hand? Whose hand? *What* hand?" Scarlett pushed him backwards and he dropped into the chair by her desk. "What the hell, Roe: *what hand?*"

"I saw a hand. I was trying to get rid of it, the house; I opened my window, to just chuck it out, but I got caught on it." He looked at his wrist, red from the tug-of-war, then began to rub his right arm, as if he was tracing a bruise. "I thought I was dying: I was being dragged out by it…"

"And this was what, just before I got back?"

"Yes, and these arms came from behind, wrapping around me. Forcing me back. I fell backwards – we crashed onto the floor."

"We? So this mystery helper… what, they landed with you?"

"No, they must've stepped back. They vanished."

"But . . . you, saw a *hand*?"

"Kind of. The skin was all silvery, like something from a museum. But alive, definitely alive."

Scarlett stared blankly. "It sounds grim. But this… thing… it wasn't trying to kill you?"

"No, but as soon as I saw that flesh... it unlocked something – I started to remember stuff, from before."

"Before?"

"When the matchbox went missing, when you couldn't find me... I remember a rope; I woke up with it tied round my feet... next thing, being dragged, inside. And cloth, forced over my head," he faltered, eyes widening. "Then being tied, to a chair... and... I can't make it out, but something happened, something horrible. The matchbox was taken, whoever took it really wanted that flesh back. Like it meant life or death."

"To who?"

"God knows, it's like I was drugged, so much is a blank."

"But where *were* you? Think about this, Roe: how could someone grab you, drag you off, like a sack of washing?" He shrugged. "It's not like I don't believe you. I saw what that doctor found, but if what you say really had happened, we'd find *evidence*, proof."

"I know, I know. I can't see some secret door in my room, so other than a few fuzzy video frames, the only thing we've got is the model. But even if they're rubbish, those films tell us something."

"How do you mean?"

"They make me feel someone *wanted* us to look at the doll's house."

"Or tease us with it?"

"Whatever, but *whoever* it was, they definitely didn't want it to end up outside, all wrecked."

"Or *you* wrecked? So, shall we look at it?"

They crossed the landing, Derek and Daisy's plight racing in Scarlett's veins. Tonight, she vowed, was no time to sleep: if they were to be rescued alive, they must punch through the fog that had swamped them since Dad first collected that stupid key. Maybe whoever had been so thoughtless as to take her old companions had done her a favour, since rescuing her snails meant unlocking the Whitecross story for good?

As she approached the doll's house, her fists tightened. Intentionally or not, this day had given her truth. And as sick and tired of fear as she was, from here, she knew, she was all fury.

"You will do it, do it for me?" The voice whispered sweet and close to his ear.

Moreton soothed his sister's brow with a cool, damp cloth. Eyes shut and rigid, she hadn't moved since Scarlett left.

"Don't do it for *her*, do it for *me*, Mort," she breathed, as two tongues jostled in her mouth. "Just take Dad's welding kit, sever it. And thereafter, by their coming, shall I be free."

Whoever asked this, Moreton knew what he must do. But the site was protected. If damaging it was pinned on him, there would surely be legal consequences? And if his defence was to say why, they'd surely section him?

"Just do it, *just do it*," she breathed. "Do, it, for, me, for. . ." she faded.

He must think hard. Maybe call Scarlett? Too late: at this hour, with this ultimatum, she'd guess his sister's delirium was infecting him. Beyond his fears for Isabel, he wished for a better time, a better place, to have met someone like Scarlett. Just his luck.

He had returned to Isabel's room after hearing a murmur. But now, watching her return to sleep, he began to raise himself so he could creep out.

But in a flash, her fingernails clamped fast to his arm.

"*You will do this!*" she wailed, rising slowly, as if pulled by strings. "*You will listen, boy, or* – Moreton, help me, she will, she will away with me! – *If not my own, then I will take her this night, and all of your sister will be husk of skin and bone!*"

Springing back, he staggered towards the door: this voice, these eyes... where was Isabel?

"*Get out, go to it, boy!*" the shrill voice commanded, Isabel's body rising upright, floating inches above the bed. Eyes shut and lifeless, her mouth spoke with a voice both outside and inside his mind.

"*And if you have not by first light, you will have no call for apothecaries... they'll be planting her with me for good company.*"

Unable to avert his gaze, Moreton fumbled for the latch, vowing that if he was to know Isabel again, the threat could never be questioned.

Repulsed by the leech within her soul, he rushed out.

Into the cold air of the night.

part three ~ the unholy ghost

going in

They crouched around the doll's house. After its near destruction, they didn't dare risk moving it.

"It's obvious where to try," said Roan, tracing a finger from the ground floor, through the roof and down the other side. "There's a tiny space, here; enough to get a fingernail in."

"Do you think the original architect made this?" Scarlett wondered.

"You mean like a three-D plan? No way," he said, face upside down as he scrutinised the best approach. "On the original drawings there was no tower. Boxwell added it later. So the model must come *after* the house."

"Maybe he got the tower built for his wife, like an ensuite prison? From what I learned from Iz, she was locked in it."

"Could be, but my guess is the model was made by soldiers, in the Great War, a hundred years ago. Many had terrible injuries and I've read that things like this were a kind of therapy."

Scarlett shrugged. "Let's get on with it. We learn from it, or we bin it."

Placing his fingertips along the fissure, he prised a facade of mock stonework. And with the tower still depressed from his struggle against the window, the house obediently cranked apart. Like a giant clam.

Drawing closer, Scarlett felt a vibration in her back pocket: a text from Moreton. Talk about timing.

If u c bright lights across Starvecrow, ignore. Just doing whatever's gotta be done. M x

"What's that about?" Roan strained to read the words.

"It's just Moreton… I have *no* idea," she shuddered. "Shut the window, Roan. It's freezing."

Roan levered the sash down, but as he secured it, he called out: "Woah! There's your 'bright lights' then! What the hell's he doing up there?"

Scarlett jumped up. Pulses of white and blue flashed from the distant corner of Starvecrow Field, cascades of sparks arcing to the ground.

"I think I can guess, but it's not important – not now."

Gently, Roan swung the two halves apart. And at last, in cold detail, they saw their life, cleanly intersected…

Hallway, kitchen, sitting room, main stairway, down to every tread, every detail… and above, all 12 bedrooms, among them, Roan's, Scarlett's. But the thirteenth room, in the tower, rested unopened, the hinged section bypassing it. Scarlett sensed this was enough for now, but Roan wanted more; something told him this was not the whole story. Witnessing the innards of their home exposed, he gasped aloud: "It opened because the window pushed the tower *downwards*… so what if we pushed it again?"

Before she could question him, he grabbed the tower and pushed. Click. Another entire layer came free. He pushed again. Click. And another…

Like secret pages, the layers swung open. And what seemed a faithful replica of their home changed: there, behind, under, between all they know, ran *another* house. A parallel one: folded like origami within their own.

Scarlett leant closer. By taking one of the new, thin sections and hingeing it back and forth, she saw a network of cavities – 'rooms', she guessed, yet barely. More like fissures, these windowless slivers of space ran between every known area. Suddenly, the space they'd grown to know since the summer was compressed, like lies trapped within versions of the truth.

"We've been living in half of a story," she whispered. "I always thought this place was a paradise for pests, but I never bargained on anything bigger than woodworm… We've been conned: Dad didn't buy one house, he bought two."

Roan laughed. "And one of them wasn't vacant? There we were thinking *he'd* tricked *us*… it's a secret network, a spies' paradise."

"Good spies, or evil ones?*"* She homed in on the section revealing her bedroom. By levering the first layer, a cavity was exposed. And as her model bed pivoted forwards, the panel beneath it disappeared, leaving a hole. An entry? As if he were reading her thoughts, Roan wiggled an insensitive finger into the space.

"Nice cosy spot, eh? Kind of like a bed *under* a bed? Cool…"

Not cool, no. Scarlett jumped up and manically dusted imagined filth from her clothes.

"That's the way they came, and left… whoever took Derek and Daisy! Can't you see? Anyone coming through the door would have been picked up on the camera – but not if they came *that* way…"

Marvelling at the craft, Roan flipped the layers: amid all his time studying the old papers, no rulers or tape measures would have revealed this.

Quickly, he saw that the hidden sections all lead to a central chamber, the dark heart of the ground floor. In the back of this space, a fireplace connected to the rear of the hearth in their sitting room, while the opposite wall bordered their kitchen. Like strands from a spider's web, unknown corridors radiated out – though they were barely that, since you'd have to negotiate them sideways? The routes zig-zagged to almost every known room. At the library, one stopped abruptly at a book case, another terminating in the main bathroom, beneath the bath, while another descended to a narrow door that led into the garden. He'd noticed that before, when he was outside, but it wouldn't open, at least not from outside.

Riddled with crawlspaces, their home was a labyrinth of lies. But now they knew. In his gut, he wished they didn't.

"Have you listened to a single word, Roe?" Scarlett stood over him, wringing her hands.

"Yes... sorry, I was just piecing stuff together."

"I'm done with that. They took my snails," she stuttered. She'd surely burst into tears if she had to say their names again. "And if they'd left through my door, they'd have been on the video, right?"

"Yep."

"So they went *that* way." She pointed under her miniature bed. "It must be a way in." In dread, he realised where this logic was heading.

"Er... *yeah*, right." Amid his turmoil, her words faded: was it not, finally, the time to spill everything to Mum and Dad?

"It's fine, Roan, if you're too young for this. But whatever these things are, they're not getting away with Derek and Daisy."

She mentioned their names. He was right: her tears flowed. Irked by their intrusion, she quickly wiped them aside.

"I'll need your torch again... you can wait and keep watch." She was too proud to beg for his company. By the time Roan had decided to follow, she was already across the landing. In truth, he knew: for snails, for sanity and for the flickering memory of Zadoc's blowtorch, it *was* time.

But if Roan anticipated she'd be careful, he was horribly wrong.

Before her doorway, she broke into a run, heading hard towards the end of her bed. Jumping like a crazed ninja, she delivered a sharp blow. The panel beneath her mattress caved in, revealing ample space to climb into the void beyond.

"So are you coming?" Cheeks flushed, she flicked on the torch.

"I guess," said Roan, touching a vestige of slime on the edge on the woodwork. Unless it was ectoplasm, he reflected, it suggested her snails had passed this way.

Glowing with anger, Scarlett was on a course he could merely follow. Her top half already within the void, he was drawn in her wake. In seconds, they were inside, Roan stopping only to replace the panel.

In the pale light of her room, it was as if they had never been there, the evening's drama all history. All was silent, save a subtle sound from Roan's room: the tidying action of deft hands, returning the model of their home to its locked state.

All secrets firmly closed.

gristle

Whitecross Hall   *December 13th, 1789*

This disease of dissent among the revolting French contaminates our peasantry. A rout marched upon Whitecross Hall tonight, waving torches, all a-clamour. No brickbats were cast, or calls, as might be fashionable of a modern mob, for the services of Madame Guillotine. But on perceiving their weaponry, my Master conceded to their idolatrous demands.

What fuels this bonfire is plainly the ever-lengthening line of short-lived servants to Whitecross. With each departure comes a litany of chattering tales of malediction and mischief.

Village tongues have wagged, some purporting to have suffered directly at the hands of the felons who, they assert, have sought refuge within these walls. The mounting belief is that the mother of their souls is abroad, and that her presence lies at the rotten heart of this devilry.

To settle this, my Master might throw his doors open to the rabble, invite them to inspect every nook, but it is not his habit to entertain a hotbraised mob. Once within, ruination would be sure and swift.

We have thus reached this accord. Tomorrow, I am to speak with the smithy. A framework will be fashioned, to be installed around her resting place at the earliest opportunity. The mob even called for the removal of the headstone, or at least all wording thus inscribed. My Master forbids this, set as it was by the Valance family, an act they contest did restore fertility to the surrounding fields. Having been unable to raise beef nor grain before they did so, the mob accepted this, their Christian grace, or some memory of pagan instincts, finally rediscovered.

Perhaps, if we adhere to their demands, we will find peace? At their behest, the Reverend Lyndon will also attend when the ironwork is installed. This device, which they call a mortsafe, commonly used to keep corpse thieves at bay, they insist upon. And by the Reverend's blessing and his adjuration of evil, the matter shall be closed. Not that I know how assured my faith can be: I grow old and weary of this position. Readily, I avow that to believe in Him is also to believe in evil and all its portent. Yet what need for the hunting of witchcraft when we find such iniquity in mankind?   C.B

Moreton feared it might not start, his heart thumping as he turned the key. How many times had he told his dad that quad wasn't fit for scrap?

Behind him, in the trailer, lay the welding kit, hissing beneath spits of rain. The flame had cut quickly through the ironwork, though he took care not to simply discard the bars. In the dark, his hands sensed that importance, even if his mind was elsewhere, in turmoil for Isabel. The remnants lay neatly beside Rosamond's grave. In the first light, his effort would show, though to the eyes that mattered, would they ever be satisfied?

Beyond the trampled brambles, dawn would also reveal the tombstone, its epitaph flaked by more than 300 winters. Now just a stub of memory, he saw it as the only positive attempt made to recognise this as a resting place for some-one, as much as some-body. Yet if he flattened his palms against the cold surface and listened through the wind, he was sure the chiselled letters might speak. Words to soothe a bitter wrong, a wrong his family carried in its nightmares, trickling down generations, searching for the weakest way out. Rest in Peace? As he powered the quadbike towards home, willing the mud-clad wheels to fly, he sensed no such reassurance.

The air in the black chamber was not frigid. A trace of warmth from a space beyond stirred a scent of straw as, beneath her fingers, Scarlett sensed what must be a mattress. They advanced like lizards.

"Point it *this* way," she hissed, fumbling to guide Roan's torch. Beyond an oblong of blankness, they saw only a brick wall.

"That makes no sense…" Roan whispered. "It's got to be straight ahead?" If there was no way forward, the doll's house had to be wrong after all – and merely the work of a bored fantasist?

Wriggling forward, he reached out to test the brickwork, inches away. Maybe it would wobble like scenery? But by extending his arm, he moved over the unseen void – directly below.

The beam of Roan's torch cut an arc as he tumbled, head-first, down the unseen ladder. Realising the brick wall was the opposite side of a narrow shaft, Scarlett wasted no time descending.

But before the final rung was close enough to check Roan, she knew they faced a setback: her brother's torch. She slapped it against her thigh; it glowed like a dying ember.

"Damn! You okay?"

"Well," Roan groaned, "I guess that wasn't the easiest way down."

In the dark, they edged along the narrow passage, turning through ninety degrees, then twice the other way. They could be upright now, but unease marked every tip-toe step. Some 20 feet further, the first sound. They froze. She denied it, but when it repeated, it was unmistakeable: chinking glasses, scraping spoons and the cutting of something resistant.

"Bad timing – they're having supper?" She retched at the image her mind built, every fibre of her body straining to retreat, but anger rooted her. "Don't you hate it when people call by, just as you're sitting down to eat?" she spat. "It's high time they had gatecrashers."

"Wait! What you thinking?" Roan held out a restraining arm. "Maybe they haven't eaten them yet?"

"Can't you *smell*?" Scarlett gasped. The air was thick with garlic.

"Congratulations are rare of late, dear brothers." Jacob wiggled a long fingernail in his mouth to prise gristle from his teeth. "But that was mighty fine." He raised his goblet and they followed suit, Jacob hammering his heels in a thudding drum roll.

"And full respect, Master Zadoc," he added, "for thinking on your feet to create such a dish. Eddie boy, you came up trumps! Necessity is the mother of good relish!"

The firelight's flicker interplayed with the glow from the candlestick. Zadoc, calmer than his twin, studied Edmund's face, knowing he has always struggled to accept compliments. Both knew that Jacob was the flag-bearer for their emotions. Were there joy to sing, his would be the mouth to sing it.

From the shadows, Zadoc chortled: "Come now, Jacob, there is hardly ingenuity in gathering and preparing *churchpigs*? I could find you handfuls in every corner, under anything you care to lift! But purloining eggs was a true bonus, and those earth-apples, with that cream? A *coup de grâce!*" He nodded to Edmund for his dexterity with sleeping Friesians. "Churchpig or not, it was an omelette to die for."

Ignoring Zadoc's taunt, Edmund lifted his glass. And beneath the table, between the brothers' wiry feet, Derek and Daisy slept on in their bucket, ignorant of their delayed execution, forced by Edmund's failure to find the necessary alum to prepare them – or even, as Zadoc had complained, "a mouldering morsel of lemon".

Poised like a primed cat, Scarlett listened, confused, temper churning. When she sprang, Roan knows he must follow. Yet still, for crucial seconds, something held her back. He was grateful for each one.

"It's nearly midnight – their lights are still on," Richard grunted as he climbed into bed. "I killed the WiFi ages ago; even took the cable out."

"I thought part of the joy of living in a mansion meant we all got breathing space from each other?"

"It's not *breathing* I worry about. That's one miracle they somehow manage alone."

Joanna let her magazine slide to the floor. "Speaking of miracles, you need to talk to them. If they don't want to leave, we've got to respect that."

"Sorry to be technical dear, but sleeping in a retail space is frowned upon, last I heard."

"Don't be deliberately stupid, Richard. I mean we'll have to move *nearby*. Roan might roll with whatever, but *Scarlett*? She's changing so fast."

"Fast? She's a new download of herself every morning. First the hair, then the make-up . . ." He lay back to massage his brow.

"Seriously!" she elbowed. "She needs stability; we must go gently."

"Yes, gentle's good. Well done, by the way," he said, through a yawn.

"For what?" Joanna reached to turn off her lamp.

"For being so selfless."

"Richard, I've always been selfless. It's because I have an infinite capacity to feel pity. After all, why else did I marry you?"

"Sweet dreams," he sighed. "Everything's just working out perfectly."

a cracking meal

"Nightcap, milord?" Zadoc slurred as he shunted a bottle of brandy across the table towards Edmund. "Their Bordeaux isn't bad, but *this*, dear Jacob, is dandy licker."

"Not for me, I shall presently retire," Edmund replied, the hands of his pocket watch bunching at midnight.

Retirement, for Edmund, usually meant the fireside chair, just feet away; any prospect of lying flat became too uncomfortable around 1901. Zadoc once shared the same area, until he found Edmund's snoring too similar to the lament of a lovesick pheasant. *His* rest lay far away, via a route that culminated in the first-floor bathroom. There, beneath the bath, he savoured his feather-lined sanctuary. There was more than meat to be gained from nature's gift of the crow, he liked to say. Sitting up suddenly risked clouting his head into the bath's iron underbelly, but he treasured the compartment. And on bath nights, now that they had company, it was eminently cosy.

"Bed? Me too, I am proper whoppered, as old Mells used to say," Jacob chuckled, eyes glinting in the fire's glow.

"It's no end of wonder," Edmund snorted, "that you parrot the words of servants who haven't graced these halls since – "

"Since perhaps those days when we lived fetter-free?" Jacob cut in, "Well, what's 300 years, between brothers?"

Zadoc sensed brewing friction. "Come now, no point getting caught up in nostalgia."

"Exactly, Zadoc," Edmund replied, as he swirled the dregs of his glass. "If I am testy, I confess it is merely for our sake. Nostalgia, reminiscence… they amount to the same: this endless regaling is as much a prison as these walls. Perhaps I may ask you both: that bucket beneath our table, does anyone understand what it contains?

"A brace of overgrown snails?" Zadoc answered, happy to fall into Edmund's trap if it might hasten their bedtime.

"No." Jacob laughed. "Our brother is the master of metaphor!"

"Bravo, Jacob. They are revolution. Liberty. *Opportunity*! If it never occurred, taking the snails was a declaration. Of war."

"Oh dear. Here we go…" Jacob mumbled.

"For sure," Edmund continued, "we may pilfer, but discretion is our signature, is it not? Yet what is discreet in this? They will notice the absence, they must have already. So *yes*," Edmund glared into the lost corners of the room, "yes, it *is* war. And war brings change. Did Waterloo teach us nothing?"

"Then why," Zadoc asked, "did you agree that we take them? What will we gain?"

"Ask, more importantly, what we *lose* in peace," Edmund snapped. "Is this a life, scurrying around in the darksome bowels of this mansion? We are more dying than living; did not just the smallest fragment of loss from Jacob's sorry skin make that clear? We grow weaker by each unlit day." He paused to gather his cascading hair.

"Yet picture this," he said, eyes brightening, "were we to drive these people away, rather than wait interminably for them to leave, what then? We could have this house once more for our own – and have it as soon as tomorrow! Think of it: to live freely, to taste liberty before our final days."

"Who speaks of dying?" I'm fighting fit." To illustrate his vigour, Zadoc interlocked his fingers and flexed his palms outwards. A fingernail pinged silently into the dark. "Well, maybe the odd loose fleshspade, but that's just maturity."

Jacob raised a calming hand. "Maybe it's just melancholia, dear Edmund? All living things are dying from the day they are born. True, you might pick a date when we *should* have died, maybe 1760, when they parked that crown on George the Third's crackpot head. By all measures, a fair innings… or let's say 1820. George the Fourth arrives and – "

" – Yes," Edmund cut back in, "a 100 years of Georges, surely that would be time to call it a day."

"Maybe more will follow…" Zadoc mumbled.

"Enough of this, get to your beds," Edmund scowled. "Forgive me, brothers, for being so foolish as to think you could ever grab destiny in your senile hands."

"Oh, I heed your offer," sighed Zadoc, "but war? You mean to upset our latest tenants enough to… what? If they flee, yes, we have the run of the house again, but we'd be back to sole reliance on your night-time scavengings. I, for one, enjoy the easy victuals the Wycherleys offer."

Edmund paused. His eventual words seem addressed to the fire.

"Better it is to burn brightly, once in a lifetime, than smoulder forever, like wet wood." Drunkenly, he jabbed the poker into the hot embers.

"Pah! Aim for your empty victories. I am not yet so desperate," Zadoc retorted, as he stood tall and swivelled to leave.

"And that precisely means?" Jumping up, Edmund swung the poker to eye level, blocking Zadoc's path. Its orange tip glowed dull, inches from his pupil. Yet Zadoc didn't even blink.

"Edmund, you jeered at my test with our brother's wart… you would slander us as 'meacocks', but I still hold a hope, wretched as you may reckon it is, that we could walk from this place, one day."

"Piffle!" Edmund scoffed, the poker menacingly close. "I ought to do you a favour – burn out what remaining brain you have."

Despite his slight frame, Jacob wedged between them.

"*Enough!* Gentlemen!" he insisted, jostling them apart. They remained motionless as, grasping the table edge, he steadied himself before shuffling away, reaching to feel for the gap that led to his under-bed chamber. Edmund looked on in shame: observing the poker in his outstretched arm, he lowered it slowly. He would never harm his own. Even in the mist of anger, he hoped.

Unruffled, Zadoc stepped around Edmund to leave for his own crawlspace as the distance between Jacob and his exit narrowed to inches – the same space in which Scarlett and Roan crouched, watching every turn in the brothers' bitter row.

"Quickly!"

Covering her mouth, Roan dragged Scarlett back. Now they knew her snails were still alive, surely for now, at least, that was enough?

But by the time they retreated to the ladder, they heard Jacob moving closer. They climbed the rungs to a chorus of betraying squeaks. And Jacob's ears missed nothing.

Opening his eyes wider to the murk, he shouted: "Who goes there?"

Beyond the ladder, he heard the panel thud shut: whoever had spied on them, whoever had the gall to pollute their sacred home, was already away. In a flash, Edmund and Zadoc rushed to his side.

"*What is it?*" cried Edmund. He still held the poker, now cool.

"Do you not *smell* them?"

Zadoc flexed his nostrils; yes, the air was thick with the scent: people, normal people. A twang of fresh air, a taunt of sunlight.

"Gadzooks! They got in, they were *here*!" Jacob cried. "They must have opened the panel, from the girl's room. Congratulations, Edmund: your dream for war appears already under way."

"But how *dare* they spy on us?" Zadoc growled.

Behind him, Edmund laughs drily. "Spying on *us*? Be flattered! And if it is so, it'll be your tomfoolery that taught 'em how. You dragged that boy in. Had you the wit to – "

" – Stop, brothers! *Please*!" Jacob implored. "Think! Perhaps we left the hatch open when we took her snails. Unless the obvious escapes you, what we took was *not* their food; the snails… they must be objects of affection?" Zadoc and Edmund grunted. "But their motive is irrelevant. What matters now is *defence*. Open war would be no use to anyone."

Still dreaming of conflict, Edmund remained silent.

"I suggest we all sleep on the hope for calm," Jacob added, "and how we best preserve it. Let us hope it is not our last night freely to do so." With that, he grunted up the ladder to his chamber.

Edmund was already so far away in the passageway that Zadoc couldn't catch his mumblings. But he knew they spoke nothing of peace.

gutting

An alarm should have sounded when Scarlett first heard her mother clattering downstairs: Mum didn't do early starts. But being so frazzled, she barely noticed the sound of her busying away.

And besides, she had bigger news. She had slept dreadfully but, somehow, they were back. Once more in their home, oblivious to being on death's menu, sat her old friends, as if nothing had happened. Only her dusty clothes, piled on her bedside chair, witnessed the truth.

Derek and Daisy absorbed her attention until she noticed the movement, beyond her window: a large pickup pulling up on the driveway. The lettering declared *Valance Farm Ltd*. By his resemblance, the driver had to be Moreton's dad. And no guessing why he'd come: Moreton had mentioned their trade in Christmas trees; lashed to the back of the truck was the biggest one she'd ever seen.

"You never said about a tree!" Scarlett called down from the landing. Richard struggled across the hall, wrestling with the thick end of the trunk as Jack Moreton followed with the crown, their plan, to whittle the end of the trunk so it would drop into the socket concealed within the middle of the hallway's mosaic floor.

"Jack offered us one," Richard beamed. "His grandfather always brought one here. And bingo, he showed me this special hole, made just for the purpose... we'd never even noticed it."

Minutes later, the tree stood proudly in place; from above, Scarlett could almost touch the tallest branches.

"Woah! Where's it from, Trafalgar Square?" Roan rushed to the balcony. "So I suppose now's not the best moment?" he whispered.

"Maybe not, but we have a result," she said. "They're back, Roe... Derek and Daisy! I just got up... and boom! There they were!"

"That's brilliant." Roan's face lit up. "I started wondering if my stick insects were next. They'd probably turn them into Twiglets? It's odd though... maybe something spoiled our friends' appetite?"

"Maybe, but it doesn't change all this," she gestured to the tree. "I mean *Christmas*? We'll all be pulling crackers while a bunch of zombie squatters spies from..." she trailed off, looking around. Roan gazed across the same space.

"Zombies?" He shook his head.

"Nah, far too quick on their feet," Scarlett agreed. "And these specimens blather on like they're stuck in some Shakespearean tragedy."

"Not vampires, either," Roan added, as if he was working through a checklist. "Even if vampires existed, snails have weird blue blood, which I doubt they'd go after. Also, consider the whole garlic thing – they had plenty of that last night, and though it was dark I never spotted any fangs or – "

" – Stop! Are we *actually* doing this, Roan? Are we chit-chatting about living, breathing ghouls, behind our walls, under my freaking bed… spying on us like pervs, planning to do God-knows what? For God's sake, they've already used you for a skin-graft!"

"Well, yeah, when you put like that, this *is* grim. But more importantly, it's also unbelievable."

"What? And your point is?"

"Think: spill all this to Mum and Dad and it just sounds barmy, like we're just out to ruin Christmas, like some kind of revenge – "

"– For being here in the first place?" Scarlett sighed. Annoying or not, it was a compelling argument. "And if we *don't* tell them, it might end up looking, in the longer run, at least a bit, well, forgetful?"

"Yeah, especially if this terrible trio pop out and butcher us."

"Have you noticed something else?"

"No… what?"

"That we're both *whispering*. Like *we're* the ones hiding?"

Roan shuddered. "There is one way for Mum and Dad to listen though," he said. "If we showed them the facts – open up the model, the passage under your bed. Maybe Dad will go in?"

"Ah, *there* you are! Lurking in the tree-tops like a couple of baubles!" Joanna called up, from the kitchen doorway. "So you decking the hall all morning or coming down for breakfast?" She was wearing a pinny. "I say it myself, but I've done a wonderful spread."

"I'll tell you one thing," Roan muttered, staring at the pinny, "ghouls are one thing, but *mum* doing a 'wonderful' breakfast? That's supernatural."

If she hadn't felt so frazzled, Scarlett would have laughed.

Sorted for the school day, they headed for the kitchen. And they'd decided. Finally, it was time to hang it all, spill everything. Or at least everything they knew. As Scarlett left her room, she forgot her phone. From her bed, it vibrated with an incoming message.

Dad's coming to yours this w/e. Have they told u? I'll come... if u feel like seeing anyone? Call me l8r? Adi X

"You sure you're up for school?" Moreton asked.

Isabel slouched over her cereal, looking badly defibrillated, her spark dampened by another feverish night. His own sleep shredded, Moreton had checked her several times.

"Gotta keep the fanbase happy, bruv," she breathed. "The price of being so popular."

"You left the welder in the trailer *again*, what you got, silage for brains?" Jack called from the hall, fighting to pull off his odorous boots.

"Sorry about that Dad, I took it up the top field, some of the new heifers have been rubbing that gate so much they broke a strut clean off."

"Ah, no worries boy. Hey, guess where I've been?" he beamed. "Up to see the lawds of the manor. Took 'em a tree. One was sincerely chuffed."

"Whitecross?" Isabel exclaimed, the word zapping her awake. "Everything okay for them? Did you see Scarlett?"

Moreton buttered his toast, feigning indifference.

"She was just getting up. You should see the fancy breakfast they 'ave, all laid out like a flippin' banquet."

"Ey! Don't you not get decent enough grub here?" Margaret chided. Emerging from a skirmish with the stove, she bore a plate of brittle bacon and congealed scrambled eggs.

"Absolutely Peg! No one fixes better grub!" he roared, slapping his wife's bottom and winking at Isabel. "How about *you*, Izzie? That lurgy finally got bored of you?"

"Oh, yeah, I'm good, Dad, good enough for school."

Moreton chewed on, wondering how much might slip beneath his parents' radar. Sure, they were aware of Isabel's occasional sleepwalking, but beyond that? Ignorance must be bliss. And they had enough to contend with. Besides, their preoccupations brought benefits: today, he had no intention of heading for the school bus.

"Is that the time?" Jack exclaimed. "You two better get a move on. Always best to be early, Moreton – don't wanna miss the seat next to the prettiest girl, eh?"

Moreton blushed. Maybe their ignorance had its limits.

"We've got something exciting to tell you, about this house… "

Joanna hoped Richard might wait until they'd all enjoyed her grand spread, but they had barely begun.

"That's funny, we've got something to tell *you*, haven't we, Roe?" said Scarlett, between gulps of fresh orange juice.

"Er, yes, I guess?" Roan faltered.

"Okay," Richard smiled, "you first!"

"U-uh," Scarlett said, "save the best for last."

"Well," Richard declared as, with a clairvoyant impulse, Scarlett instantly realised what he was about to say. *How could he even think of doing this twice?* Her realisation threatened to blot out any ability to listen. But no matter how little she might absorb, Roan knew she was heading directly towards a reaction. A volcanic one.

"So as you know," Richard began, "when we first got here, we were high and dry, with no road map for our future. And that's when a curious coincidence came along… "

"A *coincidence* to do with Adeline's father?" Scarlett shoved her plate away as if Mustard had licked it.

"Well, *yes*…" Richard paused, "After all, he's a man with his finger in a lot of pies."

"Snout, you mean," she snarled.

"If you'll just hear me out, Scarlett, before passing any death sentences?"

She folded her arms in mock surrender.

"Now as it happens, Tom was involved in a plan for a new retail centre, just up the road, in the village. We talked about it before; it was partly his reason for coming up before Hallowe'en."

"*Y-e-sss…*" Scarlett sighed, eyes rolling.

"Well, that plan got refused. So they considered other options. And that's when Tom got a bit *creative*... He had a chat with the officers and asked them how they'd judge a proposal to adapt and extend an *old* building, maybe a building needing renovation..."

"A building like this?" asked Roan. Hooray, Scarlett reflected: he was finally up to speed.

"Well, er..." Richard stuttered.

"Yes, *this* building," said Joanna, frustrated by his painful progress. "They've put a plan together, your father and Tom. If it's approved, they'll be able to sign up a range of brand names to get on board for a retail centre."

"You, you what?" Roan stuttered. "You're going to have our house turned into a *mall*?" His cutlery clanged onto the table.

"Not exactly," Richard replied.

"And how 'exactly' would that all fit in to *this*, Dad?" Roan threw his hands wide. "Is Tom Benn crazy?"

"No, he's mapped it all out. If you take out all the gubbins, maybe add a glass atrium, you'd be amazed."

"So would *they*," grunted Scarlett.

"Sorry, you've lost me," said Joanna. "They?"

"Just the people from around here," she swerved. "I just can't believe they'd want it."

"They'd actually *gut* it?" asked Roan. He could already picture a wrecking ball veering towards the kitchen window.

"In a nice way, yes... It's often the best way for problem buildings, shore up the good, chop out the bad."

"You'd certainly be doing that," Scarlett laughed.

"Precisely! No more nights hugging radiators, catching all those leaks in buckets."

"Well that's irrelevant, Richard," Joanna waded in. "There'll be no more nights here at all."

Scarlett wondered whether Roan would now deliver some truths, but his gobsmacked face took her straight back to that August bombshell, around the same table. Seconds passed. *He isn't even going to try.* She's aghast, yet her own mouth was equally useless.

"So," Richard continued, "the consortium behind the idea is offering us enough cash to buy a very nice place, maybe something less shabby, more chic? Which brings us to *where*." Joanna moved to intervene, but he raised a hand. "It could be back in London, where you wanted to be. But, if you preferred, there'd be no need to change schools again, or find your feet in a new area."

"Brilliant. All mapped out, Dad," Scarlett hissed.

"No, I know it's not perfect, Scar, but we could all end up in a better place, in every sense."

"Whatever!" The kitchen clock told her time was short. Thankfully.

"And *your* news?" Joanna asked, as she collected up the plates of half-eaten food.

"Nothing!" Scarlett snapped, thoughts spinning as she shouldered her bag. "It'll wait, it doesn't matter – not now."

peepo!

Date: December 14
From: scarlettwycherley@whitecrosshall.com
To: adelinebenn@74lincolnvale.co.uk

Adi – Don't come. I'm seriously hacked off with Dad. I was last to know – as ever. Will email. Scar

Scarlett knew she was being terse. She could have given herself more time to reflect upon it, she knew, but oldest friends or not, she was in no mood for weekends with anyone from Tom Benn's family. She was yet to learn what timetable her father intended for booking removals for a second time in fewer than five months. They would have to make some common agreement on where they might at least *like* to go? But beyond that, she realised she was equally preoccupied with something else.

    Since they'd moved, part of her strained for freedom, screamed to get away – get *back* to where everything was happening. But *now*? It felt clear the tug she'd known for so long had weakened. In its place came something less easy to square with who she thought she was. Beyond the irritation of being expected to be a textbook Obedient Daughter, beyond the effort of trying to make sense of life in a fusty wreck in the middle of nowhere, she sensed a new awareness.

    Sitting at her desk, still in her uniform, she eyed her reflection across the room and wondered how she might have missed something so obvious. And so exciting. She tingled at the prospect.

    Taking the scissors, she stepped towards the mirror. With her free hand, she twisted and furled the side of her hair that remained relatively long. The way she'd seen her world was so pinned-down. Now might it float free?

    She was stuck here, miles from life, but what did she need? Shopping? The human right to buy stuff, even if stuff bought ends up as stuff stuffed in a cupboard. Snip. The blades sliced through the first tress. If there was anything she needed, there was always the web.

Friends? Snip, snip. She squinted to judge a line of symmetry. They were all a flick of her thumb away – and easier to switch off from here.

Personal space? Snip, snip. A pile of strands began to amass at her feet. Did *true* space ever exist in London? Might London feel like a rediscovered pair of shoes unearthed from the bottom of a wardrobe: exciting, but annoyingly tight? The hand she watched, so busy with the scissors, finally stopped, the lopsidedness, lopped away. If the first cut had been a stepping stone, tonight was the other side. She stood back. She'd never had hair so short. It was a self-cut mess. A disaster.

Perfect.

Dad would hate it. She hoped. They'd both see it as a protest. Well spotted. She looked down at the dark pile of her severed self. Did all those days of what she was now belong to the past? Could she bin them? Yes, they held no currency for her future.

But then a whisper pinged into her calm: *what will Moreton think?* She hadn't seen him that day. Isabel had made it to the bus – just – looking like she'd got there via a teleporting device. With dodgy wiring. But no, no Moreton. *Where* was he? Isabel had no idea. She'd felt him like a gap in the long day.

She returned the scissors to her desk. *Whatever, it's his problem. If he wants the true me, where does hair figure in that?* Maybe he had no such expectations. Maybe he had no expectations at all. Only one way to know.

She faced her mobile. Click. It was as bad as any selfie could be, but that was just it.

Made discoveries with Roan. As you can see, am losing it. If you're okay getting out, come over. Be warned: I experiment with blades. Scar x

There was no time for regret.

No worries. Just finishing cows. Be over 7ish . . . yay! Cool cut! Mx

His reply was fluster-free. What more might she want? Nothing, but if her head trusted her eyes, her stomach wouldn't.

"Silent night, holy night . . ."

It was early for carols, but as she melted in the bath's heat, Joanna's imagination drifted to the weeks ahead.

She sipped the gin and tonic Richard had brought her, returning the heavy bottomed tumbler, with a clunk, to the edge of the bath. It steadied the nerves. Sure, another house move would be in the pipeline, post the New Year, but at least she and Richard now had a plan. A joint one. They could finally relax about this creaking pile. Joanna didn't expect Scarlett to understand, but she hoped she might one day see this turbulent patch in their life as that and nothing more.

"All is calm, all is bright," she hummed.

Steam tumbled in folding veils. He'd put too much bubble bath in. The foam was crazy. But it was as rare a moment of happiness as she could remember within Whitecross. He'd even lit a trio of tealight candles and put them around the head of the bath; so much nicer than the stark light bulb, though the limits of the room remained pitch black.

"Sleep in heavenly peeece, sleep in heav-en-ly – "

" – You will, ma'am," grated a voice, somewhere beneath the foam.

"Rich... *Richard?*" she called, looking round. "Are you there? Is this some joke?"

And then – puff! Out went the first candle, closest to the taps.

"Richard!" she yelled.

"Violent night, lonely night..." the voice chuckled. A low voice, a message from the other side. Delivered via Victorian plumbing.

"Flee from harm, choked with fright." The voice was bolder. Closer?

Puff. Another candle snuffed. Just one now remained.

She could still make out her bathrobe and towel, there across the room. It would be the longest journey of her life. But in the absence of gills, she knew she couldn't hide.

Leaning forward to grab the last candle, she resolved to dash for the chair. But as her arm reached out, a sluice of cold air washed against it – a rush of ventilation that could only come from one place: the overflow hole. Momentarily, her focus flitted to that place. Which is when she saw it.

An eye. Glinting.

A cold, bloodless iris.

As if someone has lobbed an electric fire into the water, Joanna was up and across the floor, half wrapped in the towel, legging it before Zadoc even had time to retreat from his spy-hole, re-attaching the overflow pipe to the concealed side of the bath. To anyone hearing her scream, the vision was surely the imagination of a woman who enjoyed a little too much early-evening G&T. After all, in what conceivable way could anyone look through an overflow? There would have to be a cavity behind it.

Zadoc hadn't planned it, but his temper won him over: with the bath filled and his cavity beautifully warm, he'd relished an early night. But when the infernal woman got in and began warbling, it was just too much. And besides, to the victor, the spoils: now shot of her, he pivoted the bath's side panel inwards, wormed his long fingers up over the ledge and salvaged her abandoned drink.

"Cheers, missus," he said, downing it in one slurp. "Gin's the ruin of mothers, in any case." A vague thought crossed his mind that a direct confrontation with the matriarch of the house might trigger an undesirable reaction, but perhaps Edmund's lust for confrontation was contagious? That morning, they may have agreed to return the girl's beloved snails, but peace, he sensed, was far from breaking out.

With the bath above still radiating heat, he settled back. "All is calm, all is bright," he growled. "Oh, to sleep in heavenly peace."

The knock came just as Joanna slammed the bedroom door shut, jumping into Richard's arms like a traumatised kangaroo. Amid shudders, she recounted her ordeal. But the knocker wasn't going away.

"Can you get that, somebody... *anybody*?" Richard called. Scarlett's door was shut; she was probably playing loud music, so it was down to Roan, head in his laptop, to do the honours. He shuffled downstairs, finding Moreton huddling against a slant of sleety drizzle.

"Scarlett's in her room; go on up."

They paused in the hall, listening awkwardly to strange yelps coming from the main bedroom.

"Maybe Mum's got cramp. Who knows? Scarlett can update you."

Moreton pushed the door. She was at her desk and at least looked remarkably together.

"Y'okay?" he asked, then realising her obvious change: "Oh, yeah... the hair thing... well, nothing a hat can't sort?"

"Thing? At least I *have* a hairstyle," she laughed, closing her laptop. "So how's farming? Obviously much more interesting than school."

"Nah, just needed some headspace. Had a heavy night, with Isabel."

"Yeah, we all need space. When I got your text, and saw the lights up on the tump, I thought you'd lost the plot."

"You and me both. You had to be there... wasn't like I had a choice."

His limbs were stiff as his words, hardly calming Scarlett's nagging fear that, whatever might be between them, fate was out to spoil it. She motioned for him to sit down; he moved her school bag from her armchair and committed to the edge.

"Isabel came over all strange – this time it went up a notch. As if she were someone else, someone not exactly pleasant."

A smile played on Scarlett's lips. "You're sure it's not just a girl thing? We can be complex."

"It wasn't, believe me."

"Sorry, I'm being flippant. What did your sister, if she *was* your sister, actually say?"

"In as many words? She ordered me to cut away the bars... around the grave. And if I didn't, Isabel wouldn't be with us, by the morning."

"Jeez, Moreton."

"I know. *Insane*. But it was no wind-up, for sure. I should've called you... I'm not scared of the dark, but it wasn't exactly fun."

"I can imagine." She admired his honesty.

"But no choice. Anyhow, she's loads better now, for whatever reason – more herself. I'm not superstitious, but it wasn't worth the risk."

"*Risk?*" What do you mean, Mort, are you telling me everything, because hell's let loose here. If there's anything you know that might help, now's a good time."

He sighed deeply. "Basically, Scar, my sister's *always* been as she is."

Scarlett laughed. "I guessed that, it's what makes her Iz."

"Sure, but it's dangerous when you factor in... well, the stuff I showed you: the grave, the stories she's told you. The problem is, it's *not* a story: what happened, all those generations ago, that happened to *real* people. Boxwell sounds like a baddy, but he was flesh and blood. As was Rosamond, who he married. Before she first married, in fact... before she married Jeb Tow," he says, shifting in his seat, "she was born a Valance."

Scarlett recoiled. "Talk about keeping stuff in!" Her mind reeled as she voiced a realisation out loud: "So, it's not like Iz is being got at from outside, more like she's connecting to something *inside*. In her blood?"

"That, or thereabouts."

Scarlett suppressed a shiver. Taking her hand, he pulled her to his lap.

"Thanks," he said, drawing her closer.

"What for?" Her fingers closed around his.

"Anyone else, even if there *was* anyone I'd tell, would think our whole family needs therapy. Or a deal with reality TV."

"Yeah and my family's just so normal? What's funny is the timing."

"How?"

"Well, while you're doing insurance with your blowtorch, me and Roan were back here, maybe doing the opposite? Taking a huge risk." She looked down as he placed a finger under her chin, tilting her face up. "First, my snails: one minute they're here, the next gone."

"Maybe your mum hired a hungry French cleaner?"

"Ha ha."

"So any clues?"

"Oh, just *hours* of video. It's not all bad, having a geeky brother."

"You mean... what? You've got evidence, on film?"

"Kind of: we fixed a camera in Roan's room, and my laptop... just here." She gestured to her desk.

"And you what, caught someone, like red-handed?"

"We got film, of a woman, carrying a doll's house, to Roan's room."

"A *woman*? A doll's house?" He shuddered.

"It's a perfect replica of *this* house. It turned up in the kitchen, the other morning, and we thought that was weird, but then it popped up again, in Roan's room. Come and see; it's on his floor. You can enjoy the videos, too."

"That'd be, er, nice, though you still haven't explained the 'risk'."

Scarlett shrugged. "I'm getting there, though if you want to bail out, I'd not blame you."

He looked puzzled. "No. I'm happy. I just keep thinking it'd be... well, good to hook up and not feel like we're in –"

"– a parallel universe?"

"Yeah, something like that."

enlightenment

"Ta-da!" Roan marked the spot on the recording when the doll's house appeared. Moreton watched in silence. "The model arrives in the gap between these two files."

"So if there's a *gap*, what do you have to go on?" Moreton asked.

"A cross-reference, from my laptop," Scarlett explained. "Here."

Accessing the file, Roan freeze-framed to where the smudgy form glided into view, hauling the model into his room.

"Someone's been busy! But the model itself…" he said, turning to look at it on the floor, "what's so interesting about it? Why does it matter?"

"I'll show you," Roan replied, crouching to take hold of the north tower. "You just press this like so, and it opens."

But it didn't.

"Wait," he said. "The mechanism must be sticky." He pressed again. He wiggled, levered, strained. It was rock-solid.

"I don't get it," he gasped. "Look round the edges, here, you can see where it opens, but it's like it's re-locked itself. Damn *thing*!" He gazes around the room, as if searching for hidden eyes. Scarlett read his thoughts: is someone playing with them? Is this just their dark game?

"It doesn't matter, Roe – just tell him what it shows."

Roan explained the hidden layers, leaving Moreton puzzled: "So these layers are what, places to hide away?"

"Exactly."

"Then how d'you get in?" he asked.

"If you *wanted* to get in?" Scarlett scoffed.

"We *know* how," Roan added.

"Let me guess, a book case that swivels, the back of a wardrobe?"

"Possibly. We only know one – it's the way they got into my room and took Derek and Daisy."

"Where could that be?"

"We'll show you," Roan offered.

In Scarlett's room, they raised the edge to her duvet.

"I just did a run-up and gave it a boot," Scarlett said, still proud.

"A *run-up*?" Moreton judged the distance. "Remind me never to lock you out. Then what?"

"This panel caved in. I was angry: I wasn't sure what I wanted to do, but there was no way I wasn't going to get my snails."

"So… you went… *inside*?" His eyes widened.

"We *both* did." Her chin seemed all the more defiant now her hair was so boldly cropped.

"We followed a route through the space," Roan said. "It drops down, by a ladder, into the edge of this room without windows – a space that's squeezed between the kitchen, the library and sitting room."

"Unbelievable."

"Yeah, but *that* was the believable bit."

"What d'you mean?"

"They're in there, Moreton," Scarlett said. "It's where they live."

"They?"

"Three of them," Roan added. "We watched them, sitting there, by their cosy fire, enjoying a meal."

"Oh no… not your snails?"

"I thought they'd eaten them, but then they had a row, one of them has a seriously acid temper. We legged it and they spotted us, maybe… all we know is boom: next morning, my snails are back, like nothing happened."

"A happy ending!" Moreton laughed, unconvincingly. "And this panel, it just what, comes off?" Beneath his sturdy fingers it felt solid.

"With a kick," Scarlett nodded. "Move."

Before they could stop her, she turned and flayed a heel out hard. Nothing budged.

Morton grinned and paced towards the door. "Let's show it a proper one, eh?" Flying towards the end of the bed, he delivered a crashing blow, but nothing gave and the momentum of his body continued, angling him up and over Scarlett's bed, where he landed, in a bundle of bedclothes.

"What on *earth* are you lot up to?" Richard stood in the doorway.

Moreton jumped up from the bed, looking sheepish. He'd explain, but Scarlett got in first: "Sorry Dad! Moreton popped by, and we were all just here, talking, when we thought we saw – a mouse! Yeah, it went into a crack, under my bed, and Moreton was trying to tackle it, and – "

"– a mouse?" Richard cut in, "Cuh, whatever next? You know what, Moreton, mice can get to the back of the queue," he groaned. "I'll be glad to be shot of this place. Mum's in a state – she had a scare in the bathroom. I told her, it's all in her imagination. That, or we have bigger vermin. Ho-hum. Well,

I'm going to get her a top-up and something for myself. Maybe Scarlett will sort you a hot drink, Moreton, if she remembers her manners?"

"So it was *this* panel?" Moreton whispered, with her father finally out of earshot.

"Totally," said Roan.

"Well, whoever's behind it," Roan pondered, "they've had enough. They're closed for visits tonight."

⚿

"What was that all about?" Huddling on the bed with a brandy, the glass chinked against Joanna's teeth.

"What? Oh *that*... apparently, they saw a mouse, Moreton tried to wallop it . . . I suspect teenage horseplay."

"Not poltergeists then, nor visiting aliens?"

"Nope, no more supernaturals tonight," he said, rubbing her arm. "And we're agreed, as to whatever you *thought* you saw?"

"I guess. Like you say, it'd hardly help to talk about such things, and we'll be gone soon enough."

"Exactly, darling."

"On one condition," she added.

"What?"

"That I never use *that* bathroom again. It's ensuite or nothing now."

"Absolutely," Richard soothed. But whether a change of bathroom might fix everything, he was far from convinced. Increasingly, not least whenever he sat on the lavatory, he felt a sensation of being not quite alone. It wasn't as if he expected a disembodied hand to pass the loo roll, but it was a feeling of . . . company. Every time he pulled the chain, he wondered if history was piled so high in Whitecross it would never flush away.

⚿

"So why don't you talk to them – tell'em straight?" Moreton asked, as he lifted the lid on Scarlett's glass case to witness her snails' survival.

"Yeah! They'd just laugh it off as some plot to undermine them." She stood before the grand mirror. Despite Moreton's presence, she couldn't resist checking her hair again, just to be sure it wasn't a crazed decision.

"She's probably right," Roan sighed, as he loitered in her doorway. "Before Mum and Dad spilled the beans, about selling up, we thought they'd just see all this as us trying to scare them into getting us all out. But now that we *are* going, I guess they'd say we're just spinning all this to make the house impossible to sell."

Moreton stared, aghast. "Woah! Back up a minute. *Selling up?* I thought your dad said something odd – is this true, Scar?"

"We only found out today. Dad's in on a deal, a 'business venture'."

"What, so you'll up sticks and... just go?"

"Ah, I think I'll leave you two for now," Roan mumbled, fearing he'd activated a time bomb. Gingerly, he pulled the door shut.

"No, *nothing's* decided," Scarlett said, avoiding eye contact. "Dad's agreed on a 'project' – for a shopping centre."

"You what? For here?" He was stunned.

"Yep, he says Whitecross will be *gutted,* then converted into a commercial centre, a big hall with lots of little 'boutique' shops."

'Gutted,' he repeated flatly.

"But if I can, I want to stay." She took his hand.

"But gutted? There'd be *no way* you could stay. It's the end for Whitecross, isn't it?"

"We'd have to leave, but *I* don't want to. Sounds mad, but I'm happy here. In a way..."

She leant to pull him closer. He didn't resist, but was lost in a myriad of thoughts. If the Wycherleys had stirred up so much mud for Isabel, what would a line of bulldozers do? Shaking his head, he closed his arms around her. Their thoughts lost, they moved closer still until, unplanned, unthinking, they kissed. Scarlett felt weightless.

"You said happy? Well that's something." He stared into her eyes, then suddenly snapped from a reverie: "Sod it! I've got to go – right now! I told Dad I'd be there to help out before the end of the milking."

In the doorway, he stopped. "You know I don't like you being here... this place, it feels like it's coming to God-knows-what. And with Iz... it's like we're all dragged in."

"I know, I *know*... I get it..."

"But…" he added, "maybe it's selfish: I like the thought of you going much less."

"It's not selfish."

"Why's that?"

"Because I feel the same, you idiot!" she grinned. "Now go on, get back to your precious cows!"

"What do these prattling lovebirds twitter about?" Zadoc hissed. "Tell me, Jacob; I fear the urge to vomit doth preclude my ability to listen. What is the detail of their business?"

Sandwiched beneath Scarlett's bed, Zadoc was in no mood for spying after his early bed had been so rudely interrupted. The cavity beneath the bath was wonderfully warm after Mrs Wycherley stopped by, but Jacob soon dragged him here after what he'd described as a "violent attack": a rain of blows upon his chamber that he had barely managed to repel. And with Edmund out stalking the gardens for tomorrow's menu, Zadoc had been his only recourse.

The voices were muffled. Employing a favourite trick, Jacob pressed his ear to a knot of wood, the grain's concentric pattern funnelling the acoustics of the room beyond. Yet he still struggled.

"Damn their parlance! The youth of this silly century have surrendered control of their tongues," he grumbled. "But one fact is assured: our trysting lovers are troubled, albeit impossible to determine precisely wherefore."

He shushed Zadoc with a flap of his hands. In the silence, a more distinct string of words fed through, words that struck like a slap against his wizened face: Whitecross will be *something*, she said. What *was* that word? When the boy repeated it, it was acid in the canals of his ancient ear.

Gutted.

"Oh," said Jacob, a broken little sound that convinced his brother there was good reason *not* to insist upon knowing more. Not before the three were gathered.

wheels on fire

Clammy from the night, Edmund shambled back to the fireside. Already plucked at his favourite spot, the heart of the maze, he secured the brace of crows on the hook above the hearth before rekindling the embers. It was not until he turned around that he noticed Zadoc and Jacob, sitting slack-shouldered, in a symmetry of surrender.

"You have faces like dropped pies. Is it *that* bad?"

"*That bad*, it is," growled Zadoc. "Ask your brother. He heard it first."

"So?" Edmund barked. "Sing, Jacob, sing freely. I despise suspense on an empty stomach."

"Ah, I may be wrong," Jacob began, "for our ears, verily, are not what they were."

"Nonsense. Of our six, yours are the sharpest. Pray, tell."

"Well t'is thus: the children, I heard them – the daughter, the boy from Valance Farm."

"Oh well, if this pertains to the *Valances*, forget a pinch of salt. I'll take a handful with their tittle-tattle."

"But it wasn't him; t'was *her*." Jacob's fingers writhed. Edmund sensed he may need an early drink. "They've sold the house," he finally said. "*This* house."

"Sold it!" Edmund broke into laughter. "Fabulous! At last! When shall they quit? By George! And you say *bad*? Why the scowling? You fools!" He reached for the half-drunk claret from the night before and popped the cork loose, its fall muted against the floor's carpet of matted decay. "Three glasses – gentlemen, we celebrate!"

"That *might* be hasty," Jacob added. "They've sold it to businessmen."

"*Business*-men? And what issue there? They'll perhaps not have verminous children and may be away half the time."

"But there's the rub," Jacob interjected. "Businessmen, I might subjoin, who plan to…" he looked helplessly towards Zadoc. Could he not relieve him of this burden?

Zadoc sighed. "What our brother seeks to impart, Edmund, in his buttock-numbing way, is that they are selling up, to unknown characters, who desire to fashion our abode into a mercantile cornucopia. A giant *shop*. By which means they would remove all of the, shall we say, innards. The specific verb used, as Jacob is certain, was 'gut'."

Edmund had the goblet poised at his papery lips. "Gut?" he breathed, holding the vessel still.

"Gut."

"So, metaphorically, as pertaining to a fish?" he asked, returning the untouched vessel to the table.

"Just as a fish," Zadoc nodded. "Our house, a fish; us, a kipper. There indeed lies, what did your Yankee friends call it, Jacob, the rub?

"So. This *is* bad, bad indeed." Pursing his mouth against emotion, Edmund pulled out a chair. Raising a desiccated hand, he pushed the lank hair from his face. It has been decades since he had cried, but Zadoc feared it now. It would signal a crumbling of their walls long before any sledgehammer was used in anger.

"Brothers, I believe *we* are the gut. It will surely be the end of us," Jacob groaned.

"The end of us," Zadoc echoed.

"Our goose is cooked," Jacob wailed.

"As would inevitably be any manner of bird," Zadoc gnashed, "that we might care to – "

"– oh, I do wish you two moppets would *stop*!" Edmund thundered, throwing his goblet into the fire with a smash and a swoosh of wasted claret.

"Stop what?" Jacob asked.

"Stop, for a start, repeating *everything* like clucking hens. We need to *think*, not wail like short-changed costermongers. You appear confused: we are not fish, nor geese: we are *human*, laughable as such realisation may be when I behold you."

Zadoc felt relief: give him Edmund's toxicity over his tears any day.

"First," Edmund continued, "how did we not *see* this, not *hear* it?"

He paced the room, scratching feverishly at a sore patch on the side of his head, pausing only to remove something from beneath his fingernail. Gnawing the offending item, he spat it into the dampened fire.

Zadoc closed his eyes, as if in prayer: "Edmund, you do your work splendidly as our provider. Gathering intelligence befalls us. We listen, we observe whatever, whenever, but we cannot be *everywhere*. And these people, they are unusual; they triumph in the unexpected. They are odd, untrustworthy. They have even trespassed, as we know. Perhaps we should have perceived warnings, I know, but – "

" – You *know*? You *dare* use that word?" Edmund slammed his fist upon the table. "Well, *I* intend, to know, and know *more*! Tonight I will visit the library; the master tends his affairs there. We move swiftly. Time is short."

Richard preferred to check emails when the house was asleep. He crossed the library to refill his tumbler before settling at his desk. Comically undersized for its space, it sat within the window's recess, its sides framed by long curtains, though an awkward gap remained. He was too tired to draw them closer, and besides, the view was pleasant: outside, the lights of the room revealed the beginnings of a frost silvering the lawn. Momentarily, he wondered how many previous occupants had stared out from this window to witness the same scene.

To his right, the curtain undulated gently. He put that down to the draught around his ankles. Eventually, he found the email, buried in his inbox: a file, a document attached. He scrolled through ponderous paragraphs.

Taking another sip of whisky, he returned the tumbler to the desktop, beside the keyboard. The jargon bewildered; a printed copy for bedtime reading had to be better than frostbitten feet. But he would need the correct printer lead first. A search through the spaghetti of leads Roan had left by the bookcase produced nothing. He left to try the kitchen dresser.

Finally, back at the desk with a more promising lead in hand, he failed to notice his chair, in a slightly different position. Or his tumbler, now lighter, and bearing dusty fingerprints. Most of all, he didn't spot how the document had been scrolled down to its final paragraph. He simply hit PRINT, collected the sheets and retired.

In his absence, Edmund had seen enough. The document's arcane language was depressingly clear. No law existed to stop Whitecross becoming a shop. There was even government finance to help the vandalism. Bar howling at the moon, it was all over.

Emerging from behind the curtain, he shouldered the central section of the bookcase. It rotated free and he stepped through, into the passageway. Anger seethed from every atom of his ancient body.

"This cannot be the end," he growled. "Intervention is our only recourse. What now have we to lose?"

He tugged the bookcase shut, but a trailing end of his coat tails jammed tight in the frame. From behind, muted grunts rang out as he wrestled to retract it. Finally, the garment slid free, the bookcase clunking back into place. As if he was never there.

In semi-sleep, cold fingers grappled Scarlett's thoughts. Through endless circles of monologue, she longed for the reason of daylight. But this new dimension… wouldn't the rumour of it alone send anyone sane running for the exit? Creatures unknown squatting in their home, parasites in a parallel plan, weirdos in the walls… all the same, she knew their trespass was arguable. After all, how much was this truly *her* home? True, she no longer daydreamed for life somewhere else, but could anywhere with such a patina of the past be somewhere you could feel belonged entirely to her, to Roan, to *anyone* alive? Dad wrote the cheque, but what makes her family any more than lodgers? And besides, weren't her parents now telling her to pack up and say goodbye? Above all, she wondered if she should feel more fear. A voice screamed yes: she *must* feel scared witless. Yet how could she now contemplate fear, instead of sweating it? Maybe it was Roan's fault, with his abstract logic, knitting everything into normality, but how do you rationalise the presence of those who lived and died, those who must have departed years and years ago, yet somehow, somewhere along the line, forgot to do the dying bit? Wrestling to find an easier place in the mattress, she punched the pillow into obedience.

"Prithee, mistress, let us not commence such tomfoolery again."

This time, she didn't pause. "Oh, *sorry* for the interruption, but if you hadn't been *messing* our lives up in the first place, we'd all be getting a decent night's rest."

"I recognise your contention, young lady, but perhaps you approach the equation from the wrong end?"

She sat up and gave her head a shake. Nope: it was definitely a conversation with the disembodied voice of a Shakespearean actor who'd decided to Airbnb under her mattress. In her intimate space, without so much as a cheers matey.

"The 'wrong end'?" she gasped. "And that means what? 'I was here first?' Don't make me laugh!" Given his silence, he wasn't planning to. "I think we need to talk," she finally added, taken aback by her own confidence. "I think we ought to – "

"– Indeed you do; indeed we should. The wheels of time's winged chariot are verily smoking. What we need, Mistress Wycherley, is a parley."

"A *parley*?"

"With yourself and Master Wycherley. I propose you come, you sit and you speak with us. In the interest of a mutual benefit."

Scarlett shuddered.

"Furthermore, I am sorry," the voice added.

"*Sorry?*" This *has* to be a dream.

"On behalf of myself, and my brothers, I wish it be known that we are sorry. Regarding the regrettable affair of the giant snails."

The snails? After so much, it felt as if their disappearance was history. How hilarious that whoever owned this voice could actually be *sorry*.

"Um, okay... apology accepted?"

"A mistake, on our part. It may not befit me to speak collectively, but Zadoc has the temper of a wasp in October while Edmund is a black dog walking upright. A prize pair, indeed, but they are not..." he hesitated.

"Not *what*?" The word she suspected was monsters.

"Not so... bad, t'is all. Sleep well tonight, I will quit and not dally. *Requiesce in pace.*"

"Well that's, er, relaxing, I guess."

"And tomorrow, let us be in touch again. Should I find accord with my brethren, let us convene, for the benefit of all."

"Okayyyy." Scarlett felt dazed, but within minutes, slid into a long-awaited sleep, where images of tomorrow floated unbidden into her dreams.

tomorrow

"So this voice," Roan whispered, "it suggests, *what*? Meeting... as in, what, actually *meeting*?"

Scarlett wolfed toast while Roan chased cereal around a bowl. Joanna had dashed away to find money for school lunch; today was the end-of-term Christmas dinner.

"We've nothing to lose. Whoever they are, *what*-ever, they know what's going on – they know far more of our lives than we do of theirs... and if they're as freaky as it seems, it's my guess they might need to help us." Roan shrugged. "Think about it, Roe. For them, everything's at stake. If they've been here as long as the stories say, maybe their survival depends on remaining here?"

Roan mused over all the *legend-has-it* spiel from Isabel. Mad as it was, Scarlett's pillow talk hardly tore such tales apart. But he lowered his spoon and stared with wooden detachment.

"Sorry if I'm not keeping up, but I'm trying to get my head round the idea of a sister who finds spooks living behind our walls, only to come up with the brainwave of getting chummy with them and launching some kind of diplomatic mission."

She dabbed crumbs from her plate. "Okay, perhaps think of it as more of a *deal*?"

"And *who* are you 'dealing' with, young lady?" Joanna asked, breezing back in.

"Damn it Mum, you busted our county line! Anyone'd think we had a paranoid mum, spying on her own kids."

"Very funny, but you'll understand, one day – and it's only natural to be curious."

"Nosy, more like."

"Okay," she persisted, "but indulge me, who's this 'deal' with?"

Scarlett sighed. "I was talking to Roe about Adeline: she texted to say she's coming up tomorrow, with her dad... and she's invited me to a New Year's party..."

"Yeah," Roan waded in, "and Scar was wondering how to butter you up for an exit pass to London – I suggested she offers to do some chores."

"Aah, that's touching, but no need – I'm sure we'd be fine with her coming – and there's not going to be much need for chores here, is there?"

"Yeah, seeing as Dad wants to rip our lives up," Scarlett growled.

"Well 'rip' is a bit strong. Maybe Whitecross will end up lovelier?" Joanna tidied the plates.

"Huh. Remind me, if we ever come shopping here, to the place where people lived for generations, all turned into a stupid mall."

Grabbing her bag, Scarlett flounced from the room, giving the kitchen door a medium-level slam. Mustard flapped his ears.

"Is this all just the sale?" Joanna looked at Roan hopefully.

"That's anyone's guess. We're both late though, come to think… better dash, catch ya later, mum."

In a flurry of uniform, he, too, vanished.

"*Catch ya later?*" Joanna mouthed to the doorway. Barely a blink ago, Scarlett went to bed as a daughter and woke up as a grunting imposter. Now she could see Roan sliding into a matching state. She poured more tea and settled into the armchair beside Mustard, who snored at the foot of the Aga. She'd always liked this spot, but after last night's bath, felt less sure. No: parental guilt could go hang. They *have* to leave.

Her eyes rested on the gauze covering a vent, above the pantry. There was nothing behind it; nothing she could see.

One day to the Christmas break, school spirits were high. But from the last bell all the way home, Scarlett thought only of her 'parley'. It weighed more heavily than any books lugged home for holiday reading.

Moreton sensed her state of mind; when she told him of her agreement he still wondered if a fever hadn't infected them all. All the same, he offered to go in with her and Roan. But Scarlett was clear: anyone more might blow everything. She'd already seen them erupt. And, in any case, she'd keep her phone on. If hell broke loose… he'd know about it soon enough.

In her room, the panel beneath her bed was uninvitingly ajar. Driven by determination, she led. Roan followed less surely, fingers feeling for the kitchen knife concealed in his pocket. Unaware of his weapon, Scarlett hoped a packet of biscuits, filched from the larder, might help. She has no idea what might please the tastebuds of the technically dead, but they'd no appetite for snails, and didn't everyone love a digestive?

To Roan, the hidden space felt changed. This time, there was no comfort of ignorance: something, some *things,* live within. They'd attacked him, yet the imprint of violence was somehow smudged in his memory. The details, now surfacing, knock the spring from his step. At least he knew the invisible drop that awaited at the head of the bed. In turn, they reached for the ladder down to the corridor. At the end, in the murk, they perceived the room ahead. A kitchen, styled by the Transylvanian branch of IKEA.

"Children, do not lurk in the shadows."

Before they could be seen, the voice came from the edge of the hearth. In the glow, Scarlett made out an angular silhouette, crouching but unlikely to be much bigger than herself. Almost silently, the figure drew upright and padded towards them, an arm creaking faintly, an outstretched hand. Caught in the firelight, the shape of his sleeves, a ruffled grey silk spilling from the flared edges of his cuffs, urged her to recoil. Her fashion radar was sharp enough to spot something outdated, but this was another level: the approaching figure was wearing a knee-length frock coat. She shuddered at the prospect of physical contact; it felt as natural as being able to reach inside an oil painting.

"*Scaaar-let. Ro-an*," the voice croaked. "Your names, we know already. But please, forgive my incivility: I am Jacob."

Scarlett watched her own palm extend as he bent forward. Connecting her fingers gently in a cool but firm clasp, he bowed to kiss the back of her hand. She closes her eyes, anticipating the caress of a cat's tongue, but his lips feel suede-dry, neither hot nor cold. A step behind, Roan's fingers tightened around the handle of his hidden knife.

"Come!" Jacob gestured to the chairs, "Sit. Zadoc shall join with us presently. Our brother, Edmund, too. He is yet busy abroad, but he shall not be long."

They sat in a triangle of awkwardness.

"*How* is he busy?" Scarlett asked, a voice inside her crying *Woah! You're chatting with an animated corpse!*

"I would offer you tea, but such niceties escape me," he said, ignoring her question. Scarlett peered towards the blackened urn, thankful for his lack of hospitality. Carefully, she placed the biscuits on the table.

"I brought these… maybe you'd like some?"

"I thought so… digestives! And fresh ones, too! They *will* be a treat." Jacob inhaled lustily. "Edmund, to answer your question, is our provider in all things alimentary. Zadoc cooks, he creates, but it is to the hunting hands of Edmund that we owe our sustenance."

"And you? What's your… thing, exactly?" Roan wondered if she wasn't pushing her luck.

"That depends upon whom you ask. They may tell you I provide distraction, the laughter to nurse us through the dark nights, the dark decades. I prefer to describe myself as their vision – their philosopher."

"Vision?"

"Vision is everything, dear girl, though it is nothing without humour… humour breathes life into philosophy, and the latter is what keeps us together."

Together? Jacob spoke in riddles, but the word forced Roan to think of the wart, and the brothers' urgency to regain it. And where was the humour in that? What was so funny about ghouls who went about dropping bits of themselves all over the place, then torturing anyone unfortunate enough to pick up the pieces? His grip on the hidden handle stayed firm.

No one heard Zadoc loom from the shadows. Drawing a chair alongside Jacob, his eyes make Roan recoil: an unfamiliar face, but a pale stare that jolts him to a memory. In the darkness, he began to draw the knife, desire to settle scores rising in his chest.

"*Vision!*" Zadoc chuckled. "What a huge word. I do hope my brother is not boring you."

"Steady," said Jacob, "our chat has been genteel, let us not spoil it."

Against Jacob, Scarlett senses Zadoc was a force to be reckoned with, but at that moment a cold draught disturbs the room: announcing himself more as an idea than a physical presence, she realised the final brother had arrived. For Roan, the arrival of a third entity dampened his determination: were he to seek revenge on Zadoc, the odds were now dire.

From the left of the fireside, Edmund drifted closer. A few inches taller, the oldest brother's grace and poise set him beyond question as their likely leader. More potent than the two who sat before them, more credibly human, Scarlett sensed. But as Zadoc lit a candle and threw relief upon her impressions, she saw that he shared the same paper-dry skin.

"I trust you have offered our guests refreshment?" Edmund spoke loftily to the room.

"Oh, we're okay... thanks," Scarlett said, realising Roan had remained speechless since they entered the chamber.

"You have surely much to ask." Edmund rotated a chair, straddled it and rested his sharp elbows upon the back. Setting himself a distance apart, he sat like a reptilian judge.

"No, not really," she replied. "Perhaps later. I think we have more urgent things to discuss."

"Shrewd words, young lady," Edmund nodded. "From my perusal, your father has disappointed us. Sublimely."

"Well join the club: he disappointed us from day one. After all, he chose this place."

Jacob laughs, but Edmund was impassive.

"I struggle to accept that, Mistress Wycherley. Taking Whitecross as a country seat suggests a man of taste."

Scarlett leant closer, palms upturned. "No offence, Ed – you don't mind if I call you Ed? Edmund's a bit old-school..." Roan feared she might get them swiftly downgraded to prisoners, "but what *really* gets me is this: most old houses might come with a few pests, you know – woodworm, cockroaches, but . . ." she stalled, "what sort are *you*? You skulk about, hide behind walls and one of you – I know this for a *fact* – has been spying on my bedroom. I could have the police throw away the key... this might shock you but it's the twenty-first century and we've got a word for this kind of thing, you know, it's – "

"Enough Scarlett!" Roan finally interjected. "We didn't come this far to sit and argue."

"Fret not, children, we are here to listen," Edmund said, raising a finger. "And by all means, I am not averse to the abbreviation of Ed, if you do not mind 'Scar'?" His lips twisted into a smile. "It has a certain ring." She said nothing. "Perhaps," he adds, "we can be less constrained with the use of formal epithets?"

Edmund saw Scarlett is a pot close to boiling over, but continued: "It would probably be impossible to live in this concealed domain and *not* acquire so much knowledge of your lives, but calm yourself, Mistress Scar, no one has *spied* on you. Our good brother Jacob, as I believe you know, has for years more than I can count chosen to make his quarters in the space beneath the bed, in 'your' room, but he would never, trust me, *could* never, have spied on you."

"Yeah, so how're you so sure?" she glared.

"Because, dear child, is it not plain as the light of day? Look closer. He is utterly blind."

The light was terrible, but she couldn't believe it had not been obvious: the staring into the distance, the way he smiled, as if he saw what no one else might. Suddenly, that philosophy, that 'vision' he talked about… everything was clear. She felt so stupid. For Roan, the truth painted everything in a new light: were Zadoc's actions as a kidnapper fuelled by brotherly protection? He might not rush to forgive him, but the truth blunted his anger.

"Perhaps it takes a blind person to see more than us," said Edmund. "Probably because his hearing is so annoyingly sharp," he laughed. "Young Jacob has the ears of an owl. He was first to discover your father's foul plot."

"I see," said Scarlett, instantly regretting her choice of verb.

"What happened?" Roan asked. "Were you *always* like this, Jacob, or was it an accident?"

"Perhaps, dear brother," Edmund said, reaching to touch Jacob's arm, "you can enlighten our guests? I will brew some tea, so we may savour these fine biscuits to their best potential."

Jacob's tale

"I will come to what happened, but a little context might help.

I don't think anyone contests that we have not been here for some time. Our father, Robert Boxwell, built this house. We grew up within its confines: for sleep, schooling, play… as much as he permitted. And after our mother departed, we survived as best we could.

When *he* finally passed on, a short time later, he spoke from the fever of his deathbed of his fears: mostly that *they* would come, to take the place. You see, it turned out that our father was as financially bankrupt as he might ever have been morally or spiritually. We were aware he'd always feared 'them' coming, but never the depth of his terror. We knew not of the secret places he built, where evasion and survival could be assured. Just as he had insisted on a home with a hallway from which he might check where everyone was – we were always forbidden to close our doors – he had also devised a domain riddled with opportunity for concealment, from enemies he knew he had, and perhaps those he was yet to meet.

No one confessed knowledge of this, from valet to scullion. Not even our mother, when she was alive.

In the immediate days after his funeral, we were but three young men awaiting instruction. Days passed; no one arrived. As they stretched into weeks, we came to realise no one would, there would be no unknown benefactors to adopt us, nor riot of debt collectors breaking down the door. Not even thieves prising the windows by night. It was as if some word of warning had spread, and the force of those words forbade any soul to set foot on Whitecross soil. Indeed, we learned a party did attempt to approach, one of whom was mortally struck by a thunderbolt as they drew closer. So it was that we were left alone to fend for ourselves, the three forgotten Boxwell brothers.

It was then that Edmund shepherded us into this labyrinth. Words for him alone, on our father's dying breath, told him of the secret places. Now he, in turn, revealed them to us. But Edmund knew more, something he shielded from us as long as he might, burden though it was. All that *we* knew, myself and Zadoc, was that we must keep from daylight. And he, being that margin older and stronger, would by night leave us to find food.

We settled into an uneasy rhythm, and for some time we did not question why we must cower as mice. And so it was that our first realisation came from Edmund, but only indirectly, when his hand was forced…

We hid from the menace of outsiders, but a chance misjudgement by Zadoc showed a threat was far worse: it lay within our own flesh. We knew we were living, for sure: we breathed, felt hunger, pain, fear. Even hope. But one night, Zadoc got up, restless from the moon, and ventured out. He sought to show he was as capable as Edmund. The clock in the hall told him he had an hour before dawn; he could return without fear of scorning the rules. But the clock was slow.

He found himself meddling beyond the maze when a sly bank of cloud in the east blew away. Behind it, the sun's first rays were etching the top of the tower. He ran. Not fast enough. I will not forget the seared and ruddy mess when he staggered back, nor his stricken cries. That was when Edmund unloaded his final secret: should anyone drag us into the light, death awaited us more certainly than any intent from mortal hands. Hiding, we finally *all* knew, must be our lives, since our mother had sent him to his grave with the words she wrote, up in that lofty cage, in her own blood: *all life that I give will be here, never leave.*

By the power of an oath invoked in vengeance, the light of day, we now knew, would enforce that. So we have remained, confined, yet not ignorant to the outside. We have, after all, seen many occupiers come and go. And with them, witnessed three full centuries of news, watched this empire rise and fall, known the folly of man. From Trafalgar to the Crimea, all the way to the Transvaal, we certainly learned enough. Or so we thought.

There was none before and none since like that war, a century ago. War is always the same, but 1914? More bloody than man had ever known, it reached so far beyond the battlefields. All the way to our door.

They kept coming, the injured, the dying, the dead. Room upon room, packed with beds, these walls teeming with nurses and doctors. I would not disturb either of you by describing their state, but the sorriest were those who bore invisible scars. And it was one of those poor soldiers of misfortune with whom I became acquainted.

In the short winter afternoons, many would be wheeled out, or walk, to savour the sunset. And Private Tom Parkin had more reason than any to feel wary that evening, days before Christmas. Earlier that day, they discharged him as medically fit. By night, he would cry for his mother, but they took no note. I felt his torment, though. You see, they gave him the same bed you sleep in, Scarlett.

The morning of his departure, he rose at dawn, polished his boots, put on his uniform and walked out. A truck would collect him for the station. Yet he departed before light. And left a note, at his bedside.

It said they would find his body in the grounds. He thanked them for his reprieve, but said no death could be worse than that place borrowed from hell, once more in the trenches.

I was first to read it, and knew where he would go: through the woods, to the lake. You'll find just traces there now, they drained it at the beginning of the following war. I left the note at his bedside, but crucial minutes passed and no one came. In my agitation, I looked out of the window and watched daylight harden. There was no time to lose: if I could reach him, maybe I could persuade him of another way? It was foolish to reason with a mind driven senseless by war, but it had to be better than standing by? Just nineteen, he was. My age, the age I had reached when my own life ceased.

Young Tom had spent months building a model of this house. Each day, piecing together the fine details. Each night, I added, modified, making sure of *every* detail, not just the ones you see from the other side. It was a wordless conversation; he knew of my work, yet said nothing. The doctors probably saw it as therapy; they might have wondered what he was doing, creating this folly, riddled with fanciful layers. It was finished the day he was called back up.

I could see him in the morning mist, standing waist-deep. Maybe the sight of me would scare him into the depths; all I knew was that here was a soul with the gift of choice, a choice only reached beyond the battlefield, but he had a chance. I raced forward, but the sun kept rising. We had years of experience, knowing how fine to cut it. I felt the warmth, on the back of my head, but kept advancing.

He was still afloat, but his hair was wet, eyes rolling – had he been under once, twice? There could be no third attempt. I threw myself in, dragged him out. He choked and spewed as he rolled onto his side. *"Do not do it,"* I whispered, *"You can still choose."* But that was all I could say – I had to run as fast as my legs could obey.

I remember my feet pacing, head down, the whiteness leaching in... I remember running on fire, and Edmund, at the door, beyond the shadow-line. He seared his hands reaching to me as I fell in. I was safe, but the damage was done. Thereafter came the whiteness, for a few days, like a taunting, before the black.

It was 1918, though I know not of Tom's final fate. I like to think he walked free. It is but a footnote to our story, but perhaps shows how we have survived. By defying her invocation of enforced eternity, the gift bestowed on me is black.

Greater chances have been for others. Roan: you have felt the hand that saved you when you tilted from your window? Scarlett, your own mother owes so much to the same hand that freed her when lightning would crush her. Who would have considered Edmund such a force for salvation?

I digress, and Edmund's is no breast upon which to pin medals; he would have nothing said. My only hope is that these words offer clarity. Give or take the wear and tear before you, we are as we stood on the day of our father's funeral. Hardly sweetmeat, for sure. There is no hiding it, for we have travelled through time less harshly than time has travelled through us."

night song

They left by the basement door to the garden. Zadoc ahead, ushering them through the draughty cellars. Having been so long in their 'parley', they calculated it would be wiser to pretend they had been out.

Awash with understanding, if not forgiveness, Roan inhaled the open air. At the porch, they paused and locked eyes, a new level of understanding between them. Their pretence was wise: Joanna was in the hall. Wielding a garden rake, she was busy trying to coax the Christmas lights into the highest boughs of the tree.

"Hello you... getting some fresh air?"

"Yeah, Roe thought he spotted a barn owl, by the maze... we went over, sat there for ages, saw nothing."

"Ornithology now? We seriously have to stay in the sticks." She balanced an awkward strand. "There's pasta bake in the oven; if you want to carry on I'll wait for your father, he's just popped to Whitecross to get a couple of things for tomorrow."

Tomorrow... as she dollops her mother's concoction into bowls at the kitchen table, Scarlett couldn't believe Tom's visit with Adeline had crept up so quickly. The last weekend before Christmas was often a get-together to exchange gifts – but bigger spoils were obviously at stake this time.

"It's a bit chewy." Roan said, his mouth full.

"What, Dad's deal?" He prodded the congealed pasta as if the memory of their parley turned his stomach. "I know, Roe, but just focus on the prize."

"And what's that, exactly? Have you stopped to consider it? Say this 'genius' works: say our new friends scare Adeline's dad witless, so he bins his plans and legs it. Then what? Mum and Dad agree to live happily ever after, all comfy, knowing what they thought was the perfect place is actually a semi-detached house of hell – one half ours, the other owned by three..." he whispered, "*undead people,* creeping behind the walls? One of which, if you didn't notice, lists kidnapping and DIY transplants as his skill set."

She had to admit, genius would be stretching it. If, as they'd agreed, the brothers emerged to eject Adeline's father, Mum and Dad would surely find out everything? Even if they already had suspicions, it'd be catastrophic. But Roan's realism was too much: "I dunno, how about we take this a day at a time? Sort the immediate challenge, then see what we have to do?" He grunted as Scarlett helped herself to more pasta. "In any case, I've got ideas for how we might bring them out, help them towards some sort of life."

"*Bring them out*?" he gasped. "You sound like a social worker. Didn't you *listen* to Jacob: they *can't stand* daylight. They have medical needs."

"Medical needs! Who has needs?" Joanna beamed. She ought to have a bell, Scarlett reflected, so they could hear her coming. Like a Swiss cow.

"Eh? Oh, it's no big thing." Ah hell, she thought, it's never too early to start preparing ground. "I was just saying to Roe, my year has some foreign exchange students coming... and they've bungled their sleeping arrangements... a few are stuck with nowhere to stay... Can you *believe* it?"

"Oh my, how tragic. And don't tell me," Joanna scoffed, "they said 'If only there were a big house with loads of rooms going spare'?"

Scarlett smiled. "I promised *nothing*, but seeing as we aren't going to be here long... and seeing as Dad might fancy some help tidying up, you know, packing, etcetera... "

"You didn't *promise* this teacher, did you?" Joanna sighed.

"They'd not be here long, Mum. They're due in the New Year..."

"Well your father'll have reservations." Scarlett sensed her account at the Bank of Guilt was massively in credit. "So where are they from then, these students of yours?"

Roan couldn't look at his mother. Scarlett's scheme sounded lame, but he marvelled at her speed.

"That's the *funny* bit, they're from a far-flung community. In Patagonia." The word tumbled into the conversation like a clown. "Their people descended from English settlers – so they speak English, kind of."

"How d'you mean?"

"Kind of Shakespearean... ish," Roan offered. "All of them a bit odd, by all accounts..."

"Well, that might help with your English," Joanna laughed. "But what are they like?"

"A bit quirky?"

"Yeah, they speak like they swallowed an old dictionary," Roan added. "We saw them on a video link this week."

Scarlett laughed: "They'd probably make Dad sound up-to-date."

"That I'd like to see. This is a man who thought an emoji was a cocktail," Joanna groaned. "They sound intriguing, but no more than three. The drains wouldn't take any more."

"Cool. I'll tell school. Come to think, I know they have three that are brothers, so it'd be nice if they could stick together."

"And I'll talk to your father."

"Sure, Mum, that's great." Scarlett nudged Roan beneath the table. "And there's just one other thing…"

"Oh?" Joanna stopped in the doorway.

"It's the really weird bit. They're from a community of cave dwellers."

"Cave-dwellers! Images of hairy troglodytes in loin cloths filled her mind. Richard won't cope with that, she reflected. Let alone the dog.

Roan's eyes widened.

"And after so many generations, a lot of the younger members of the group have developed an allergy… to sunlight. So… they avoid it," Scarlett hesitatingly added.

"So what do they do? Wear hoodies and slouch about in the shadows?"

"Yeah, I guess so."

"Dearie me, so how will we tell them apart?"

"From what?" they both chorused.

"From you two?"

Roan finally exhaled as their mother left. Scarlett's incredibly unbelievable scheme was emerging. Rapidly. No point debating, he decided, now so much was out there. But he felt no faith. Not a morsel.

Jacob woke with a start, as if a voice scorned his storytelling, as if he'd broken an unspoken rule. He guessed it was the usual stirring in his ancient bones. For so many years, nothing had happened, and then *this* family arrived, bringing so much, so quickly. A season might be punctuated by nothing more than cutting each others' hair; a year by a tree falling in the grounds. Whole decades, uneventful. But this? The Wycherleys turned the front door key and unlocked what may well be their final days. Whichever way he weighed it, were they not doomed?

Then the voice returned. Alien but familiar, within him yet outside.

Jacob… Jacob.

Several times, she breathed to his inner ear. And then began to sing. In cold beauty.

The way is clear now, you can come to me.
You can come home, my boys, my treasured three.
Shake off your bonds of fear, from dark iniquity,
Still warm, my arms await, in final sanctuary.

    The lyric beautiful, the voice soulless, but as much as hearing, he also saw: words writ large, flowing across the void of his soul. Finally, he knew… and in knowing, all hope of sleep burnt away. Careful not to disturb Scarlett, close above, he shuffled from his bed to negotiate the crawlspace. By the fireside, he would remain, holding the echo of the words until morning.

    The longer Zadoc and Edmund slept, the longer they might be spared their meaning.

the phasm

Transformation complete, Adeline's father *was* a robot. How else could someone be so preened? From his slick hair down to his boring brogues, he was a genuine robomoron, Scarlett concluded. As she observed her father greet him in the hall, she wondered who else might see all this. Might they share her distaste?

Having moored his obese Range Rover, index plate TB1, close to the front door, Tom Benn deposited his and Adeline's suitcases, along with four Christmas presents, before he stepped back to admire the decorated tree. Scarlett, Roan and their parents stood before it like a welcoming delegation.

"*Tree*-bloody-mendous! he gawped. Adeline, lost in his shadow, held a carrier bag.

"Sorry I didn't have time for wrapping, it was last-minute. It's not from me: it's from Roan and your, er, 'friend'? They plotted with me... said you'd want them straight away?"

Scarlett didn't want to be disappointed, at least not in public, but she definitely couldn't delay the gratification – and opened the bag with a squeal.

"Doc Martens... and fourteen-eye originals! Yessss!" Roan could see the idea, hatched with Moreton, was spot-on. He feared she might even get carried away and hug him.

Tom grinned as Scarlett explained how the only Doc Martens boots were *this* type, not girly patent... in black vegan leather, with yellow laces. Richard saw how they completed the look his daughter nurtured. She looked fabulous, he decided, as she rushed to get the boots on, her cropped hair ruffled from sleep. A look that, he knew, Tom hoped his own daughter would never adopt. Despite all the door-slamming, all the curt replies, he loved her style, her flair, her fire. But just how much of that energy came from *where* they now were? If coming here made her angry, introspective, hadn't it also forced her to somehow dig deep? And here she was now, emerging, like a butterfly. With guns blazing. All of which made the contract a prospect far more weighty than a scribble on a scrap of paper? Yet he'd already signed, and now they were here, trussed and bundled into the back seat of a plan being driven by Tom Benn. At whatever speed he liked.

Tom shook him from his reverie: "You know, I'm *sure* I smell coffee! It'd go splendidly with these bad boys we grabbed at that little bakery down the road."

"Absolutely," said Richard, though something in his smile told Tom that, although their paperwork now needed just a solicitor's rubber stamp, his old mate still had barely enough appetite for a mince pie. From a crack opposite, an eye observed his determined smile, pondering his height and body weight.

Mort: they're here, it's tonight!! Things may be v different by morning, might be a weird Xmas Eve. Scar x

Scarlett pressed send. With Adeline being ever-present, as soon as she headed to the bathroom, she could waste no time. No need to tell anyone else: Roan knew full well the brothers were resolved. Tonight, it was time.

Tom Benn cursed that final extra glass of port, coming, as it did, on top of that second bottle of wine. Temporary or not though, it was a surprisingly comfy bed. It bore his weight without complaint, the pillow pert as a cherub's bottom. The arrangement was hardly five-star: their fifth bedroom, a vast space stuffed with furniture festooned in dust covers. Helpfully, Scarlett and Roan had scooted items aside, salvaging a bed from the abandoned furniture.

He reached for his bag and swigged a glug of gastric medicine, but his gut seethed. It was not until two hours after they all retired that he finally drifted off. Shortly after, his bladder woke him. Fumbling vainly for a light, he lumbered off for the doorway. He could have sworn it was closer, but in the murk, he moved further and further away, wrong by 180 degrees, following a walkway that led deep into the labyrinth of furniture. On into the valley of bric-a-brac he stumbled, cursing the clutter. Eventually, he discovered a handle to a door, tugged it, and felt inside for a light. There was none, which was entirely logical, given he had entered an eighteenth-century wardrobe. Amid flailing and cursing, he guessed where the lavatory must logically be and proceeded, without further delay, to full flow.

Relieved, he staggered back out, turned the wrong way again and wandered deeper into the morass. Finally, he gave up. Slumping to the floor, he grabbed the nearest edge of a sheet for cover and tugged it down for warmth. Deep sleep came quickly, but before long, the stagnation of boozy breath that enveloped his gasping body was stirred by a change in the air.

"Tonight it is!" Edmund barked. "Our greatest weapon is fear. We must use it." The house still, their time to act had come. Sucking the last drop from his goblet, Jacob observed his glow of happiness, a change he struggled to comprehend. "There will be no mercy for the quarry, no quarter for those who wish us harm. We must be quick. We must be *crushing*."

"And what of his daughter? I guess we are not 'crushing' her?" Jacob asked, as Zadoc methodically placed tools into a bag. Hating unavoidable violence, he shuddered at what the night might bring.

"No strategic value in targeting her," Edmund replied. "Our focus is him. And from what we have seen, we will be doing society a favour. Should he live to tell, by the telling may he be a changed man."

"And if he doesn't live?" asked Zadoc. He had several tools to satisfy the purpose.

"Death is preferable to what he continues to be, alive."

Zadoc hoisted the bag onto his bony shoulder and fell into line. At the back, Jacob reluctantly joined them. Together, they headed for the panel that opened directly into bedroom five.

"*Help me… help!*"

The voice rose. Even to the ears of a dead-drunk beast, sleep was no barrier. Lying moist and lost amid the junk, Tom stirred. It would not stop, a terrible wheedling from… a woman… a *girl*? He sat up to decode the direction, somewhere beyond the landing, beyond the door. He must go, he *had* to. Then, as a hammer to his heart, he knew – Adeline!

A bullock buffeting a hedge, stomping and flailing, he mounted the covered piles of furniture, tumbling over the first peak before falling into the next valley. From where he faces the same climb again.

"I'm coming, Adi!" he bellowed. Cresting the next ridge, he wobbled and began to cascade towards the floor, an avalanche of pink flesh and big, white underpants. The fall was long, the floor rushing up to meet him. With no chance to shield his head from the stop.

They stood like driftwood figurines. Ahead of him, Zadoc watched Edmund's hand poised on the panel. He'd tested it earlier and smoothed the lock with grease. All he need do was pull. His fingers tautened, yet for seconds the doorway stayed shut.

"Don't dally!" Zadoc hissed. "My blood rushes for open slather!"

"I can't do it," Edmund stuttered. *That's a relief*, Jacob reflected.

"If you won't, let a *real* man through." Zadoc elbowed him aside.

"I can't do it, fool, because the infernal door won't open! You try."

Zadoc insinuated his fingernails. They cracked and bent as he prised. But it was rock-tight.

"Maybe we are not *supposed* to get through," Jacob murmured.

"*Supposed*?" spat Zadoc. "What tommyrot do you spout now?"

"I fear this is *her* doing. She spoke to me, last night. She said *the way is clear*."

"Ah, soothsayer Jacob," Zadoc sneered. "Well, we'd best go back for extra supper and a cosy sleep, if dear ol' Mama's looking after us."

"I wouldn't scoff, Zadoc, I feel something, too; something afoot," Edmund added. "We may not be the actors tonight. More likely, we are merely the audience."

Tom raised his fingers to meet a gluey smear around his temple. He landed hard, but could still move, still think. And *still* hear... the voice continued. Delirious, he dragged himself towards the covered edge of a sofa, grappling to get up. In the gloom, he made out a sliver of light, beneath the door.

"Help, please save me… *please!*" The voice weakened.

From the landing, he was drawn left, down the long corridor – Adeline must be behind *one* of these doors? He tried every handle. All locked. How? One after the other, he grabbed, kicked, bashed. Each door solid. And while the plaintive cry continued and he called back, assuring Adeline he *was* coming, not a soul stirred. Finally, the corridor's end, the last possible door.

It opened freely. Immediately, the cry was louder, swept down with the draught from high above. He had never ventured there before, yet his feet moved with certainty. Finding the guiding rail, he drew on unknown reserves. At the spiral's final steps, the wind was harder, pushing him back.

Moonlight pooled into the room as he caught his breath. He could make out iron bars, criss-crossing the unglazed windows; little wonder it was so cold. The air whistled through, an endless wail. Yet where was she?

"Adeline? Are you here?"

Wading through a thick bed of scattered straw, he kicked and flailed, scooping armfuls high into the air. Nothing, though a mound, piled in the corner, escaped his notice.

He hung his head. The sound *was* here. He approached a window. For minutes, he stared out and, as the moon bleached his sweaty face into a ghostly pallor, a shape, in the straw behind him, began to rise.

Despair rising to anger, he grasped the bars and pushed. A rough edge to the ironwork sliced into the side of his thumb, splitting it like a blade across fruit. He gasped and punched at the metalwork. To his surprise, the entire frame gave way, tumbling into the void below. Leaning forward, he strained to see where it had landed; despite his anguish, he feared it might have smashed onto the roof of his precious car. And as he leant, the face of Rosamond Tow took form.

Behind his shoulder, outstretched hands swam towards him, eyes glinting sapphire steel, metallic hair floating in an electric blaze. Closer she drew, so close she might kiss his ear.

Sorry to text so late. Is all OK? Moreton xx

Light flickered from Scarlett's phone, briefly illuminating her face. She rested, sound asleep, beside Adeline. Set to silent, the light made no difference; they had talked until late; it would take far more to wake her now. And little use if she did: the sheets were clamped fast around her. As for everyone present, meddling in the work of this night would be no option.

Jacob was the first to identify the scream. It ripped the night. To Edmund, it was a raptor, closing on the kill. To Zadoc, a taunt. He clenched his fingers as he sat beside his brothers, adrenaline coursing as if it might set him alight.

"Perhaps, when she said 'the way is clear', she was anticipating whatever is now afoot?" he ventured, still dwelling upon the song in his bedchamber. "To her mind, this man must surely have been an impediment, to be tidied away?"

"Well it hardly sounds *tidy* to me," Edmund groaned. The shrieks ebbed and flowed in waves, beneath them, the faint cries of her victim.

"She's making a meal of it," Jacob groaned. "The whole house will rise. Like a vixen in a god-damned henhouse."

"Unless, Jacob, it is we alone who can hear?" Edmund suggested. "We have no need to remind ourselves of her powers, but since that fool of a farmboy cut away the cage, perhaps tonight she is blossoming?"

"She's dangling him. Up in the tower, that's my guess," said Zadoc.

"So why not let go of the wretch?" Jacob asked, voice quaking.

"Isn't it plain?" Edmund laughed. "She is having her moment, because she *can*. Even if you could, what fool might try to stop her?"

peace & goodwill

If strangulation didn't kill him, the drop would. Not that he could look down. The force that ejected him left him dangling, feet-first, his only restraint a pair of wiry hands clasped around his neck. Struggling helplessly, he wondered how he wasn't dead already.

"Do be patient," the voice shrieked. "Not long now, dear Daddy." Her voice was the exact tone of his daughter's before it disintegrated into uncontrollable cackles.

"*Help!*" he croaked. "Dear God, I'll do *anything*, just let me go!"

"*Let you go?* Your final wish is granted, on condition you never trouble this place again," Rosamond hissed.

"Yes, yes, I promise. Not never, ever." He wheezed for oxygen.

"And so: I release you."

The voice howled as her fingers slackened. Gravity surging through his body, he hurtled down, accelerating towards the moonlit roof of his Range Rover. Unable to look away, he saw every detail as it closed on his sweaty head.

The bump jolted Richard from his sleep.

"What the blazes was that?"

"Who cares?" Joanna murmured.

"*Who cares?*" He fumbled to free the duvet tangled tight around his limbs. Then he realised. "Probably just that hippo falling out of bed. I knew he'd had far too much."

Checking his watch, he lay back. His wife was probably right: if anything *had* happened, they'd know, soon enough.

Tom tried to focus on the hand before him. Eventually, the image sharpened. It was his own. It was covered in blood. *His* blood.

Sitting up, he struggled to absorb where he was. Or wasn't. He wasn't on top of his car, he wasn't lying in Richard Wycherley's flower bed. He was in a mess of tumbled furniture and sheets, somewhere near the doorway of his makeshift accommodation. He rubbed his head and discovered the source of a pain that was fast becoming sharper: a spongey matt of hair and clotted moisture behind his left ear. That'll need stitching, he winced.

Feeling little relief in being not dead, he scrambled to find his clothes; all he wanted was to grab Adeline and floor it from this hell-hole. He dressed with such haste that getting his trousers on the right way around was a pure fluke. Stealthily, he crept to Scarlett's room and eased her door. Adeline opened her eyes – enough to see his urgency. Silently, he motioned to her to grab her bag and shepherded her down the creaky staircase.

"We're going, *now!*" he whispered, by the side of the Christmas tree. "Talk later!"

Forcing the backs down on his highly polished shoes, he tugged his coat from the overloaded pegs, then motioned to Adeline to wait, before he unlocked the door. Shaking a match from the box on the hallway mantelpiece, he drew from his briefcase a sheath of papers, flinging them into the hearth. Adeline glimpsed a heading: *Whitecross Mall.* In seconds, the contract was cinders.

For a while, their outlines were cast by the flames. And from behind the portrait of Robert Boxwell, his eldest son approached a convenient hole, and looked on. With deep satisfaction.

As her father wheel-span away, Adeline glanced up to the North Tower. That memory repelled all questions over their sudden exit.

"*Must* have been something I drank," Tom said, gingerly touching his head. A patch of scalp that should feel firm has the consistency of a fried egg. "I fell while trying to climb the junk in that blasted room, and then I…" She breathed relief as they left the front gates. "Well, I think I ran down the corridor." The acceleration pushed her back in the seat. "I was looking for you; there was this voice, calling out, and before I knew it I was climbing – "

"– What, in the tower?"

"Yes, though now I'm beginning to realise it was all a crazy dream. All the same, I can't go back there, not even if it *was* my imagination. It must have been, or I'd not be here now."

Fleeing felt rash, but Adeline felt no regret. From what she'd seen, it was as if Scarlett had been there for years. A sense of distance saddened her, but maybe the best Christmas present her oldest friend could have was to be left alone? She jiggled the button to recline the seat and began to doze as her father carved through the lanes.

A mile further on, Tom sighed with relief and was only vaguely aware of a dark patch of shadow ahead, beneath a tunnel of overhanging trees. As the car whooshed on, its automatic headlamps activated.

And there, picked out from the gloom, perhaps thirty feet ahead, a woman was standing in the road.

He had no time to hit the brakes. When the headlamps first found her, her back was turned, but as they ploughed closer, she rotated. And in those milliseconds, he stared into a haggard face. One he knew too well.

"Dear God!" he yelled, wrestling with the wheel as the car lurched to a sharp stop, two wheels across the muddy verge.

"What is it?" Adeline yelped, rubbing her jolted neck.

"It's nothing, nothing. There was something, someone… in the road… a woman," he said, turning to look. "She turned to me, but I couldn't make out her face."

Couldn't or wouldn't? Adeline shuddered. She watched her father, his eyes fixed on the rear-view mirror as he rubbed his fingers.

"What've you done to your hand?" Pity welled in her eyes; so far, Daddy was having a rotten Christmas.

"Sorry? Oh *that?*" he said, looking down. "No, it was last night…" He was lost in thought, "I cut my thumb, it's just a bit sore." And then, in a flash, reality hit him: the bars on the window, the sharp lip of metal.

Shoving the lever into drive and flooring the throttle hard, he didn't look back.

graffiti

Flushed from a glass of mulled wine, Scarlett was glad to see the best part of Christmas day digested. Over a jolly lunch, little was discussed of Tom and Adeline's abrupt exit, or their radio silence. And nothing on the idea of a house move being as likely to see the light of day again as Roan's hand-knitted socks from Aunty Emily. To her amusement, he couldn't suppress a groan when he opened them.

If she'd pushed her father, Scarlett sensed he'd admit it: the unravelling of his grand plan was best for everyone. But from the look on his face, post-turkey and trimmings, she knew it was a conversation for another day. They both looked so carefree, slumped semi-conscious before *Chitty Chitty Bang Bang*. It marked an ideal moment.

At the garden gate for the meadow between their homes, they met, sauntering arm-in-arm, heading south, towards the lone chestnut tree at the field's far end.

"I never really thanked you for the boots." She squeezed his arm. "You nailed it; you must be telepathic."

Moreton smiled. "You did mention the idea a few hundred times... and Roan was relieved. He said he hadn't a clue what you'd like."

"And you do."

"Sorry?"

"Have a clue."

"I like listening to you," he shrugged, "maybe I just remember stuff."

"Well, I remember *everything* you say. Seeing as there's so little." Laughing, she broke free and ran ahead. Half way to the dilapidated tree, they were drawn to its listing mass, fuzzed beneath a veil of late-afternoon mist. Moreton didn't run after her, but stretched his pace. When he reached her, she turned. He pulled her close, with a kiss more certain than before. Fizzing at his proximity, she didn't close her eyes, as if doing so would be wasteful. But as he moved back to look at her, her gaze was drawn away. Through a brief window in the mist, a parchment moon edged over the trees that fringe Whitecross, the lofty roofline notched within a tracery of branches against the weak blue. And then, piercing the silence, a skein of geese, thirty, maybe more, clattered a wobbly V across the space. She thrilled as their feathers sawed the still air.

"They know where they're headed." Moreton's gaze was fixed west. "Escaping the cold… they'll land at the Severn."

Watching their mass shrink to dots, Scarlett wondered at the ease of being animal, of life mapped to destinations hard-wired, of existence free from the gravity of choice. She hugged him closer.

"So what *happened*?" he asked, watching the eastern sky darken, his touch warm at the nape of her neck. "Did they save the day then, your oh-so-old mates?"

"I guess so, I've heard nothing though…" she faltered. "I was too exhausted to start more conversations. I left them a tray, a Christmas lunch, bits and bobs. It's like having pets… " She laughed, then felt relieved they were out of earshot. "They're not 'pets' though, I know that."

"No, human in flesh and blood, just like us."

"Yep, but just extra mature, like three fine old cheeses from Whitecross market."

"Vintage," he corrected.

They walked on. Drawing closer to the tree, Scarlett wondered why she couldn't speak about the brothers without veering into flippant jokes. Then her thoughts froze: there, in the bark, she saw a subtle pattern of marks, caught by the sunset's slant.

"Well fancy that!" Moreton stooped. "All those times I've climbed up, yet I never noticed… it could be mistaken for a line, from the way chestnuts corkscrew upwards, but… it *is*, isn't it?"

She traced a finger along the shape. It was no more than a blurred relief: a stroke across the top, a parallel, longer flourish below, an oblique slash tying them together.

ᘔ

The realisation sent their eyes darting around. Before long, others jumped out, concertinaed, stretched, yet obvious:

E　J

They tugged back the undergrowth. And there, cut deep, draped around the folds of bark as they merged towards the roots, a final proof:

Boxwell, 1722

Scarlett pictured the hands that carved them, the hands of three boys, skin tanned by summer sun, risking the wrath of their father, doing what any three young boys do: living life, out there, out here. Her tears welled.

"Is this what you wanted, Scar... I'm guessing *not*?" He held her.

"Eh? God knows." She spluttered. "But life goes on." She pulled a tissue from her pocket. "At least for *us*... but for *them*, I'm not convinced it's *any* life – trapped inside... more dead than alive." It was a messy answer, but Moreton understood.

"Perhaps this contact, with you and Roe, is a step towards something better? Maybe you can help them . . . maybe *we* can?"

Scarlett nodded. "I've thought about nothing else. And I have an idea, mad as it might sound... I've told Mum something. It sounds barmy, but..."

"Just spit it out, Scar!" he laughed.

"I said we might be having visitors. Some odd people, from abroad."

"You mean..." he struggled, "you've been paving some way for them to do . . . what? Come out, like into normal life?"

"I guess. She heard something I said to Roe... and I had to think on the spot. One thing kind of led to another..."

"One thing? More like one lie?" he smirked.

"Yeah, well the end result is we've got three – don't laugh – Patagonian students, who speak like a Shakespearean English... they're due to come and stay with us... and they're a bit albino, because they're from a tradition of cave-dwellers."

"Genius!" Moreton smiled to the sky. "You went for such an epic lie there's no way it's made up! It's total rubbish, but if it works, maybe it's best."

"Best for everyone?"

He hesitated. "Well you know what *I* care about, so for my part, well, I'm happy if – "

"– I'm not talking about *you*. Of course you're happy, seeing as I'm not going! But what about your sister... what about Iz?"

He'd hoped to leave her out. "I still worry, I can't lie. She's like an open channel; she picks stuff up, from thin air. Or stuff picks *her* up."

Scarlett was yet to speak to the brothers, but already knew Moreton's fear. After all, they'd played little part in ridding Whitecross of Tom Benn. So who had? And what would that obvious answer mean for Isabel?

"Maybe things will settle down now? Maybe *she'll* be happy?"

Moreton shook his head. "Your 'Patagonian lodgers' never sorted Tom Benn... she's out now, and she's never going to stop. And all this? She was just clearing the way."

His words ripped the needle from their Christmas soundtrack. With a sense of carrying something broken, they began to walk back as the darkness crept in.

"I should never have cut those bars." He gazed north, towards Starvecrow Field. She won't stop now, not 'til she gets *everything* she wants."

Yet of his deepest fear, he said nothing. Rosamund may have saved Whitecross to spare her sons from immediate danger, but what if she'd duped him: what if those bars had never caged her spirit in the first place? How could they ever have contained her when she'd shown her presence through such a willing shell as Isabel?

It was a fear to nail him to insomnia: Rosamond surely wanted the cage destroyed to create a wider gateway for her sons.

And now that he'd obediently done it, who else would she suck in?

"Brothers, is it not beginning to feel somewhat akin to Christmas?"

Zadoc raised his goblet to lead the toast. Scarlett's delivery had been a feast; far more than they would ever normally take, not without risk of making it obvious the house had crime issues. Zadoc held clear memories of Christmas 1831, when he acquired two guinea fowl. They had barely provided a meal for one, yet in the ensuing investigation, a scullery boy was flogged. He'd never again savour the taste of that meat.

They clunked vessels, filled from a bottle of claret Scarlett had supplied. But a crack in one made the sound dull to Edmund's ears. He was polite enough, but as he jabbed at his turkey even Jacob knew he was far from happy. Wet wood, hissing in the fire, only enhanced the silence.

"May I guess," said Zadoc, when he eventually spoke, "what it is that weighs upon you, Edmund?"

Edmund struggled. He would freely express his disappointment, though today, of all days, was no moment. "The night before last was a victory," he said. "We cannot contest that. But it was not *won*. It was bestowed. It is fresh illustration of how nothing has changed."

"I understand," Zadoc replied. "I shared your appetite for battle. The feeling coils in my stomach and has lain there 300 years."

"No, my appetite is sharper than ever," Edmund countered. "Excuse my melancholia; I assure you both," he said, looking to Jacob, "I am not testy, just truthful. Brothers, there are three possible lives upon this planet. Life external, the life of normal beings, life internal, the life of anyone confined by whatever force of circumstances, and the life eternal, which, bereft of the bookend of death, is really… nothing, a senseless existence, starved of the punctuation of events. A road," he added, "without turnings, choice or return."

"And a merry Christmas to you too," Zadoc laughed, refilling their goblets. "Stare into your umbilicus long enough and it becomes a bottomless abyss." His casual mirth snapped Edmund back; with a shrug of his shoulders he mustered a smile.

But Jacob dwelt upon Edmund's words. And decided that they held an inescapable truth. Perhaps the bravest choice of all still awaited? Had they the guts, wouldn't they face the release of death? Embrace it? Embrace her wish, even despite her? Obviously, she was waiting.

They continued the meal, but within the colourless confines of Jacob's imagination, Edmund's logic shone bright.

That night, he decided: come the opportunity, he would take these words. Like a knife, to his heart.

death's miracle

"So they won't," Roan whispered, "think it *a teensy bit* weird, as in three cranky English-speaking Patagonian brothers rocking up, all blessed with a skin condition that makes them allergic to daylight?"

Perched on Scarlett's bed, he itched with disbelief. They'd been over this before, but for Roan it repeated as badly as Mum's herb stuffing. After the drama of the Benn's visit, tonight marked his first true opportunity to speak to his sister – and his scepticism gushed. In practice, Scarlett's plan for their new-found allies would surely fall apart. Would the brothers even comply?

"Well, I've been Googling." Scarlett squinted into her laptop. "Apparently, there's a condition called..." she stalled, "Erythro-poietic proto-por-phyria... it's all on here, see?" She swivelled the screen. "And besides, Dad always says people our age hate daylight, so why should Patagonians be so different?"

Roan snorted. "They'd have to be so covered up they look like muggers. And what about going out? If they're exchange students, they can't just hang out here. Do you take them to school? Ride on the bus? How's that going to work – plaster them in sun block?"

Scarlett jolted upright. "*What* did you just say? Sun block? *Suncream!* That's it!" She screamed and bundled her brother sideways. "You're still a genius, Roe, just when I think you've reinvented stupid, you think of a *brilliant* idea! I could almost love you!"

"Jacob, if you're awake... I guess you're there?"

Scarlett spoke to her pillow, eyes wide in the dark. It's well past midnight. "I hope your day went okay. I always think it's a thing to survive, Christmas..." This felt foolish.

No reply. She persisted: "I've been thinking... Well, *planning*... I was hoping we might sit down, again, tomorrow? We've an idea that might help everyone." He really *was* quiet. She wouldn't drag on: "Okay, till then, sleep well. I'll try not to fidget..."

But Jacob had already left, reversing his bedtime journey to sit at Edmund's writing desk.

In the corner, Edmund slept on; he knew it would take more than mere shuffling to wake him. Fumbling for the bottle at the side, he poured a little of the crows' blood, trickling it into a dumpy pot. Then he took a sheet of vellum from the drawer and selected a quill.

How can a blind man write? The question tormented as ever: but he *could* do it, he knew; had he not proved as much, with Edmund's guidance, when he finished Roan's homework, those few weeks ago? His brothers declared the script perfectly legible.

His hands obeyed a memory of the strokes. For a moment, the ink would not flow, the nib dry to his touch. He shook it and a gob of fluid spattered the page, like coughed anger. Feeling gently, he paused to contemplate the irregular blotch, imagining the way it leeched into the white. Finally, he found the thought. Tearing away the spill, he began.

My dear brothers – I believe we do not need eyes to see how far we have travelled, nor how far we may be prepared to go. And though I have only you as my eyes, I see death more clearly now. I have run from it, but it is a race no soul can win. We are the quarry.

Death is what it is: a black excrescence, hacked from nowhere onto each pristine page of allotted life. When it comes, when we finally see the point it randomly marks, we feel it as a ruination. Yet without it, what if the pages of our lives keep turning? What if it were an infinite ream, an endless white of life? What life is that, without the miracle of death?

More and more, with every day of late, I have craved the mark, the blemish, the full stop. And that craving is a scourge, gnawing my soul, reducing me, day by day. Its progress is not hindered by any effort to cloak it in humour. As another year approaches, I hope you will forgive me, but I call time upon myself.

Our mother, I know, awaits us, but I feel no draw to her cold breast. My own end, I wish to be mine, of none other. And gladly I go to it. For one hundred years, my eyes may have not seen, yet tonight? The path is beautiful. It shines.

In leaving you, I love you yet more for the distance we have covered, shoulder-to-shoulder, brothers in arms – fratres in aeternum. If I take any dream for slumber, it is that we will be together, at another place and time; I pray providence carry me there and watch over you. Until that glorious day when I see you again.

He signed the letter with a simple J, adding, in the last edge of space, two Xs, simple runes that speak more than all his words. Leaving the paper close to the fire, he departed, following the route that led down to the garden door. There, he awaited dawn. Once bright enough, he would walk out, head high. Into the furnace of a final peace.

Her sleep had been so dreamless, Scarlett felt it had been stolen. She blinked, blurry-eyed at the clock: nearly eight, though the grey beginning to Boxing Day made it barely light. She could sleep on, but something disagreed. Before she could question her intuition, her phone rattled from the bedside table.

"Moreton... you okay?" she mumbled.

"Sorry Scar, I know it's early, but it's Isabel..."

"She's not – " Panic pulsed.

" – Too right: she walked out overnight. I thought she was fine, but she's gone. I've checked the grave and all around Starvecrow – no sign, and then, when I stopped to think, I worked out she's got to be headed your way."

"Why?" Scarlett began to throw on her nearest clothes.

"We know our friend Rosamond's been working overtime, and we know she can hijack Iz, mind and body." His voice cracked with fatigue.

Still dressing, Scarlett thrust Roan's door open. The movement didn't stir him. She yanked his curtains wide but, before she could prod him, a sudden movement caught her eye: out in the gloom, in the heart of the maze, a clump of hair, bobbing into view between gaps in the ragged hedge. Dark blonde, curly, wild.

She phoned back fast as she can. "She's here! In the maze!"

"Don't rush, she's probably not even awake." The phone distorted his voice. "I'm coming!"

Scarlett gave up on subtlety. "Get your shoes Roan!" she yelled. "We've got visitors, *outside*!"

Were Rosamond, by virtue of Isabel's body, paying them a visit, Scarlett knew it must be for good reason. As she dashed back to her room to grab her boots, something instinctive gripped her: Jacob! Last night: what did he actually *say*? Horror pooled in her stomach.

The sun crept up like an assassin as they closed on the heart of the maze. Masked by feeble strands of cloud, its rays seared ever closer. A low wailing stemmed from deep within. Hesitating to calculate the best way, Roan pulled Scarlett back.

"Come on, Roe, if Jacob's here, he's dead meat!"

Taking separate paths, Scarlett ran headlong. But as she sensed the distance closing, the moaning faded. Then she heard Moreton: "Iz? I'm coming, Iz! Stay there!"

From opposing directions, they converged on the obelisk that marked the heart of the maze. But while Moreton saw a sister stooped over the limp body of a boy, his face covered by her distraught form, Scarlett watched a grieving mother, floundering in the face of a lost child. The two visions jostled for reality as the crouching figure twisted her head, fixing Scarlett in her cold stare.

This was not Isabel.

Moreton fell to his knees, knowing she was now merely a vessel.

"Get back, you wretch!" Rosamond hissed, eyes glowing. "There is nothing you can do now, for he is *my* son, *my* flesh, *my* blood... aroint thee, foul varmint!*"*

As if freed from gravity, Isabel's dressing gown glowed like a protective cloak around their bodies.

"*Aroint*?" Roan whispered, now at Scarlett's side. "It's a word to banish a witch . . . seems a bit ironic?"

"*Wiiiiiiitch*?" Rosamond screeched. "Curse your vile tongue, boy: I be no witch! I have done no more than any mother, so foully wronged."

"Well you could've fooled me," Moreton raged, from behind. "D'you think one wrong makes *another* right? Do you think it fair – *hacking in* to my sister... using her like a puppet? For what?" He stepped closer. Rosamond flinched, barely perceptibly, but enough to bolster him. "Didn't I do what you wanted, Rosamond? Didn't I cut away the bars, so you'd be set free, and leave us? Set free for what?" he sneered. "So you can suck up even more people?"

Fixing him with fire in her eyes, Rosamond drew proud as the belt on Isabel's dressing gown loosened to fall free. Taller than Isabel, her pyjamas hung upon the fleshless frame unblemished, though Isabel had tramped across fields the night long. The form stood back to drape the dressing gown over Jacob. Where his flesh was exposed, it has the texture of roadkill. Surely they were too late?

For a while, Jacob's mother remained motionless. She did not retreat, but Scarlett wonders if Moreton's words have changed something. Then, without warning, she lunged directly at him, spewing spikes of anger.

"I am *no witch*, Master Valance, as well you may learn!" she spat. "I thank you for your willingness to set me free, your *kind intention."* Moreton flinched, her breath scouring his skin. *"But I have always been free, always,"* she roared, "free to be trapped here: stuck, waiting for my own to return. When you cut the bars, the freedom you gave was merely my resolve: I knew that once the cage had gone, their path lies clear. They can come, the day is nigh, is now!" As she spoke, her voice multiplied to a chorus of tongues.

Scarlett froze, yet burst to say *something* for Jacob's plight.

Finally, and with a measure of control, she drew breath: "And why would they? I mean, just *look* at him . . . doesn't this show your sons would rather *die* in daylight than crawl in the dark, back to a mother who loved them so much that she cursed them?"

"Curse!" Rosamond screeched, rising into the air. "I never cursed them, fool! Isn't it plain? *He* cursed us all, and his hatred has held those walls between us ever since. Then *you* come, your clever family with your clever ideas. You wished to destroy their world! Let it rest upon your soul: you alone brought them to this!"

"But wait! I know…" Scarlett stood firm. "I know that whatever drove you, the force of the words came from you… because *you* wrote it… that 'the lives that I give him will be here, never leave'." Stupid as it may be, Roan was aghast at his sister's bravery. The words pinned her like a dagger.

"Who said this to you?" she screamed. Scarlett gulped. Even the dead had nerves to press. Overcome with rage, Rosamond flew towards her, razor nails flailing.

"Never leave until *I* return to claim them!*"* she railed, rising tall above Scarlett's cowering head. "I… and no other!"

From Scarlett's side, Roan watched the form circle and surge, face-first, body flowing behind, like a hornet breaking free from a cobweb. And in watching, he decided. Enough: *one thing that I will never be again is a flipping spectator.*

"Get back, you wretch!" Square between them, he crossed his forearms in defiance. Scarlett couldn't process his reaction and Rosamond, too, seemed momentarily taken aback, her form freezing, as if Roan's intervention and Scarlett's words, quoting her very blood, sucked her energy from the air. Slowly, with a glint of tears, she glided back, towards Jacob. And by now, the light was so strong Scarlett doubted what protection the dressing gown could offer.

Crouching to kiss his brow, the entity turned, fixing Scarlett in the eye. A low breeze lifting her hair, a sudden beauty shone in her face, like an echo of her mortal past. Her lips parted to speak, but she tumbled forward, beside her son, face-down into the grass.

Moreton wasted no time. Bounding over, he turned the female form, exposing her to the day. Beneath the shock of hair, Isabel's face was untroubled, sleeping with the abandon of a discarded doll.

Scarlett knew they couldn't waste a second. "Go! Take Iz back!" she urged. "We'll get Jacob inside."

Scooped his sister up, he looked back as he retreated: "I'll call you, as soon as she's safe to bed."

Roan urged Scarlett to help and, together, they began to drag Jacob's limp frame into the shadows. Beyond the edge of the basement door.

tea & sanctity

"Shall I be mother?" The Reverend Diana Allway removed the cosy from the teapot and poured. "Seeing as I can't *really* be father," she smiled.

Four days after Jacob's misadventure, an impulse for another perspective, beyond the suffocation, drove Scarlett to Whitecross's vicarage. She hadn't a clue why, still less how to begin a conversation. Meeting a woman threw her further still, but she rebuked herself. After all, wasn't this whole mess down to a woman's thwarted will?

"So what brings you, my dear?" she gently asked, "Not that you need any reasons . . ."

"Probably easier to say what *doesn't*," she sighed. "It's a long shot…"

"How intriguing! Well, I don't mind being a long shot. Have a slice of Christmas cake," she urged, "Can you believe it's New Year's Eve tomorrow and we've still got acres of the stuff… all kindly meant, though I do prefer a nice Victoria sponge."

"Thanks, I'm not hungry," Scarlett replied, knowing she was all bones. Again, she questioned being here. She didn't seek confession, she wasn't a jot religious, but life had become a choke of bindweed, snaking around parents, brother, boyfriend. And there, in the tangle, ever-present, those eyes, some blind, some ever-seeing. *I can't free them*, she said, only to realise her words are no more than streaming tears.

"Oh, my dear child!" Diana rubbed her forearm, reaching for a tissue. "What a funny way to meet. I hoped to see you at Christmas, maybe in jollier circumstances." Scarlett sobbed freely. "You know, if something's weighing on you, there's always tea in the pot. Now, what can we do? How about we start from the top?"

"So how does the infernal unguent come out?" Standing before Roan at the fireplace, Edmund squeezed the bottle as small gobs of lotion spat into his cracked palm.

"As you're doing," Roan said, "though it's usually easier – we tend to do this in daylight, at the beach."

"Beech? So... you do it beneath a tree? The boy speak such riddles."

"No, the *beach*... you know, the seaside? Donkey rides? Ice cream... when we go on holiday... ugh, forget it."

Edmund's eyes lit up. "*Holi*-days? Ah! Days of celebration in the memory of the saints," he laughed at some dim memory. Roan blew his cheeks into a pout. Maybe there was fun to be found in conversations that straddle centuries, in the right time and place. But where on earth was Scarlett? Even *if* trying his random suncream idea worked, actually integrating the brothers was a touch more complex than a slap of Boots factor fifty and shoving one foot before another.

Having squeezed too much, Edmund's hands and face were smeared so much he looked like a wooden doll coated in mayonnaise. Watching in awe, Zadoc grabbed the bottle, squeezing it impatiently.

"So how do I look?" Edmund stood back. His arms shone with a creepy translucence.

Like a greased alien, Roan decided. "Perfect," he said, "though try to avoid your hair. And maybe get a hat?"

"Or a hood? Scarlett said she can purvey *hoods*?"

"No, Edmund, hood-*ie*, which is like a jumper, with a hood built-in."

"Hood-*ie*?" Edmund laughed. "Ingenious."

"Not necessarily worn by the ingenious," Roan muttered. No one, however, laughed.

"And how about me... are my Hollywood looks still obvious?" The drawl came from the fireside chair: Jacob was evidently well enough to seek attention. The sunlight appearing to have cost his face its uppermost layer of skin, he had a complexion of freshly grated beetroot. Rosamond may have covered him against the sun's worst effect, but Roan judged it would be another day before he might walk. As advised by Scarlett, they prescribed a bottle of calamine lotion, with the direction to keep slapping it on. So far, Jacob appeared beyond severe pain and his brothers, aghast when they found his note, now hung on every small sign of recovery.

Roan wondered if his rescue marked a breakthrough: from that point, had he and Scarlett not proved they were genuinely on their side, clearly putting themselves in danger for their protection? In the firelight, he caught a glint in Edmund's eye. If there could be a bond, could he be the key to it? But such questions when meaningless when one remains – where the hell was Scarlett? To kill time, he explained the significance of the bottles on the table.

Factor fifty was essential; they must *never* risk anything less. There was also a small container of pills.

"And what's this?" asked Zadoc.

"Vitamin D. Strengthens the bones."

"Never trust the apothecary. Are our bones not strong enough?" Zadoc replied. "They've kept us from flopping all these years . . . I like *this* though." He squinted at the label on another bottle. In bold, it declared: ANTI-AGEING. "We could all do with a bit of that, eh?" he chuckled. "One finds one gets to a certain age when, despite the obvious radiant charm, a little medicinal assistance is welcome." Jacob echoed his laughter.

"Maybe," said Roan. "A pill a day might boost you up – especially *you*, Jacob."

Edmund slipped the vitamin bottle into his pocket. He'd inspect it more closely at his leisure.

"She is back now, your sister, from wherever," Jacob said, his eyelids tightly shut.

"How'd you know?" Roan asked.

"I felt a disturbance; the front door. I hear those Apothecary Martin boots; I've known quieter horses."

"Right, then I must away!" Roan said, shivering at the thought of their archaic tongue infecting his own, "Maybe tomorrow, we can see how our plan looks – put it to the test?"

"Aye, tomorrow," Edmund repeated, lost in contemplation of his fingertips and their creamy, softening skin.

But the plan – to receive their long-awaited 'Patagonians' the following evening – felt ambitious. So much so, neither Scarlett or Roan dared remind their parents. By the following afternoon, Jacob showed good signs, but after more than a couple of paces, his legs rebelled. Passed through her under-bed panel, Scarlett sent chicken soup, which Edmund poured from the carton into his old pot. Once heated, Jacob sipped it slowly from the fireside chair, his brothers supping the rest at their table.

"Would it bother you, Jacob," Edmund asked, "if we left for a while, this afternoon?" Zadoc looked bewildered – the sun cream has surely yet to be tested? He shuddered to think of a trial with so little warning.

"Edmund, I'm your brother, not your giddy aunt," said Jacob. "Should you wish to go dip a toe, indeed any appendage, into the light and see how far your 'protection' goes, I will be delighted to refrain from such gambling."

"So be it." Edmund slurped his bowl dry. "The children will meet us at the basement door. We shall see how events proceed."

"Just don't dive headlong," Jacob added. "Trust me on that."

Edmund reached for a bag, beneath the table. "She also sent this through." He shook out the contents: three hoodies, three pairs of sunglasses. Zadoc pawed through the items like a magistrate viewing exhibits from a petty crime.

"Good grief, is this modern fashion?"

"Apparently so," Edmund snorted. "And all the more fortuitous, too, if we are to cheat the sun. T'is the mode, she informs me, to wear this hood in all seasons. These darkening spectacles complement the apparel."

"Will this not signal brigandage is our business?" Zadoc asked.

"Certainly, but that, she said, is good: it is all about being *sick*."

"Sick?" Zadoc gasped. "Don't be ridiculous: I haven't been *sick* since 1943 and have no intention of doing so now."

Zadoc sighed. "We must bend to their world, not them to ours."

"Did you bring more sunblock?" Scarlett asked, peering into the basement's gloom. Edmund and Zadoc stood within the shadows; Jacob's absence came as no surprise.

"The prescribed balm?" Edmund grinned, confidently patting the pocket of his breeches.

His breeches! Scarlett panicked. There was something beyond bizarre in the combination of hoody, sunglasses and trousers that looked like they'd been binned from Whitecross Village Dramatic Society's staging of *The Three Musketeers*. Maybe, she hoped, the exchange excuse could save the day again? After all, who was to know what Patagonian trousers looked like?

"Okay, Roan, do it now," she said. He opened a stripy beach umbrella and held it over the doorway. Given the clouds, they were hardly under ultraviolet attack, but they decided extra cover was sensible.

"Just a little," she said, reaching to beckon Edmund forward. He clasped her hand, mindful that he hadn't walked in daylight since his mortal years. Standing behind him, Zadoc squinted, anticipating the spectacle of a lamb to the slaughter.

From outside the shadow, Scarlett gently pulled. The line progressed to her wrist; its edge wasn't sharp, yet as it neared his own flesh, Edmund was sure it was a burning blade. First, the tips of his long fingernails, then his clasped fingers, were drawn cross the divide. Scarlett let go. To his humiliation, his hand trembled.

"D'you *feel* anything?" Roan asked. In daylight, his skin had the tone of overworked pastry.

"It feels... just *warm*," he replied.

"Just warm?" Scarlett didn't dare breathe.

"Better than that," he declared, moving further, "it feels... *good!*"

She urged Zadoc out and moments later, Roan lowered the umbrella.

"How about *now*?" Scarlett asked. Three minutes had ticked by.

"Yes. We are fine," Edmund declared. Lost in the moment, Zadoc studies his hands.

"Right, let's go," she insisted. "There's something this way. A surprise." Roan looked as baffled as they were.

From the grounds, they headed through the field towards Valance Farm. Edmund and Zadoc were eager to drop their hoods and remove the irritating sunglasses, but respected the rules. By the time they reached the lane, Scarlett saw how Edmund was more capable, more poised. Thousands of night-time sorties had given him a confidence. At the stile, she helped Zadoc down. Through his clothing, his bones feel like a bicycle frame.

"Where are we now?" Zadoc wheezed, pausing to regain breath.

"Starvecrow Field," Edmund offered. By now, he knew.

"Ah . . . So they must be here already." Joanna was at the sink, tackling an obstinate residue of pasta on an oven dish.

"*They,* dear?" Richard replied. He'd been given a digital radio for Christmas and was trying to tune it in. Without success.

"The Patagonians. The students – do you listen to nothing?" She reached across to prod a button marked 'Autotune'.

"Ah, from the school exchange?"

"Yes, that's the ones, as opposed to the other Patagonians we usually have over." Her voice trailed as she watched Scarlett and Roan disappear around the side of the house. Two strange-looking figures were walking close beside them.

"Very odd... both wearing hoodies and sunglasses... and the *weirdest* trousers you've ever seen, even on a teenager – baggy in the backside, skinny on the legs... ending half way up the calves, with long, grey socks... they look like extras from *Poldark*."

"Ah, probably top fashion in Patagonia. Maybe you shouldn't be staring at young men's bottoms anyway."

"I'll set the table for seven," she said, sighing.

"Seven? I thought we were eating at eight?"

"Seven *people*, clot. Can't see the third one... perhaps he didn't make the trip? Or he's got jet-lag. They're all brothers, apparently," she added, placing the scrubbed dish on the side.

"Well, that's nice, I'm looking forward to hearing about their home. And maybe they wear hoodies because of their condition?"

"Condition?"

"Now who's the one with memory issues? The light sensitivity thing? Scarlett explained it. And I *listened*," he declared. "See? There's life in these old lugs yet."

"Why bring us *here*, of all places?" Sunglasses on or off, she registered Edmund's unease.

"I wanted you to... there's something I arranged... "

"You wanted us what? To come to..." disbelief made the air too thick to speak, "our *mother's* grave? The same mother who trapped us in this excuse for life?" He turned squarely. "What did I give you credit for, girl?

What brainsick trust might I place in someone who would value this folly?" He snapped: "Zadoc! Come hither."

Yanking his confused brother to his side, he gestured with a long forefinger. "Beyond that hedge, up there... *that* is the place I always told you about; the place where our mother lived, before she met our father, where she died, and now *lies buried* – when she chooses. Here endeth the discourse." he spat. "I thank you for your favours, but the hour is late and we must away. Good day to you!" With a crimped sneer, he bowed, swivelled and strutted off in the direction of the stile, Zadoc, more confused than upset, in his wake.

"That went well then," sighed Roan. "Honestly, Scar – what was the plan? See if they combust and then, if not, nip up to nose around their mum's burial plot? That's a genius day out."

Scarlett sighed. "I just wanted to try, well, *something*. I rushed the idea, I guess."

"The *idea*? Well feel free to let me in on it, rather than giving me the, what do they call it, *mushroom* treatment? Keeping me in the dark and feeding me on – "

" – She's coming!" Scarlett pointed to a figure, moving at the bottom of the field. "She just missed them. Oh well, maybe that was for the best?"

Roan squinted to make her out: a woman in a long skirt, which suggested more impending drama, given the muddy state of her Wellington boots. At 100 yards, he also made out a detail that parted his lips in wordless surprise. Around her neck, she was wearing a vicar's collar.

"What hand of mischief is upon her?" Zadoc staggered through the mud in Edmund's furious wake.

"I know not," Edmund snapped. "Perhaps naivety controls her fopdoodle brain. First, she plays the apothecary, prescribing curative lotions, next she believes we can be wrested free of this miasma of mortality, purely by consorting with *that* spirit. I'd sooner a dialogue with the devil and . . ." He stopped short as they reach the stile. Beyond it, a woman waited politely.

"Afternoon boys, lovely day!" she breezed.

They mumbled a greeting as they pass, heads down. Had it not been for their breeches and a pungent mix of dust and suncream, the Reverend Allway might have thought them textbook teenagers.

"Did you not see?" Zadoc whispered, a few paces on. "Did you *see* what she was wearing – *a cleric's collar*!"

"And did you not remark that *she* was a woman? So be not so doltish: since when was there such a lunatick entity as a woman of the cloth? Heavens, Zadoc, you clearly confuse religious apparel with modern fashion."

Zadoc had to agree; all further speculation was insane. As he trailed behind his brother, he noticed the task becomes less difficult; by the garden gate, something about Edmund was amiss. Watching his hand reach for the latch, he blurted: "Edmund! Your skin! It's burning… quickly, inside!"

Edmund raised his fingers. A crimson tracery ran the length of each digit, and on the back, where until now the cream had been a barrier, the light had burned through, scoring outcrops of tiny blisters. Knowing the reaction would soon overwhelm every inch of exposed skin, he sensed foothills of discomfort, but felt sure a mountain of pain awaited.

"So much for their lies made liquid," he growled.

On balance, he reflected, as they shut the door and sucked the familiar dank air, it had not been a good day out.

Roan heard the quad bike before it came into view, surging into the field from behind the hedge, jetting plumes of mud.

"Oh dear, I hope that's not an angry farmer – you *did* warn them we were coming?" Diana asked Scarlett.

"*Him*? No, that's Moreton, he's my… well, 'boyfriend', I guess… it's his family's land," Spoken out loud, Scarlett marvelled at how curiously alien the B word felt.

"And the girl?"

"His sister, Isabel." In leather jacket and jeans, wild ringlets trailing in the wind, she looked convincing – as if she'd never dream of wandering outside the twenty-first century.

"Ah, the poor girl who's been so troubled. Well, let's crack on."

Cracking on was hardly what Scarlett expected, but she admired the vicar's confidence. After a few awkward hellos, the five of them crossed the fence and began to pick through the hawthorn and hazel, ascending the gentle dome of ground. Scarlett eyed the sky for portents: maybe a sudden squadron of crows, their aerial formation perfectly depicting a rune of doom, or a rogue cloud harbouring a precision thunderbolt. Perhaps old Mrs Tow herself, back by unpopular demand, swooping down, teeth and fingernails flaying in a display of spittle-flecked rage. But no. A robin sang carelessly, a lazy scribble of smoke unwound from the far chimney of Valance Farm and, best of all, Isabel was just… Isabel. So far, so weirdly okay.

Moreton led his sister by the hand. To her conscious mind, she did not know the path with accuracy, even if her shoeless feet might faultlessly trace it in the black of night. She wasn't even unnerved by what he told her of Scarlett's idea, though she doubted it was of any value.

In a semi-circle, they closed around the grave. Moreton wondered if the vicar might ask about the pile of broken iron bars, but she said nothing, merely reaching into her rucksack to produce a bible and a glass vial.

"Well, thank you, all, for coming. Before we proceed, I wanted to speak about why we're here and what we might hope from this. Scarlett has drawn my attention to an issue she feels is a source of unhappiness, an unhappiness that lingers today, yet lies rooted deep in the past. A wrong which, if not tackled, raises questions for the future."

Blimey, Roan reflected, *she more politician than preacher.*

"Now I don't come to you today with a magic wand, just faith. But faith *can* change the world, both the physical one we see and feel and the spiritual one God oversees, the one many of us often sense. Some," she cast an eye towards Isabel, "more than others."

Spirituality, she continued, can be like a radio station. "Once you know where it is on the dial, it may be easy to tune in. All of which brings me to a question I have often been asked whether I, and the church I represent, believe in ghosts. The answer is easy: of course! We have the holy ghost, the supreme spirit who watches over us, and that is core to our faith. We believe, too, that all of us are spiritual beings and I like to think that, as much as we talk about human rights, we can also only benefit ourselves by thinking of *spiritual* rights. That might sound airy-fairy, but it brings us to the truth of where we are, today."

Scarlett checked the sky again. No sign.

"I've been digging into records, and much of what Scarlett tells me appears to be supported. There was, indeed, a burial here, in the early 1700s, the details of the woman buried going unrecorded – she was given no ceremony, no opportunity to be judged by God, in accordance with faith… no, she was judged by the people. And, condemned as a witch, she was consigned, with contempt, to the afterlife. It's a picture of a woman wronged against, and a church that endorsed that wrong, at the behest of the powerful. And, a generation later, the judgement was reinforced by these iron bars, which Moreton recently, and rightly, saw fit to remove. This cage…" she said, gesturing at the severed bars, "appears to have been designed to fulfil some superstition, that an 'evil' spirit might escape so as to carry out acts of mischief. It's a sorry illustration of the mistreatment of so many women, and it's my regret that the Christian faith played a part in such episodes."

Scarlett wished Edmund had not lost his temper; how could he be angered by such words?

"So… we can't undo the past, but we can act for the present, and show where we stand against such moments in history. Rosamond Tow suffered a wrong, and her soul may easily have been charged by some hunger for revenge. Revenge, of course, holds no place in our faith, but I am equally sure she was no 'witch'. For that reason, we come here today," she said, stepping forward, "to offer our prayers and ask God to recognise this place of burial as a holy place." For a moment, she fumbled with the top on the vial. Eventually, it freed, with a dull pop. *"O God, whose son Jesus Christ was laid in a tomb: bless, we pray, this grave as the place where the body of Rosamond Boxwell, once Rosamond Tow, once Rosamond Valance, may rest in peace, through your Son, who is the resurrection and the life; who died and is alive, and reigns with you now and forever… Amen."*

They repeated her final word as she sprinkled holy water onto the grave. "We're more than 300 years late, but that's a blink in God's eye. And now that we've offered a blessing for Rosamond's soul, perhaps we might share a moment in silent prayer." She lowered her head.

Like the others, Scarlett guessed it could do no harm. But what to pray for? If Rosamond was pacified by their good intention, would she trouble their world no more? Yet what of her legacy, her living legacy?

What prayers for them?

live & let dine

"You never said we had guests, Scarlett!" Joanna called across the hall.

That's it, she thought, *the game's up: they must have seen them.*

"Well I'm doing a turkey curry – they'll eat curry, your Patagonian friends?" Standing in the kitchen doorway, she brandished a tea towel.

"Curry? Sorry no… I mean *yes*, I guess?" Scarlett stumbled. "Sorry, I never said: they turned up this morning, you and Dad were out – the flight landed earlier, thanks to some mix-up… "

"I see, but no sign of their luggage? I didn't see anything by the beds we made up?"

Scarlett wondered how long this could drag on. "Yes… they've been, delayed, typical of Air Patagonia!" she rolled her eyes. "They've got cabin luggage – they'll survive for now."

"So tell me their names! No, don't, we'll learn everything over supper. Your father's *so* looking forward to it!" she beamed. "Turns out he did a trip there as a student! It must have changed, but I'm sure there'll be *lots* they can share. And he can dust off his rusty Spanish!"

"No! He can't do that!" Roan interjected, having finally removed his boots. "Well, probably not," he added, more calmly. "They speak English, or something like it – we said, remember?"

"Yes…" Joanna nodded uncertainly. "Ah well, I'm sure it'll all be fascinating. Your friends belong to a lost people, you say? Fascinating…" She trailed back to the kitchen as they scurried towards the stairs.

"I think we might need to get our guests up to speed," Scarlett whispered. "What do we know about Patagonia?"

"I'll ask my mate Wiki."

If it wasn't all based on lies, Scarlett would have been moved to tears. Her mother had made every effort: the table, in the middle of the library, lit by candles, dressed as if to welcome world dignitaries. Crisp, white cloth, silver cutlery, cut-glass goblets, even hand-written menus, one for each place setting. They'd begin with soup, followed by turkey curry (plus a vegan option for Scarlett) and, to finish, ice cream and Christmas pudding. Richard had lit a fire, put on calm but jolly music and the stage was set – for an evening of torture and misery.

"Did you speak to them, what did they say?" Roan whispered, as they hung back in the doorway, "Do they have the right clothes?"

"God knows: what'd be 'right'? Edmund barely seemed to care. He was still stroppy from our walk. I sneaked them a bottle of wine, a peace offering. He just grunted and got stuck into it. He did say one thing though…"

"Oh?"

"Our 'experiment' failed. He's covered in red blotches."

"Oh hell, Scar! Is he suffering?"

"Not quite, but on a scale of one to 10, I'd say their mood's in the minuses and sinking. I said be ready by now, but… I dunno, Roe, it wouldn't shock me if they didn't even turn up."

"Bugger. Then what?"

"We'd have to just tell all. I can't do this much longer."

Roan sighed. Their absence would spell disaster. Mum and Dad would pull the house apart. And the brothers? He pictured them locked away in a government research lab, all official existence disclaimed by the authorities. Case conveniently closed, they'd face eternity as live specimens. However he saw it, the endgame was grim.

Ding-dong, ding-dong,
Dong-ding, dong-ding,
Ding-dong, ding-dong…

The grandfather clock in the hall sounded with a papery clunk, its unfinished phrase hanging in the air. It was a quarter to the hour.

Scarlett glanced to Roan in shock: "Hang on, the clock… Since when was it working?"

"Since I took the liberty, Mistress Scarlett, to reset the weights." The voice comes from the doorway. "Horology can be most rewarding, when one has the time to study it."

It was Edmund. And he looked incredible.

"Forgive me, your counsel was to dress for dinner?" he asked, looking the two of them up and down. Roan couldn't believe the transformation: patent shoes buffed mirror-clean, a crisp tuxedo, precise bow-tie, popstar dark glasses and some unknown product liberally applied to his slicked-down hair – so liberally, that his customary bag of rats' tails was marshalled into the coiffure of someone... what *was* the word? He struggled to pin it down.

"Cool!" Scarlett exclaimed. "What the hell, Edmund! You look bang-on, cool!"

"One tries, my dear, one tries." He punctuated his reply with a click of his heels. "American officers in the second world war left this garb here. We have little occasion to wear it, but we thought it might one day be useful, so we kept it safe from the moths. My brothers will join us presently. Jacob has been in need of assistance, as you will appreciate; some of these buttons are fiendish." A slight slur suggested he may not have equally shared the smuggled wine.

"Aha, so you must be?" Richard stood behind Edmund, extending a hand. Swivelling seamlessly, Edmund readily clasped it. In the candlelight, Scarlett prayed her father might not perceive their guest's deathly pallor.

"Buenas tardes, signor Wycherley, mi nombre es Edmundo," Edmund declared, with a gracious bow, "Puedo entender que han visitado nuestro maravilloso país?"

Looking stumped, Richard could only mutter: "Uh, si, me-o, uh . . ."

"Oh, I *do* apologise, Signor: your delightful daughter intimated that you had been a guest in our homeland?"

"Aha!" he laughed. "My wife, Joanna, loves to exaggerate. *Technically*, yes, I've set foot in Patagonia, but only to change planes, at Terra del Fuego. My Spanish, sadly, is more kindergarten than schoolboy." They all laughed, awkwardly, though Scarlett felt a fraction less tense. "And it's Richard, *please*... do make yourself comfortable."

"Thank you, and might I propose we converse," Edmund continues, "In the King's English?"

As he spoke, Zadoc materialised from the hall, Jacob at his side. Scarlett wondered if he could mask the fact that he was actually propping his brother up, but with her father tending the fire and her mother busy in the kitchen, she was able to get the brothers to their seats without scrutiny.

Roan gulped: thanks to their evening dress, the aura of decay that surrounded the brothers has been swept away by a sheen of confidence. Swagger even, when it came to Edmund. Even Jacob, frail and unsteady, appeared plausible. He guessed the sunglasses would help them appear less ancient. Scarlett took her seat at the end of the table, beside Jacob, shooting her brother a wide-eyed look that said it all: they were, were they not, totally amazing? Could it be, she wondered, that they might, just *might*, pull it off? The night was young.

Happy New Yr Morrie! Meal great. Mum & Dad swallowed mega helping of Patagonian nonsense along with rehashed turkey. Still working out resolutions tho. Sx   11.46pm

Good stuff. Isabel's back to her mad self – sane mad, hopefully. So yr secret bros can go free now? What's the deal? Mx ps HNY2U2! 11.49pm

Not quite. Turns out suncream useless :(Not sure where to now? X 11.51pm

Hmm, new yr res: run away, find life in normal place? X 11.55pm

Steady! I have vicar on speed dial. X 11.57pm

Hang resolutions, hang goals. How about normal? Love u, Scarface X Love u 2 HNY X   11.59pm

The grandfather clock clunked in the new year as Scarlett read her texts. How strange, this night: she had envisaged a menu of wooden conversation, ugly revelation and bitter indigestion. At some point, she'd have bet serious money the fire would have fizzled out as Mum, perceiving a crone's face hovering at the window, clenched her glass too tightly, peppering the cloth with a thousand exploded shards. But no: their meal was polite and easy. Even normal, which was hardly normal at all.

    And Edmund was a total star. Lubricated by an unknown quantity of wine, he'd smoothed a pathway through the evening's conversation. And all the while, her father, relieved from his escape from Tom Benn's plans, positively revelled at meeting three young men who came from a world so quaint yet so cultured, so civilised. Talking to them felt almost like stepping back in time. He toasted them as a credit to Patagonia. Three times. As for her mother, Scarlett became convinced that, as the evening and the wine wore on, she was so relaxed as to actually be flirting with Edmund. To her relief, the misbehaviour went one way only.

All the same, she'd not wanted to push their luck. When Roan asked Edmund if jet-lag didn't make them yearn for sleep, Scarlett reinforcing the hint by nudging his rickety leg, the brothers compliantly nodded. And so, some dreaded scenario of a midnight rendition of *Auld Land Syne* was consequently sidestepped.

She presumed the brothers had retired to the beds they were expected to take, but didn't check – judging it perhaps insulting. In reality, Edmund insisted they simply ruffle the sheets to simulate occupation before returning to their usual quarters. Historical habits die hard.

Besides, for his part, Edmund suspected the growing heat in his flesh, smouldering deep beneath his skin, would ensure he would not sleep comfortably *anywhere* that night, whatever century the bedding.

hellfire

Numbed by wine, Jacob was back beneath Scarlett's bed. Having seen him safely there, Edmund drew comfort from evidence of his recovery. And by putting his ear to the cold water pipe that led to the main bathroom, he determined Zadoc was snoring steadily.

He sat at the table, holding his hands close to the candle: it was difficult to be sure in such feeble light, but what he first thought superficial ran deep, deeper than any effect he thought sunlight could have. Against all previous mishaps, this was different: as if the flesh beneath were ablaze, consuming itself. As if yesterday's sun had merely been a catalyst.

From the shelves, he found a residue of brandy, downing it quickly. It scorched an instant pathway from throat to stomach, a flush of distraction pulsing into his blood. But it made no difference. *I am burning up, and so I am to meet the fate our dear father would most probably have wished upon her. Maybe this is what he now exacts upon us? If that spirit were trapped here, would it not be vengeful?*

Uninvited questions churned. For a while, he reclined in the fireside chair, aching for sleep. When fatigue finally took hold over the mounting heat, his slumber was fitful. By dawn, he stood at the basement door, his hand on the handle. Resolved to finish what fate had begun, he stepped back and, in one concession to fear, began to undress.

"If I am to finish this dying, I beg providence just this: that the moment might be quick and merciful."

Joanna woke with a hangover she knew can only be remedied by two paracetamol, limitless coffee and a day without human interaction. Her brain pleaded for peace, but her thoughts raged like Punch and Judy. She staggered to the kitchen, filled the kettle and dumped it on the Aga. From the sink, she watched the approaching light of the first day of the year. Oblivious, Mustard slept on.

Edmund cursed a cowardice he believed he never had. Deeper even than the fever in his flesh, it now surfaced, rooting him to the spot. The basement door ajar, he was transfixed, unable to command a muscle. For minutes, there he remained, the fire within rendering him immune to the draught around his limbs. What finally freed him was what he least expected: a scalpel blade of sunlight, slicing apart the grey belly of a January sky, began to burn yellow-white across the lawn; growing quickly, a majestic force to rudely disagree with the year's dull start.

"That will do me fine," he cried, legs jumping to life as his torso tilted forward, every sinew and muscle springing. By the edge of the lawn, 15 yards beyond the doorway, he reached a momentum not known since childhood. Skidding and diving into the patch of light, he willed it upon his skin, thrusting forward to bask in every second before it might fade. But the shaft held steady and, rolling onto his back, Edmund Boxwell stared up, into the alien sun, feeling it burn, willing it to transport him to a place beyond pain.

Seconds passed. He squinted on at the searing orb, anticipating a supernova of his self, wondering if this was how death makes itself known.

Raising his head, his vision was dazzled, but something never seen before, never recalled, defied his eyes...

His flesh, it was changing. It was the colour of... *flesh*? Pink, cream, red. The colour of life? Gently, he ran his fingers along his legs. The sensation was different, alien. New. Sitting upright, his mouth opened in disbelief. The pain... vanished, evaporated, yet he had not. And the not feeling edged away as his nerves awoke as a tingling, fizzing mass. Charged with a rush, he jumped to his feet and thrust a strong forearm up into the light.

"I, am, *alive*!" Tears rolled down his youthful cheeks. "You hear me? *I am alive!*"

Well I say, that's a fine figure of a young man, Joanna gasped as she peered from the window, her mug dropping with a resounding smash. *Really though, someone should explain we don't do that sort of thing in England. New Year's Day might be like that in Patagonia, but we tend to take sandwiches to the beach, maybe go to the sales...*

A blur of buttocks and limbs, Edmund exited the lawn. As she reached to pick up the remnants of her broken mug, Joanna wondered how to prevent any repetition of this shocking dawn ritual. *Oh well, they're not staying long – maybe the other two can keep him under control?*

Then he was back. With the other two. And they were naked, too; all three, holding hands.

"Oh my God alive!" she cried, almost covering her eyes. "They're *all* at it now!" This was a terrible hangover cure.

In the kitchen doorway, Scarlett scratched her ruffled hair.

"Mum, what's all the noise… what's happening?" She feared hearing the answer.

"Cover your eyes, young lady! Your guests are doing some sort of naked Morris dancing out there. All of them – not a stitch!"

"*Really? In broad daylight?*" Scarlett craned her neck. "Ah, Yes…" Gradually, she realised: the sun had finally shone on the brothers' fate. And for some fantastic reason, it apparently agreed with them.

"Turn your head, madam! And you know what, Scarlett? I think you and I need to talk!" Joanna scowled, cradling her forehead. "There's something that's just not right about this!"

"Yes Mum, I know… " Scarlett pulled out a chair. By now, Roan and her father had descended. Joanna gestured for them to sit.

"These so-called *boys*… your father and I have been talking. This isn't easy, so I'll come right out with it." She took a deep breath. "It doesn't add up. And the bottom line is this: they're not *really* from Patagonia… are they?"

Roan glanced at Scarlett in resignation.

"*Technically?* Nope, not at all." She smiled.

"So where the hell *are* they from?"

"From a type of hell? If I tell you, if we *both* tell you, will you try to believe us?"

"Every word," said Richard.

"Okay, every word." Scarlett looked at Roan and the beam of sunlight streaming across the room. "Though we'd best to go back to the beginning."

four months later

7.45pm, April 23
From: scarlettwycherley@whitecrosshall.com
To: adelinebenn@74lincolnvale.co.uk

Hi Adeline – hope you had a BRILLIANT birthday, yay – the big 16. Darn, you beat me by a week. I'm sure that happened last year ;) Sorry, I know it's been sooo long. After you left, what with Christmas and New Year, everything's zoooomed. I guess there hasn't been much need to state the obvious: the chances of us moving are zero. I hope your dad didn't feel too bad about things not coming together?

Moreton's still around – going 'steady', Mum calls it (cringe)... We're happy though – I think?! And you? What news from the city?

Weird fact: Dad ended up talking to the local council and he's working for them now, on some rural regeneration thing... made Mum laugh, but he's way less stressed, which has got to be good. Mum's gone mad decorating. Amazing what a bit of paint does. All still crumbly underneath, but it's begun to feel like home.

Speaking of makeovers, note updated selfie. Hair less short now, decided I didn't need to keep shocking Dad, or anyone else. Still love my DMs, saving for a pair of purple knee-lengths. Maybe escape to London to get some soon?

I could also bring Iz... She's still hyper, though no more sleepwalking, Moreton says, dealing better with school. Suppose I am, too – have started to make one or two friends.

That's about it. Roan's still Roan – he's given up researching Whitecross. He went right through a journal from the 1780s, discovered enough for a horror festival, but in the end whoever wrote it was probably carted off to an asylum – or at least that's all we know – the journal Roan found suddenly ended, the final pages ripped out. Anyhow, it's back where it belongs – in the dusty library.   See you soon! hugs + kisses Scar X X X

ps nearly forgot! We've got lodgers! Students of ancient history, they say. Three brothers. A bit old-fashioned, but they're very outdoorsy and seem pleasant – Edmund, Zadoc and Jacob... odd names, I know! Funniest thing is their surname... Boxwell! Apparently, they might have family connections with the guy who built Whitecross – remember, your Harry Styles bodydouble? Mum was worried about three extra people, but they keep themselves to themselves. In fact, you'd barely know they were here.

It felt good to reach out to her oldest friend, though she felt the distance had grown, perhaps finally to what it always really had been.

It was a slow, spring evening as Scarlett headed across the field. He would have shut the chickens away by now. As she walked, she thought about her birthday, two days ahead, and the two interlocking Rs, glinting even in the slightest light. It didn't fit perfectly, but somehow felt right. She vowed to treasure it.

To be fair, the ring wouldn't *entirely* be from Moreton: the brothers, after all, had passed it to him. They'd always kept it, secreted away. Their wish, Edmund declared, was that he do whatever he liked with it. And though unsure if it was good or bad, Moreton seemed typically philosophical, save one request: that it would never, by anyone's measure of a lifetime, make contact with Isabel.

What then to do with it, he wondered aloud, as they sat beneath the chestnut tree, looking back at the outline of her home. Was it a gift, or a curse to fling into oblivion?

"No, I'll wear it, I'd love it, if you like… for my birthday?"

He raised his eyebrows. She laughed.

"Okay, we know the history, but I've a feeling, call it an *inkling*, the past is the past. And it's… beautiful…" she hesitated, "to my eyes."

In its dull glint, Scarlett sensed something reflected of herself, tangled within the embracing letters. Saying nothing, Moreton studied the shape in his palm, as if he was weighing it against the late sun in Scarlett's eyes.

Finally, he looked skyward, smiled and closed his fingers.

Folding it into darkness.

BY THE SAME AUTHOR ON AMAZON

Polar Nights

"This is a warning for all sea areas north…" Like the convulsions of a dying moth in a paper cup, the thin voice on Long Wave washes in and out of reception's static wash. "Fair Isle, north-easterly seven, seven to severe gale nine, closing slowly from North Utsire, Viking…" a warning of the hard limits that lie beyond the harbour, out there within the infinite black merging of saltwater and sky."

Hitching a ride on a chunk of melting iceberg, a polar bear washes up on the north coast of Scotland and immediately causes havoc within a small fishing community. Intent on the media scoop of the decade, TV journalist Rebecca Riposte is on its trail.

But so, too, is Lord Tobias von Hindmarch, a man desperate to settle an old hunting score and bag the one trophy that's escaped his collection. Meanwhile, scientist Dan Travis flies in, his mission to play down the government's melting green reputation.

As the action converges and the body count rises, each must face challenges more deadly than their darkest fears.

"A sumptuous read."
Thriller of the Month, USA-UK website e-thriller.com.

"All the hallmarks of a best-seller…"
Northern Times.

"Packed with twists to keep you gripped to the final chapter…"
Cheltenham Echo.

Printed in Great Britain
by Amazon